S.T.O.P.

Stop Terrorising Our Planet

James Moclair

Grosvenor House
Publishing Limited

This book is published by
Grosvenor House Publishing Ltd
Link House
140 The Broadway, Tolworth, Surrey, KT6 7HT.
www.grosvenorhousepublishing.co.uk

This book is a work of fiction. Any resemblance to
people or events, past or present, is purely coincidental.

A CIP record for this book
is available from the British Library

Paperback ISBN 978-1-80381-007-2
Ebook ISBN 978-1-80381-008-9

Chapter One, Anniversary

With the covid 19 virus still throwing up new variants, life on our planet had never really returned back to normal. We now had a new normal, that was without a doubt life in covid chaos. Booster jabs were always being issued for new variants and lateral flow tests and PCR tests were a part of our normal lives. Despite many, many protests, Covid passports had become compulsory in the UK. The mandatory wearing of face masks in all shops, bars, restaurants, and public places had been dropped, it was now left to the individual's discretion.

Despite all of this, there was some good news. Holidays at home and abroad had begun to pick up. Travel firms, airlines, and cruise ships had added precautions and it was now relatively safe to travel, or at least that was what we were told. Obviously, all these covid safeguards came at a price and certain companies had made billions and billions out of the covid pandemic.

We, that is me and my family hadn't taken a holiday for a few years now, and with our twenty-fifth wedding anniversary only seven days away, I bit the bullet and booked a surprise, an all-inclusive ten-day holiday to the Canary Island of Tenerife.

In the past, we had always made every life and holiday decision together, and have to admit, I was a little nervous about telling my wife Shelia about this. I chose the moment carefully. It was a Sunday afternoon and we were watching a TV program called A Place in the Sun and as it went to its first commercial break, stumbling over my words, I blurted it out like a kid who had a big secret to tell. To my delight, Shelia kissed me passionately and said it was a really romantic thing to do. This pleased me and the icing on the cake was, we were going on holiday for the first time without our two now grown up, but always when it comes to money, dependant Kids.

Excitedly over the next week, we both did a bit of frantic holiday shopping. We bought a couple of bottles of high factor suntan lotion, mosquito repellent, anti-bacterial wipes and spray, disposable face masks and gloves, a couple of boxes of covid relief tablets, new shorts, and a few tee shirts. After that, we spent a couple of hours packing and repacking. The reason for the repacking was we only had a twenty-kilo weight allowance and we both struggled to keep our luggage below that. However, after deciding that we could rinse through most of our essential clothing, we left lots of extras out, and then we were almost ready. One last thing to do was check-in online and print out our boarding passes, latest covid test certificates, and Spanish locator forms. That all took quite a few hours and then we were ready for what I would class as the holiday of our lifetime.

I have to say we were so excited the night before our departure that we both couldn't sleep and, in the morning, we were ready with our "less than" twenty-kilo suite cases in the hallway well over an hour before the taxi came. After that, everything went like clockwork, the flights were all on time and when we got to Lanzarote airport, we passed through customs quickly and was then transferred to our hotel by a limousine that I had booked as an extra surprise. Shelia smiling from ear to ear said everything was perfect, she then grabbed me, kissed me passionately on the lips and whispered; "thank you, I can't wait to get to the room."

To add to our overall excitement, as soon as we arrived in our five-star beach fronted hotel in Playa La Enromada, we were told that the Hotel management had upgraded us to a tenth-floor executive suite. The suite was extravagantly furnished with a sumptuous king-sized bed, hot tub, and a large lavishly furnished balcony that overlooked the beach that was mostly black volcanic sand with splashes of volcanic rock. It looked spectacular.

After a quick, hot, steamy sex session, we unpacked and spent the rest of the day relaxing by the pool in the warm Mediterranean sun. That evening, we dressed up a bit. Shelia wore an elegant off-the-shoulder black dress, a white pearl necklace, and earrings to match. Wow and double wow, after all these years, she still looked fabulous. We then had a candlelit five-course dinner that was served to us on our spacious balcony. After that we went down to the hotel's bar had a couple of drinks and as we looked into each other's eyes, we instantly decided to head back to our room.

For our wedding anniversary day, we had both made up a fun day bucket list. As a man, mine was fairly simple. Number one was sex as soon woke up. To my delight, this also was Shelia's number one, or at least that's what she told me. So, our wedding anniversary got off to a fantastic start, with a steamy, early morning sex session. We were just like a pair of young lovers, we hadn't done anything as outrageous as this for years, but we both crept naked out onto the balcony and had sex as the sun was rising.

After that, we both cooled off in our large walk-in shower. Then it was number two on both our lists, a full English breakfast on the balcony. The hotel management was fantastic; they brought us a chilled bottle of half-decent champagne and a beautiful bouquet for my wife. With breakfast out of the way our lists changed, all I wanted to do was relax by the pool until lunchtime. Shelia, however, was on one of her 'on holiday' fitness campaigns and wanted to go to the hotel gym first. To be fair, we both enjoyed a healthy lifestyle and as we owned a small chain of martial arts and fitness studios in the UK, we had ample opportunity to work out. Although I had gone a little grey and gained a few lines around my eyes, my beautiful wife had aged extremely well. She still had a youthful face and a nice slender, firm but shapely figure that still turned men's heads. So, I was pleased that she still wanted to work out on holiday.

Once Shelia's workout was out of the way, she wanted to do something she had never done before, and that was go parascending. I have to admit, I am a bit of a coward with heights, so Parascending wasn't on my bucket list. However, we agreed to both meet up by the pool and then venture down to the beach. When I say venture down to the beach, it makes it sound like we had to travel a vast distance. The large jetty for the Parascending was on the sandy beach and it was almost opposite the hotel.

We walked bare feet across the black sandy beach, it was only ten-thirty in the morning, and the beach was almost empty. As we got closer to the rock-made jetty, I commented to Shelia that it was a bit windy today and maybe we should leave the Parascending until another day. She laughed and said;

"Don't you know that there is always a breeze in Tenerife and it's always a bit windier by the sea?"

I just nodded and looked to the skies. Over the sea the sky was clear but to the back of us were some tall hills and Mount Teide where dark thick clouds were hovering. I pointed to them and again Shelia smiled and said;

"B.J, you know you're a right worry gut. If it's unsafe, I am sure the people who run the Parascending will let us know."

When you have been married for twenty-five years, you instinctively know when to keep your big mouth shut and this was one of those occasions. Besides that, I didn't want to spoil Shelia's fun.

As we stepped onto the jetty, we were greeted in good English by a man named Carlos who told us he was the owner and that this was a beautiful day to see Lanzarote shoreline from the air. Shelia looked at me, smiled, and in that 'I told you so smiles.' I smiled back and asked Carlos how he knew we were British? Carlos had a deep brown suntan and teeth whiter than white. With a big toothy grin, he answered;

"Senor, British look like British, Germans look like Germans and Spaniards look like Spaniards."

Not really agreeing with Carlos's ethnic analogy, I then casually asked Carlos what he thought about the darkening clouds over the mountains. With a big toothy smile, he replied;

"Senor, this is the island of Tenerife, in the morning, afternoon, and evening we often have clouds over the hills, mountain's and even more over our famous Mount Teide."

OK, I said I'd keep quiet about this, but when I have concerns, I sometimes find it hard to keep my big mouth shut. Shelia just gave me another 'I told you so smile.' And then Carlos inquired if we would be Parascending in tandem or solo? Shelia answered and told him it would be just her. Carlos gave a knowing nod, looked at me, and said in what I would say is a sneering tone;

"Senor, perhaps you would like to ride in the safety of my speed boat? To you my British friend, it's no extra cost"

Feeling that the all-smiling Carlos was trying to make fun of me, I declined by just shaking my head from side to side. Carlos thrust both hands into the air, smiled his toothy grin, and then proceeded to give Shelia a broad explanation on Parascending safety procedures. After that, he fitted Shelia into her harness.

Salvador, as we were told is Carlos's brother-in-law and second in command. Apparently, according to Carlos, he was the best speed boat 'Capitan' in all of Tenerife. As he was sitting in the driver's seat in the speed boat, I could only see his back but he seemed to have a fantastic tan and I bet amazing white teeth. Another chap was also in the speed boat, this was their cousin, Marcus. Marcus was there to control the parachute's winch. Salvador fired up the twin-Yamaha engine speed boat and then slowly positioned the boat to take up the slack on the towing line. Shelia was then positioned so she stood halfway down the edge of the jetty and Carlos ran to the rear and adjusted the multi-coloured parachute. He then gave the thumbs up and with a roar; the double engine speed boat headed for open waters. Once there, I could see Shelia's parachute open and within seconds, Shelia was soaring over thirty metres above the crystal blue calm sea. I eagerly waved and then snapped off some photos in sports mode with my compact digital camera and then turn the switch to video mode.

Suddenly, without warning, there were several tremendous loud bangs to the rear of me. As a firearms certificate holder, I am used to hearing loud bangs from regularly visiting my local firing range. However, this was something quite different, each bang sent shock waves that shuddered the boat jetty and then vibrated through my body. As I swung around to see what had happened, another tremendous long-lasting bang filled the air. It was one big thunderstorm and it was right on top of us! I immediately looked at Carlos, but he was on the ball. He had a two-way radio and was shouting something down it repeatedly in Spanish. I guess it was, 'Salvador, come back in immediately'.

As I looked out to sea, the waters had instantly turned from a millpond into a raging sea. The speed boat was bouncing along as it battled against the high waves and to my horror, in the air, Shelia was being jerked violently up and down and side to side! Frantically I called Carlos and said;

"Use your radio and tell them to winch her in."

Trying to remain calm, Carlos replied;

"Senor, that is too dangerous, if we try this now, she might crash into the sea or our boat. If the storm does not calm down soon, we will attempt to bring her in for a shore landing on the large beach a little further up the coast."

At that, the heavens opened up with torrential rain. Even at a distance, I could see Shelia's parachute canopy begin to sag as it absorbed the sudden deluge of rainwater. Abruptly, her overall height began to drop rapidly. To compensate for this, Salvador increased his speed but then, a bolt of lightning struck Shelia. In a millisecond her parachute plummeted into the raging sea. It was at this point, I wished I had swallowed my foolish pride and had agreed to ride in the speedboat.

Without hesitation, I dropped my camera and ran to the end of the rocky jetty, and dived into the turbulent sea. Despite the now heavy waves, I began swimming as fast as I could towards the speedboat. Distantly, I could hear some shouting, but I ignored it put my head down, and swam for all I was worth. I don't know how long it took me to reach the now-stopped speedboat, but with the rough seas, it felt like an eternity. Marcus immediately helped me on board and I could see that they had already retrieved Shelia. She was lying motionless on the deck. Salvador was crying and saying something in Spanish, however, although I don't speak any Spanish, I had a good idea of what he was saying;

"Senor, your wife, I am so, so sorry, I think she is dead!"

As I looked at Sheila, I could see all the metal on the harness had melted and there were massive burns across her arms and chest. As a qualified first aider, I knew a little first aid and quickly knelt beside her and immediately checked her pulse, there was nothing. Just as I began to give her mouth-to-mouth resuscitation, a lifeboat vessel turned up with a paramedic on board. It was a young Spanish lady. She politely ushered me out of the way and then began to work on my wife. After a few minutes, she looked up at me and shook her head from side to side.

The whole thing seemed dreamlike; Shelia was dead? I knelt, scooped her limp body close to my own, and just wept, I kissed her repeatedly and said;

"Please Shelia, please wake up."

When that didn't happen, frustration and anger kicked in and I began yelling and swearing at Salvador and Marcus. Both men said nothing, with tears in their eyes, they just lowered their heads and made signs of the cross.

While this was going on, I hadn't realized that the speed boat had been taken into tow by the lifeboat vessel. We had made our way through the turbulent seas and we were now close to the jetty where an ambulance and several Spanish police officers were waiting. As we docked, the lady paramedic sympathetically told me in English that Shelia needed to be put in the ambulance. I just nodded, let her go, then two ambulance men boarded the speedboat with a small stretcher. They gently placed Sheila on the stretcher and then put a blanket over her. One of the ambulance men pulled the blanket over her beautiful face, I couldn't have that. Shaking my head from side to side gave him the message and he re-adjusted it so it was just under her chin. Once we disembarked from the speedboat, I walked beside her, holding her hand as they took her to the ambulance. I hadn't noticed, but the rain was still hamming down and a thoughtful police officer rushed over and held an umbrella over Shelia's exposed face until she was in the ambulance.

To my surprise, a Doctor was waiting in the ambulance and he again examined Shelia. This only took a few minutes and then he formally pronounced that she was dead. Well, that was it, I just lost it. Carlos was standing close by the ambulance and I leaped out and charged at him, knocking him forcibly down onto the sandy beach. Gripping him by the throat, I was just about to punch his lights out when I heard Shelia's voice! Calmly she said;

"B.J, it was an accident. Please don't hurt the man. Now, let him go."

Carlos lay motionless as I looked around, but Shelia was still lying dead in the ambulance? Confused, I released my grip and stood up. Carlos scurried away saying;

"It's OK Senor; understandably, you are upset, I have brought your camera back."

Even though the rain was still heavy, a small group of onlookers had gathered. However, the police were very efficient. They had cordoned off the area and were shouting at some insensitive people who were trying to take pictures or videos. I guess if they hadn't been stopped my beautiful wife's dead body would have been paraded all over Facebook and YouTube. I just wanted to go over and punch their lights out, but then one of the police officers walked over to me and in good English said;

"Senor Jameson, this is a tragic accident, please accept my condolences. For our records, I will need some details and a statement from you. But we can do that later. They are going to take your wife away now; would you like to accompany her?"

Without even asking where they going to take her, I just nodded and he escorted me to his police car and said;

"Please get in, we will follow the ambulance."

While all that had happened seemed surreal, as I sat in the back of the police car, I could feel that Shelia was there with me and in some bizarre way, it kind of comforted me. I don't know how long this lasted but the next thing I knew was, we were at Tenerife Hospital and it was the morgue entrance! The police officer had opened my door, but as I tried to get out of the car, my legs went to jelly. He could see what was happening and helped me out and thoughtfully supported me as we walked behind the wheeled stretcher.

After that, everything was a mental blur and before I knew it, I was back in my hotel room with my new friend the police officer who somewhere along the way had picked up another police officer? Both men were sitting and drinking coffee and then in a sympathetic tone, my police officer friend asked me;

"Senor, if you're up to it, we can make a statement now."

I nodded, and then I went through the whole dreadful nightmare again. At times, I just burst into tears and had to pause, so that I could compose myself. With this latest ordeal over, the two police told me a grief therapist would be calling soon. The police officers then said their farewells, and I was left alone! Or was I?

The patio doors were open and, in the distance, I could hear people laughing and enjoying themselves. For some reason, I felt angry at them, and at the top of my voice, I yelled;

"Shut the frack up!"

It didn't help, my emotions were on a roller coaster ride and then I could not help it, I burst out crying. Above my loud sobs and my utter surprise, in one of her calm reassuring voices Shelia said to me;

"B.J, my love, I'm OK. I know you are upset, but you have to be strong."

Well, that freaked me out. I nearly jumped out of my skin! I quickly looked around the room, but Shelia wasn't there. Next, I ran out onto the balcony calling out her name, but again she wasn't there. As I re-entered the room, my doorbell rang. This got the hairs on the back of my neck to stand up. As fast as I could, I ran to the door calling;

"Shelia I'm coming."

However, as I opened the door, a man from the hotel desk greeted me with a smile. He could see the shock and disappointment on my face. He could also see from my red swollen eyes that I had been crying. Just to be careful, he stepped back a few paces and said;

"Senor Jameson, I am Pedro Iglesias, the hotel manager, please accept the condolences of all the staff and guests in the Hotel and on the island of Tenerife. If there is anything we can do to assist you, just ask and it will be done.

We have been contacted by the local and international press who wish to speak to you. I have told them you are not available for any comments at this point in time. Is that OK?"

To be quite honest, I wasn't listening to him. I had poked my head out the door and was looking up and down the corridor for Shelia? Seeing that she wasn't there, I was totally confused, I'm sure I heard her voice, or was I in shock and just imagining it? To be courteous to the manager, I just nodded and before he left, he added"

"Senor, if you need to contact anyone back in the UK, I have arranged that you can make any phone calls directly from your room free of charge. The internet is also available for you and here is the access code."

As he walked away, his last words began to sink in. I then realized with horror, that I hadn't informed anyone back home about what had happened! Oh my god! What was I going to tell my daughter's and Shelia's parents?

We both had mobile phones with us and an iPad for face time calls, so I began the arduous task of contacting our families. Under normal conditions, I am quite cool and collected, but each time the phone connected and I heard a voice, I burst into tears. I then tried face time......that was even worse! As soon as I looked at my daughters, I just broke down and sobbed! However, they did the same. In between the crying and sobbing, they said, they would fly out to Tenerife with Shelia's parents as soon as possible. As soon as we finished our face time chat, I contacted the hotel manager and asked if they had any rooms available for some of my family. He couldn't have been more helpful and said that all I needed to do was let him know their flight numbers and he would make all the arrangements for airport picks ups and hotel accommodation.

As I put the phone down, I realized that the sun had set and it was night. Feeling mentally and physically exhausted, I slumped on the bed and closed my eyes. Although I was tired, my mind wouldn't turn off and the events of the day kept repeating themselves, over and over again. Just as I drifted off, my phone rang. Instantly I was awake and then I heard it was a reporter from the Daily something! My blood boiled and I yelled down the phone 'piss off' and hung up immediately. I began to pace around the room cursing and swearing and ranting about them invading my privacy. It was then I heard Shelia clearly say;

"B.J, just calm down, they are only doing their job. Just turn off the mobile phone."

Although it was my wife talking, goosebumps covered my body and I began to tremble. Almost in the quietest of whispers, I said;

"Sheila, where are you?"

I then repeated the question. When I got no reply, I turned the hotel room light off, sat still, and slowly looked around. I don't know what I was expecting; perhaps a luminous apparition, but there was nothing. I laughed to myself and said;

"B.J you fool, you have been watching too many movies."

Once again, my emotions kicked in and I began to weep. Sobbing, I lay back on the bed and then drifted in and out of sleep. The same nightmare kept repeating itself, Shelia Parascending and being hit by lightning with me frantically swimming, but never getting close to her. As I woke up, I was covered in sweat and could see that the sun was about to rise. With a feeling of complete emptiness and an inner ache that only those who have lost someone will know, I slowly made my way into the shower room and took a shower. As the water cascaded over my body, I mentally told myself that I had to be strong. I then repeated this several times and added B.J you know Shelia would want you to be strong.

As I stepped out of the shower, I could see Shelia's toothbrush and toiletries neatly arranged by her sink. I repeated my mantra, B.J you know Shelia would want you to be strong. I then dried myself and shaved. After popping on a clean pair of pants, shorts, and a tee-shirt, I walked out onto the balcony. Instantly, my eyes were drawn to the Parascending jetty. Even at this distance, I could see several dozen candles flickering in the light breeze and lots of floral tributes placed on both sides of the jetty's walkway. Well, that was it, my lower lip began to quiver and my eyes filled with tears. To ward off the oncoming storm, I scrunched my face muscles as hard as I could and repeated my mantra, but it didn't help. In about a Nanosecond, I was crying and shaking uncontrollably.

After a few minutes, I once again composed myself and decided to phone home and see if there was any news on my family flying out to me. The first thing I found out was the whole family and a few close friends had been inundated by reporters wanting the family's reaction to the tragic accident. This made me mad, but I calmed down when my eldest daughter told me they had booked a flight and it would be landing in Tenerife at three-thirty this afternoon. She then gave me the flight number and without delay, I informed the hotel manager of this. As always, he was extremely helpful and told me he would have a car waiting outside for me at two o'clock. He then said;

"Senor Jameson, I don't think you have eaten anything since yesterday morning, so breakfast is on its way up to you."

Although I wasn't hungry, I thanked him and within a few minutes, there was a knock on the door. As I answered it, I was overwhelmed by the number of flowers that lined the hotel corridor. Tears once again filled my eyes, but to my surprise, the two young women who had brought me my breakfast rushed forward and hugged me. They then insisted in extremely good English that I go and sit down at the table while serving my breakfast to me. As I picked at the food, one young lady served me a cup of coffee and offered her condolences on the loss of my wife. I thanked her and as she walked away almost shouting, I heard Shelia say;

"B.J, you must contact the girls right away and tell them not to get on their flight today!"

The shock made me expel a mouthful of coffee all over my food and embarrassingly some also went on to the white table cloth. As the one young lady was close by, she ran over and started patting me on the back and said;

"You must drink slowly Senor Jameson, or you will choke."

After coughing a few times, I asked her;

"Did you hear that voice? That was my wife."

Smiling, shrugging her shoulders and making the sign of the cross, she replied;

"Your wife is now with the angels. Angels can only talk to one's close to them."

Unruffled by my bizarre behavior, she then proceeded to clean up my mess. Now my mind was in utter confusion. I was sure I heard what I just heard, but what the hell did Shelia mean? I am not a religious man or one that believes in ghosts, spirits, ghouls, or monsters, but this and the other vocal instances had me on edge. My body began to tremble. All I wanted to do was call out to Shelia and ask her to tell me more, but with the two women in the room, I know I would look like a right idiot.

Chapter Two, Delay

For the next ten minutes or so, the message kept repeating itself in my head. I mentally argued with myself that this was just shock, grief and I was imagining this. However, another side of me then argued what if it's for real and what could it possibly mean? The one thing I did decide was as soon as the two ladies left my room, I would phone home and even at the risk of sounding barmy, I tell my daughter about this. Before this happened, the phone in my room rang, it was the hotel manager, he said;

"I am very sorry to disturb you, Senor Jameson. We are getting reports of delayed and cancelled flights from the UK. Could you please telephone home immediately and see if it has affected your family's flights?"

Stunned with my heart pounding and hands trembling, I replied;

"Yes, yes. I will do it right away.

Within a minute or so, I was speaking to my eldest daughter again and explained what had happened. She was quite cool about her Moms voices and sympathetically said;

"Dad, you like all of us are in shock. What's happened to mom is worse than terrible."

She then began to cry and added;

"You have always been very protective of me and my sister and to be honest, I think you might just be panicking about us traveling."

Trying not to upset her more, I conceded for a moment and then asked about the flights being cancelled from the UK? Emma replied that earlier this morning she had seen on the BBC news that the Bardarbunga volcano in Iceland had kicked off again. Iceland had issued a code red and it could affect certain UK air flights. She then added that I didn't have to worry, only transatlantic flights were disrupted and she had contacted Ryan Air, and flights out of the UK to Tenerife were running on time.

Hers and Ryan Airs' reassurances didn't alleviate my concerns, so while she was talking, I had turned on my iPad and began to look up the Bardarbunga volcano. Now my skin began to crawl. Google came up with lots of instant facts like; the volcano's eruption has caused thousands of minor earthquakes deep beneath the Vatnajokull glacier. With the water and magma interaction, there will be lots of ash thrown into the atmosphere and if it gets worse, flights across Europe could be disrupted for several months.

It seems to be a family trait that both of my daughters are as stubborn as I am. Talking them out of flying out wasn't going to be easy, so I needed to put my foot down and elaborated on what Shelia said. In an uncompromising voice, I then told Emma;

"Look, my interpretation of what your mom said is, the plane is going to crash! We must heed her warning; I am not joking, none of you can get on the plane today!"

This stopped Emma in her tracks, after a few moments she replied;

"OK Dad, we cancel the flight, but we will fly out as soon as it is safe."

By now, I knew that my whole family must have thought I had totally lost it, but I didn't care. I thanked Emma, told her I loved her and her sister, and then put the phone down. Instantly, the debate began to run inside my mind, but before I knew it, I was verbally shouting and asking Shelia if I had done the right thing. However, disappointingly Shelia didn't respond.

Feeling aggravated by everything, I decided to give myself a B.J blast, that's a long run followed by some intensive gym exercise. I slipped on some trainers and headed for the beach. I only got as far as the hotel lobby and was met by an armada of journalists and photographers waiting to pounce on me. Pedro Iglesias, the hotel manager must have seen me out the corner of his eye and instantly beckoned the news-hungry fleet to his desk. Inwardly I had to smile at Pedro, he certainly knew his job. With the journalists distracted, I managed to slip by and without warming up, I ran flat out on the sandy beach until my legs gave out. My martial arts training had taught me how to make a quick recovery by doing some deep breathing exercises.

Within minutes, I was ready to continue. I pulled off my trainers and tee shirt and plunged into the refreshing sea. With each stroke, I could feel my body and mind begin to relax. Time seemed to slip by and as I exited the salty water, I realized my fingertips had gone wrinkled. Away from the shoreline, the sand was too hot, so I hastily retrieved my tee-shirt and trainers and started jogging back along the water's edge.

In the not to distance I could see someone running towards me, it was Carlos from the Parascending club? As he got closer, he started waving his arms in the air and calling;

"Detengase Senor Jameson"

I guess from his gesturing that he wanted to stop, so I halted until he came close, and then excitedly in Spanish he said;

"El Avion Tiene Estreallado!"

He must have instantly realized that I hadn't got a clue what he said, so he slowly repeated it in English;

"The airplane has crashed!"

Without warning, my legs gave way underneath me and I collapsed on the beach, I was speechless. Carlos helped me to my feet and then continued;

"Your daughter telephoned the hotel and told them. Now the airplane crash is on every news channel. Television crews have turned up at the hotel. Senor Pedro Iglesias contacted me and told me to find you and warn you of this."

Carlos could see I was in total shock and told me to sit for a while. I just nodded and sat on the wet sand. He then sat beside me and to my surprise put his right arm around my shoulder and said;

"Thank god you stopped your daughters from being on that plane."

I just looked out to sea, sighed and nodded several times, and then inquired;

"Do you know if there are any survivors?"

His right hand now patted my arm and he replied;

"It's too early to say, but Pedro Iglesias told me the news reports say all are lost!

Senor with the loss of your wife and now this, it's just too much."

Maybe Spanish men are more emotional than British guys, but then Carlos began to weep. Well, that was it for me, I couldn't help myself, I was an emotional wreck anyway and I joined in.

After a few moments, as if in agreement, we both nodded a few times, sniffed to clear our noses, and then got to our feet. Carlos then inquired;

"If you don't mind me asking, what made your daughters cancel their flights?"

Without holding back, I explained about Shelia's voices and her warning. Carlos listened intensively and then to my surprise in a very positive tone, he said;

"Senor, you are not mad. What you are hearing is your wife."

I was now puzzled, I suspected that Carlos put this down to a spiritual event, but I had to ask;

"How do you know it's my wife and not a grieving husband's wishful figment of the imagination?"

Carlos gave me one of his big Spanish toothy grins and replied;

"Let us walk back slowly and I will explain."

Chapter Three, Energia, (energy)

Although it was a calm day, Carlos paused and asked if I could see the small waves breaking. I nodded and said "Yes." He then continued;

"If those small waves were bigger, they could be used to generate electricity. In fact, in various parts of the world where the tidal flows are stronger, the tidal forces are harnessed for that purpose. Electricity is one of many forms of energy. Now, Senor Jameson, what creates the tides?

Before I could attempt to answer this, pointing to the sky, Carlos answered his own question;

"It's the moon and it does it through its gravitational pull on the earth. I'm sure you already know that gravity is one of the weakest yet most powerful forces of energy in our universe?"

I just nodded and was now a little intrigued as to where this was leading. Seeing that he had now captured my interest, Carlos then added;

"Our planet earth resides in a solar system that is controlled by a massive energy source, the sun. Further, the sun lives in a galaxy, and in that galaxy, there are billions of other stars, all churning out massive amounts of energy. If you look further out into space, there are billions and billions of other galaxies and that's one hell of a lot of energy. Now the big question is where did all this energy come from?"

The first answer that came into my mind was the big bang or string theory, but I didn't know if Carlos was religious and believed that God created everything, so I acted dumb, thrust my hand into the air, and said;

"The stage is yours, Senor Carlos, please enlighten me."

Carlos gave me another big toothy smile, patted me on the shoulder, and said;

"Senor Jameson, I think you know the answer, but I will continue. In the world of physics, one theory is all energy was created at the time of the big bang. Another newer theory, well hypotheses is something called the string theory. However, both schools of thought understand what happens to every form of energy. Let me give you a quote from Albert Einstein, 'Energy cannot be created or destroyed; it can only be changed from one form to another.' Now you might be wondering what this has to do with you hearing your wife's voice. Well, for me to continue, you must understand that this might be upsetting for you."

Carlos paused and waited for me to say something. Well, one thing was for sure, any theory that could make sense of the voices in my head was better than nothing. So, I braced myself and asked Carlos to continue;

"OK, when people pass away through illness or old age, their life's energy dissipates as their body slowly shuts down. This, however, is not true for your wife, she was fit and well and died instantly. I think when your wife was hit by the bolt of lightning; her life's energy was trapped in some kind of electrical energy field."

In some odd way, I was not shocked by Carlos's hypotheses. However, Carlos missed out on exactly how Shelia was communicating with me and that was now the least of my new worries. If Carlos was right, where exactly was Shelia's energy field? I asked Carlos this and after a moment's thought he replied;

"Senor Jameson, I'm sorry, but I have no positive answers to both questions. I can only guess that her energy is attracted to you and when you need her, she somehow breaks through her energy field and telepathically talks to you."

Carlos then began to laugh at his own words, threw his arms into the air, and added;

"Senor Jameson this sounds loco, si."

I politely smiled and replied;

"Yes, Professor Carlos, what you said does sound loco, but it's the best answer I've had so far."

We both walked in silence for a few minutes and at that time, my head was running and re-running Carlos's energy theory. I then paused and said to Carlos;

"You know Shelia was right about the airplane."

Nodding Carlos answered;

"I know that's the frightening part. Perhaps now she will be able to rest?"

I shrugged, sighed, and replied;

"That is something we will have to see."

I continued,

"It's a shame her warning couldn't have saved all the other passengers and crew."

Carlos nodded and said,

"Si, it is indeed, but what is meant to be, is meant to be."

Changing the subject, I asked Carlos how he thought I should handle the press. He answered;

"As far as I know from Pedro Iglesias, your family has declined from speaking to the press, it looks as if they are leaving that up to you. Personally, I think it would be wise not to mention your wife's voices and warnings, they will think you are loco. Just tell them that your wife's body isn't going to be released for a few days and you thought it would be better if your family came out then to accompany her back home."

Before Carlos had finished, a chill went down my spine. I hadn't thought that far forward and up until now, the thought about plans for Shelia's funeral had not entered my head. Carlos could see from my reaction that he had struck a raw nerve and said;

"Forgive me Senor Jameson; the last part was insensitive of me."

Despite my first impression, Carlos was a decent fellow. I told him that my friends called me B.J and I would prefer it if he called me that. Well, the next thing I know, he flung his arms around me and gave me a big manly hug ......I guess this is another Spanish manly thing.

As we continued to walk back, I asked Carlos how he knew so much about energy; he once again surprised me as he answered;

"Not just energy B.J, I know a great deal about physics, I have a university degree in it.

"Wow" I replied and then jokingly, I added;

"You're a lot smarter than you look."

Carlos laughed out loud and said;

23

"Si, I have heard that said many times before, mostly from the students I used to teach in Spanish academy. Now, I earn lots more money and go to work on a beautiful beach, not in a stuffy classroom."

I smiled and commented;

"You know, that's a fair trade-off, many years ago I gave up a job working in a factory as an engineer and opened my own fitness and martial arts clubs."

Carlos paused and did a Rei (bow) and with a larger than ever smile on his face he said;

"B.J, I teach Tae Kwon Do at the local sports centre and I am third Dan black belt. I take it from what you just said, you are also a (Sensei), instructor?"

It was now my turn to bow and answered;

"Yes, I am a sixth Dan Black Belt in Karate and also have black belts in Ju-Jutsu and judo. My wife Shelia was also a second Dan Karate black belt and a qualified fitness instructor."

The hotel had now come into clear view and our small talk came to an abrupt halt as dozens of reports, cameramen, and the technical bods that accompany them came running across the beach to try and get a news scoop. Carlos looked at me and said;

"Stay here B.J, I will handle this."

He then ran with his arms in the air to halt the onslaught of news teams. I could hear Carlos talking to them in Spanish and amazingly they all turned around and headed back to the hotel. When he came back, he said;

"I have just told them that you will do an orderly interview with all of them in fifteen minutes. At that time, you need to go and put on a shirt and trousers. Sadly B.J, lots of people have died on that airplane, and addressing them in shorts and a tee shirt is not respectful for the families."

Of course, Carlos was right and I thanked him for that. While I went up to my room and quickly showered and put on a shirt, trousers, a pair of socks, and shoes, Carlos said he would organize the press conference he was true to his word. He and Pedro Iglesias greeted me in the hotel reception and then ushered me into the hotel's conference room. As I entered, the room lit up with hundreds of camera flashlights. Carlos guided me to a table at the top of the room where several microphones had been attached and then he called everyone into order.

Within seconds silence filled the room and looking at all the solemn faces I began by offering my condolences to all who had died on the airplane. One of the press then told me that the flight was full and reports were coming in that there were no survivors. On hearing this I paused for a moment and said it would be appropriate if we held a minute's silence. Everyone agreed and with lowered heads, the room entered a deadly silence.

After that, the press dug in and things began to get a bit chaotic. Questions were being fired from everywhere, and truthfully, I just couldn't think of any answers. Pedro Iglesias stepped in this time and told everyone that this was an extremely difficult time for me and they needed to calm down and ask one question at a time. I thanked Pedro for his intervention and asked for the next question. A woman who was a sky news reporter stood up and said;

"Mr. Jameson, through all the commotion earlier, you may not have heard that we are all extremely sorry to hear that your wife passed away yesterday. Do you hold anyone responsible for her death?

It was a clever ploy, blindside me with an offer of condolences and then hit my grief and emotions and see what venom comes out. I took a breath and calmly replied;

"The death of my wife was a tragic accident. As you are aware, a freak storm started from nowhere and as she was Parascending, she was hit by a bolt of lightning. The odds of being hit by lightning are extremely high, I believe it could be one in three thousand over one's lifetime. So, I will repeat this again, the death of my wife was a tragic accident.

Before I answer any more questions, I would like to commend Carlos's Parascending club, the lifeboat team, paramedics, doctors, and police officers for their professionalism in handling this tragic accident."

The female reporters' claws were now out and she fired back another question;

"Come on Mr. Jameson, with a storm brewing, don't you think it was irresponsible of the Parascending club to allow your wife to go up in the first place?"

That touched a raw nerve and the only thing I could hear in the room was me taking deep breaths. I composed myself and then replied;

"Yes, I am angry and extremely upset at what happened and truthfully, I and my family want to blame someone for the death of my wife. However, we understand the meaning of the words 'tragic accident' and that what it was."

Another women reporter stood and asked;

"As you are aware Mr. Jameson, the Boeing 737 your daughters and in-laws were going to travel on tragically crashed with no survivors. Was it the risk of flying through the volcanic dust cloud that made them cancel their flights or were there other factors that you would like to share with us?"

I looked directly at the reporter and answered;

"My family cancelled their flights under my advisement. As I understand it, we cannot take my wife's body back home until the appropriate paperwork is done and transportation is arranged. It was simply luck that saved my family and nothing else."

After that, we had several rounds of 'what if' questions that I answered with almost the same answer;

"Please understand, I and my family have suffered a great loss, but we are counting our blessing that this loss was not greater still."

The press eventually got bored with this and began packing away their equipment and I was allowed to leave the conference room un-harassed. Carlos was waiting in the hotel reception and as he approached me, bowed and said;

"B.J, thank you for what you said in the press conference about my Parascending business, but you were wrong. I should have never allowed your wife to go up."

Honestly, I wish Carlos had stopped Shelia, but I remembered what Shelia said to me just after the accident;

"B.J, it was an accident."

Tears had started to form in my toothy Spanish friends' eyes and I could feel the same happening to me. Before it got embarrassing for both of us, I told Carlos what Shelia had told me. He just nodded, but I guess it's one of those decisions he would have to live with for the rest of his life. Carlos then said;

"I think is time to go and have a chat with your family, they will desperately need to talk to you about what has just happened."

Of course, he was right. I headed up to my hotel room and for the next hour or so we just talked on face time about all that had transpired. None of us had any answers as to how Shelia knew about what was going to happen, but it was just felt great knowing that her warning had kept them alive.

Chapter Four, Wake up

Within less than a minute of turning off my iPad, my mind and body felt exhausted. I flopped onto the bed and began to doze and then in less than a minute, I went into a deep peaceful sleep. My dream took me to when Shelia and I were first dating. Although she was a few years younger than me, we met in primary school; she was the sister of one of my mates. We hit it off straight away and as she was a bit of a tomboy so she started hanging out with us. It wasn't too long after that, that we had our first kiss and that was where my dream started to go crazy, everywhere went dark, then there were sudden flashes, followed by some very loud bangs?

In one almighty effort, I dragged my mind from its deep sleep and opened my eyes. That's when I realized a tremendous storm was raging outside. I jumped out of bed and ran to my patio. The skies had turned black and the rain was thundering down. Within seconds the rain turned into hailstone the size of marbles. The sound they made was deafening and then the rate they fell at intensified so hard that I decided to make a hasty retreat before I got pummelled to death.

Back in the safety of my hotel room, it was dark and yet it was only mid-afternoon. I turned on the main room light and nothing happened. I then tried all of the light switches and everything was dead. The only light on was the emergency light above the front door. After that, I then wandered out into the hotel corridor, and once again the only lights that were on were the emergency ones. The only logical explanation I could think of was the raging storm had knocked the hotel's power supply. With the power out, I used the stairs instead of the lift and proceeded down to the hotel reception area and it was in chaos. There were no lights, rainwater had flooded in and everyone was ankle-deep in muddy rainwater.

Behind the reception desk Pedro Iglesias, the hotel manager was swamped with angry guests. They were yelling that their holiday was being spoilt by having no electricity, the bad weather, floods, and lots of other inconsequential things that Pedro Iglesias had no control over. Well, I just couldn't help it, I just started to laugh. If this upsets them, they would have a triple heart attack with all that was going on with me.

To ride the storm out I popped into the gym on the first floor to do some loose weights and to my surprise, Professor Carlos was in there. He greeted me with one of his big white toothy smiles and said;

"Hola Senor, it's raining dogs and elephants outside and we have this lovely gym to ourselves."

Laughing I nodded and replied;

"Yes, it's great when you get to use a nice quiet gym. Now as to the weather, surely this cannot be the norm for this time of the year?"

Carlos moved his head from side to side and said;

"B.J, this is not the norm for any time of the year. Tenerife is known for its all-year-round clement weather. Saying that the north has more rain and can be a little cooler. But you know B.J, this is the first time that this and many other hotels in this resort's ground floors have been flooded."

To acknowledge what Carlos had said, I just nodded. But strangely, I was kind of pleased to hear that the whole resort was under a surge of rainwater and not just this hotel. Now that would have been bizarre.

Carlos and I finished our workouts in silence and then headed back to the hotel reception. It had stopped raining and a big mop-up operation was taking place. However, several male and female guests were still showing hostilities towards the hotel's staff. Pedro Iglesias the manager was doing his best to calm things down. Suddenly one big guy threw a punch and hit poor old Pedro Iglesias square on the chin and instantly knock him out.

Within a Nanosecond of this, fights broke everywhere. It was chaotic, people were now throwing heavy tables and chairs at the staff. One smashed into the large mirror at the back of the reception desk sending shards of glass everywhere. This seemed to fuel the crowd's fury and they began repeatedly kicking and punching the unconscious manager. That's when I stepped in. Well not stepped in, rushed in.

Running forward, I shoulder charged a man who was repeatedly kicking Pedro Iglesias and knock the fellow to the ground. The crowd then turned their attention to me and it was mayhem. One blow hit me so hard on the side of my face that it knocked me clean off my feet. As I staggered back on meet feet, I looked around for the culprit and realized it was a middle-aged woman who had had sucker punched me. You don't always remember the exact details of a fight but you do remember the bruises and injuries. This was one I wasn't going to forget. Taking a fighting stance, I readied myself for the next onslaught, but to my amazement, the wild crowd just stopped their frenzy. They just stood there looking confused.

Dumbfounded by what had just happened, I too took a few moments to look around. The hotel reception looked like a bomb had gone off in it. But my main concerns were for the hotel staff. Most were unconscious or possibly dead from their severe beatings. Pedro Iglesias's body was so badly beaten that his head was just brain pulp! However, I could see one young lady receptionist that was semi-conscious, she lay on the floor only yards from where I stood. So, without hesitation was I rushed over and gave her first some basic aid.

My god, she was in a very poor state. It looked like someone had slashed her throat and chest repletely with a sharp implement.

Looking at her jagged wounds I guessed a piece of glass from the broken mirror had been used. Desperately I tried to apply pressure to some of the wounds, but there were way too many. I just could not contain the bleeding. Sadly, the blood loss was too much and she died in my arms. Taking a deep breath, I looked around at the chaos and my emotions got the better of me, I began to cry.

It's strange how our minds work, I wasn't thinking about the carnage around me, it began to replay all that had happened with my beautiful wife Shelia. I then felt a strong hand on my shoulder and as I glanced around it was Carlos. His face and t-shirt were covered in blood. He too had tears in his eyes and all most whispering he inquired;

"B.J, are you alright my friend."

I looked around the hotel reception at all the carnage and answered;

"Carlos, this is a total fucking nightmare. Am I, OK, no I am not! What the hell has happened here?"

Carlos just shook his head from side to side and said;

"B. J, I have no answers. It is indeed a living nightmare."

At that, the reception lights flickered a few times and then the hotel's power came back on. I lay the dead young lady to the floor and stood up. Looking at Carlos, I asked;

"What do you think we should do now?"

With a grimace on his face he replied;

"I guess we must wait for the police to arrive. In between times, I am going to the bathroom to wash some of this blood off my face."

He then asked;

"Does my nose look out of place? I think it could be broken"

Over the years of doing martial arts I had seen lots of broken noses, so I looked closely at Carlos's nose and visually it looked OK. In my best Doctor B.J manner I told him;

"Your nose looks OK. You're still a handsome bugger."

This brought and big toothy smile to his face;

"Wow." He said. "I was worried that my good looks were destroyed. By the way, you have quite a big swelling on the side of your face. That's going to turn into one humdinger of a black eye. How did that happen?"

Truthfully in all commotion, I had forgotten about this. Then feeling the big swelling on the side of my face I replied;

"Sucker punch from a middle-aged woman who could hit harder than Mike Tyson."

Carlos frowned, paused for a moment, and said;

"My bloody nose was from a young girl who I tried to move out of dangers way. As I picked her up, she hit me as hard as any man could have."

I laughed at the thought of Carlos being punched by a little girl and replied;

"I have an idea of what might cause this superhuman strength. Adrenalin pumps through our system when we feel we are in danger. It's called a fight-or-flight response that enables your body to immediately respond to a threatening situation with a short-term burst of strenuous physical activity. As soon as the threat passes or you realize there was no real danger, everything returns to baseline within a few minutes."

Carlos took a moment to reply, obviously gathering his thoughts, and then said;

Si, what you say is plausible, but what happened here is pure evil. I'm taking Satan evil. We all imagine Satan to be the biblical devil. But Satan meaning "the enemy" or "the trouble-maker" in Hebrew can also be an earthly scoundrel."

To be honest, I wasn't sure where Carlos was going with this, but I had to agree that the event that just happened was bizarre in the extreme and things got even more bizarre. Before we could debate this anymore, a man started shouting;

"Quick everyone, Tenerife is on the BBC Worldwide News!"

Carlos, I, and everyone ran over to the now only working TV in the hotel reception area. The BBC headline was; Breaking New and the male presenter stated;

"Good afternoon I am John Claymore. The BBC new channel is receiving lots of independent reports coming in from all over the island of Tenerife that a major weather storm has hit the island and tourists have been rioting in almost every hotel on the island. We also have unconfirmed news reports that several hundred have been killed.

The storm took out all the electricity on Tenerife and also all of the telephone communications. As I speak, the authorities assure us that they are working to restore power, but say in certain areas this could take several days.

We do now have some video footage and pictures, but we have been advised by the British Government not to air these until they have been reviewed by the Spanish Authorities. Although this request is unusual, we will, of course, comply with the British Government.

What I can confirm is, the Spanish Government has declared Tenerife a state of emergency and will be seeking immediate assistance from the United Nations. They have also asked that UN troops be deployed to Tenerife to help maintain law and order.

I can also confirm that all flights in or out of Tenerife have been suspended and the airports are closed until further notice. British citizens are advised to contact the British Embassy on the following number."

While we all tried to take in what had just been reported, we all stood motionless. Then people began to react. Some cried and hugged others. A few began debates on being stuck on the island and how they were going to get back home. Others rushed off to make calls to the British Embassy and loved ones back home. But, a couple of streetwise guys began to search for the hotel's surveillance equipment. They had realized that they had just taken part in mass murder and wanted to destroy the CCTV evidence.

Carlos whispered in my ear;

B.J this is very bad, we need to get out of here right now."

Also realizing that the situation was really bad, I nodded and whispered back;

"Shall we go to my hotel room?"

Carlos returned a nod and we quickly exited. The power had gone off again, so we took the stairs to my hotel room and once inside I said;

"This is just unreal. Carlos, I know you're an intelligent man, but all these killings across Tenerife defy any logical explanation."

Looking very concerned, Carlos sat on the edge of the bed and replied;

"Si, you are right, the anger, beatings, and mob murders challenge any rational explanation. I am struggling to understand how it was only hotel staff that were attacked? And what is even more baffling is, this mayhem happened all across Tenerife? However, for the time being, I suggest we leave this up to the Spanish and UN authorities to sort out. What we need to do is look at how we are to live until law and order is restored. I see lots of initial problems. So, my English friend, we need to put together some kind of plan to get us through the forthcoming days and nights."

Carlos was right. I too could conceive all manner of difficulties that we were going to have to overcome and a plan of action was needed. I nodded my consent and then said;

"OK, the first thing I want to do is try to contact my family in England and let them know I'm fine."

Picking up his mobile phone, Carlos glanced at it and said;

"I think you will find like me that you do not have a signal."

Hell, he was right, no signal! My heart began to race. I knew as soon as my family got the knew of what had happened on Tenerife today, they would be going into a mental meltdown.

My Spanish friend could see my frustration and calmly said;

"B.J, don't worry. They will restore power soon. Your family knows you as, the fighting man. They will know you will contact them as soon as you can.

The fighting man analogy made me smile inwardly smile. The simple truth was, deep down inside I was cracking up. To Carlos and others, what they have seen on the outside was not what was going on inside me. With the tragic death of my wife and now this hotel bloodshed, my mental core had been shattered. I kind of guess that I was feeling sorry for myself, then my whole body began to shake and I just wept.

To my surprise, Carlos came and put his arms around me. In a calm voice he said;

"Over the last few days, you have gone through too much. This is not just your body telling you this, it is also your mind. Don't worry or feel embarrassed at this, it is completely natural. Grief and emotional shock manifest themselves in many ways and it will take time to come to terms with this. When you get back home you might want to consider some counselling."

Smiling, I wiped away the tears from my eyes and nodded. I knew he was right. Composing myself I said;

"OK, time to put the emotions aside, fighting man is back. Carlos, you have been a great help. Now, you need to get to go home and be with your family, they must be worried about you?"

I would not have believed this unless I had seen it first-hand. Carlos's face turned from a super Mediterranean tan to a deathly grey in a Nanosecond. His shoulder slumped forward and in a trembling voice he replied;

"I do not have any immediate family. My wife Isabella was killed in the La Rambla terrorist attack on the afternoon of 17 August 2017. She was carrying our first child at the time, so they both died."

Bloody hell, I didn't see that one coming. I had been so wrapped up in my own world that I never thought to inquire about Carlos's family. I had just assumed that when he told me of his brother-in-law Salvador, the best speed boat 'Capitan' in all of Tenerife that he was a happily married man. Oh boy, was I wrong? Looking at my Spanish friend I said;

"Oh Carlos, that's terrible. I am so sad to hear this. Please accept my sincere condolences. You must have gone through hell."

Carlos tried to smile, but a raw nerve had been triggered and I could see the sadness in his face. He looked at me and said;

"My friend, there is not one second in one day that I do not miss Isabella. To me, it was a needless act of violence, and one I cannot forgive. Both of us have suffered a great, great loss and I do appreciate your kind words. However, I was party to your wife's death and I wish with all my heart that I could undo this."

At that, the words Shelia first spoke to me popped into my head again. "B.J, it was an accident." I took a moment to reflect on this and replied to Carlos saying;

"What happened to your wife and child was a deliberate act of terrorism. And yes, I can understand that you cannot forgive this. However, the death of my wife was a freak accident. Believe me when I say this, both I and Shelia do not hold you and your brother-in-law responsible. And if it helps Carlos, we both forgive you."

Slowly I could see the colour returning to Carlos's face, he stood up and made a gesture of a martial arts bow and said;

"Thank you, my friend. Forgiveness under such hard circumstances is very difficult and I truly appreciate it."

There was one question burning in my head. I know it was going to sound strange, but I had to ask;

"After your wife died, did she communicate with you?"

Carlos sat back down on the edge of the bed, half smiled, and responded;

"To hear her voice just once again would make me very, very happy. But sadly, the answer is no. What you have experienced is special. B.J, I do not know of anyone else who has had this kind of experience."

Chapter Five, No law or order

Before I and Carlos had a chance to discuss our plan of action, the hotel's power was restored. Although our mobile telephones still did not have a signal, we were able to turn the TV on. I immediately turned it into BBC Worldwide News and the same male reporter was re-accounting what had happened and was giving some updates on the situation in Tenerife. In his normal professional tone, he added;

"We can now go live to Tenerife where our reporter Gillian Townsend can give us a first-hand report on what's happening on Tenerife."

The cameras immediately switched over to Gillian Townsend and it looked like Gillian Townsend was standing outside a large hotel. In the background, we could see the blue lights flashing on several ambulances. The Spanish police had cordoned off the area and a few fire trucks were dealing with a blaze on the second floor. Holding her microphone Gillian said;

"This is Gillian Townsend reporting for BBC Worldwide news. Today at approximately three-thirty local time, the whole of Tenerife was hit by several massive thunderstorms. Although the storms only lasted just over one hour. It is estimated that over three hundred and fifty centimetres of rain fell. This has caused widespread flooding in both homes and businesses across the island.

Electrical outages have been reported throughout the island. I am told that electricity has now been restored in the south and engineers are working on the restoration of power for the rest of the island."

The screen then switched back to John Claymore who asked;

"Gillian, what do you know of the murders that have happened across Tenerife?"

Keeping her composure Gillian answered;

"John, what I do know is as the storms raged, guests in almost every hotel across the island started to attack the hotel staff. The motive for these attacks is unknown and is being investigated by the police. That being said, an early estimate puts the death toll into a few thousand.

As you can imagine, the police in Tenerife will not be able to cope with all of these investigations Therefore the Spanish Government is bringing in police officers from the mainland. I also have unconfirmed reports that the Spanish Government is requesting assistance from the British and European Countries."

Once again, the screen switched back to John Claymore who inquired;

Gillian, I am a little confused. How does the Spanish police intend on questioning all of the suspects?

It was obvious that this was going to be a massive problem and poor Gillian hadn't got all the answers. But she replied;

"John, all I can tell you at this point in time is, the police are asking everyone to stay calm and stay in their hotels until they are contacted."

John thanked Gillian for her report and then stated a victim helpline and contact line had been set and the telephone numbers flashed up on our TV screen.

Truthfully, I found all of this difficult to take all of this in, in frustration, I looked at Carlos and said;

"Fucking hell, what a mess!"

The Spaniard moved his head from side to side and with a solemn face replied;

"B.J no swearing. Swear only when things get really bad."

Then he just burst out laughing and added;

"Yes, fucking hell, with bells on it. This is bad."

We both laughed, but that laughter was soon wiped off our faces as the next news item hit the TV screen. The title headed, Breaking News;

"Plane crash investigators rule out that Volcanic dust caused Ryan Airs' flight to Tenerife to crash."

Then John Claymore was back on the screen. He began by introducing himself and confirming that;

"Civil Aviation Authorities crash investigators have ruled out that Volcanic dust caused Ryan Airs' flight to Tenerife to crash.

Following that shock announcement, he then added;

"After retrieving the airplanes black box and analysing its data. The crash investigators have concluded that it was a massive electrical failure that caused the Boeing 737 to crash killing all one hundred and forty-three passengers.

What was even more chilling was he then went on to say;

"The cause of electrical failure has not yet been fully disclosed but the Civil Aviation Authorities and British Government are not ruling out that this could have been an act of terrorism."

Carlos and I sat in silence while we digested this information. I looked at Carlos and said;

"Do you think it could have been an electromagnetic bomb?

Shrugging his shoulders, he replied;

"Your guess is as good as mine. However, the implications of a terrorist attack on an airplane carrying holidaymakers have far-reaching consequences."

He then paused for a big breath and continued;

"B.J, if they can do this with one plane from England. What's to stop them from attacking passenger planes all over the world?

With what has just happened on Tenerife and now this. Globally, until this is sorted out, we may be looking at the end of tourism as we know it. We have only just started to get over the covid 19 pandemic. This on top of that will be an absolute financial disaster not only to Spain but also any country that depends on tourism."

We all know the expression; "things can only get better." Well in our case, that's not true. Before I could make any comments on what Carlos had just said, BBC's John Claymore said they now had an update on the situation in Tenerife.

Once again Gillian popped up on the TV screen and was still standing outside the now blazing hotel. She went through her normal BBC introductions and then stated;

"The Spanish Government has declared a state of Martial Law in Tenerife. From a legal standpoint, Martial Law may be declared in response to a crisis, and Tenerife is in a major crisis. Under Martial Law, everyone has been ordered to stay in their homes or for tourists, in their hotels. I can also confirm that an order has been put out that anyone caught looting or disobeying the rules of martial law will be shot on sight."

The screen then went back to John Claymore who asked;

"Gillian we can see that the hotel Sol Tenerife in your background is almost gutted in flames. Can we assume that the firefighter lost control of this fire and what has happened to the hotel guests?"

Gillian's composure broke down, tears weld up in her eyes, and with a trembling voice said answered;

"What you are seeing with the hotel Sol Tenerife is what has happened all over Playa De Las Americas. Looting and robberies have been going on for hours. The hotel Sol Tenerife is not the only hotel to be set on fire. We have been informed that over ninety hotels are now on fire.

John as to the hotel guests, with all the fires, most will be homeless. But I can also confirm that shootouts have been happening and several tourists and locals have been shot dead. At this point of time, I cannot confirm who shot them?"

At that, the screen switched to numerous scenes of hotels ablaze and in the background, we could hear the distinct sound of gunfire.

It was John's turn again to ask a question. However, he had realized that Gillian was more than shook up by what she has seen so he inquired first;

"Gillian we can see this new report has upset you. Are you alright to continue?"

Gillian nodded and John asked the one-million-dollar question;

Gillian, has anyone indicated why all these hotels have been set on fire?"

Gillian's face looked sombre and holding back the tears she responded;

"Oh Jonh, it is believed by the Spanish police that they have set fire to the hotels to burn the evidence of all the murders!"

This news was unbelievable. I looked at Carlos and before I could say anything, he said;

"B.J now is the right time to swear."

Chapter Six, Billy-bob clan

It was only logical after listening to the TV reports of numerous hotels being set on fire to conclude that ours might soon follow. What was even more worrying was, I was on the top floor in my executive suite. I knew it was now too risky to stay, so, I and Carlos decided for our safety we had to get out of the hotel as soon as possible.

Carlos told me that he lived on a boat that was moored in the marina at Puerto Colon and I would be welcome to stay there until I could book a flight back to the UK. Under the circumstances that sounded like a reasonable plan. Without losing any more time, I packed some essential items and then we both headed down the stairs to the reception area and the main exit. That's when we ran into the Billy-bob clan.

One of my jobs as a professional martial artist was instructing and SIA certifying doormen and women. With the odd exception to the rule, most applicants had none or very little experience in actual fighting skills. What some had going for them was, they were massive in size. And yes, this sometimes deters drunks and would be trouble makers. Others gained bulk through gym work and popping a few steroids. These gym giants thought that by flexing their bicep muscles it would stop a bottle or glass from being smashed over their or some other poor soul's head. These muscle warriors were some of the hardest to teach, but you step up a few gears and you get a Billy-bob.

Billy-bob is a name that I gave to a person who fits the profile of a shaven head, lots of tattoos, and a large beer belly. These attributes make them think that they were good street fighters and great doormen. Believe me, none of these attributes help in any defence situation. However, one must never underestimate anyone.

So, the first thing to bear in mind is, Billy-bobs are often extremely vocal and violent. And the second is, Billy-bobs attract other Billy-bobs, and we had a clan of them to face.

As I looked around the reception area, I could see six Billy-bobs, I also did not discount that there might be a few others lurking around. However, it looked like the main Billy-bob had set up a throne area by the reception area. Two were armed with baseball bats and were guarding the main hotel exit. Another two armed with what looked like meat cleavers were by the lifts. That left the kitchen knife-wielding Billy-bob who greeted us and we came down the hotel stairs.

In a Brummies' accent, stair Billy-bob called out to King Billy-bob and said;

Nevil, we've got two more mugs ere."

He then pointed his kitchen knife at us and motioned us to seek an audience with King Billy-bob. Whose girth was so big he must have struggled to fit into his throne chair. As we walk over, I could see that his arms, neck, and part of his head had an abundance of skull, bones, and other goulash tattoos. He had squeezed into some jumbo-sized jogging bottoms. But I would put some serious money on a bet that his legs and other cancelled parts of his body also had plenty of other goulash tattoos. As we got within earshot of this twenty-five stone hulk, he said;

"Right ladies, me and my lads have taken control of this hotel. Your asses are mine now. Here's what's going to happen."

Before he could say any more, Carlos interrupted and protested;

"Senor, I am Spanish and a good catholic. My ass is mine, you and your lads are not playing sexual games with my ass today or any other day."

47

Hearing this, I just couldn't help but burst out laughing. Carlos also joined in. King Billy-bob didn't find what Carlos had said one-bit funny. His face turned a fiery red and he tried to lift his massive bulk out of his throne, he roared;

"Think that's funny, do you, you Spanish bastard. You won't be laughing when I and my lads kick your asses."

Yoko Geri is a sidekick and it's one of my favourite kicks. That's what I hit King Billy-bob in the throat with. He crashed back into his throne and then he and the chair toppled backward. Seeing what just happened, the other Billy-bobs decided to rush in and help King Billy-bob. Carlos's spun around and caught one Billy-bob with a spinning roundhouse kick. I have to say his timing and accuracy were fantastic. The back of his heel hit this Billy-bob right on the side of the jaw. Instantly, several teeth flew out followed by a bucket load of blood.

When Carlos's kick landed, all the Billy-bobs backed off and simultaneously grimaced. I have never worked what stimulates anger, but seeing their buddies' teeth being knocked out did just that. At first, we both got lots of verbal threats, and to be quite honest we both just laughed at them. This only added fuel to their anger, they then started throwing a few chairs and anything else they could get their hand on at us.

We easily dodged this barrage and after a few seconds, they all realized this was futile and stopped. It was Stair Billy-bob with his kitchen knife that made the next move. Screaming obscenities, he rushed forward trying to thrust the knife into my stomach. I avoided this attack by employing a manoeuvre called Tai Sabaki. This is a way of manoeuvring the body to both avoid a strike or attack whilst at the same time positioning oneself into a position to execute a technique.

It was bad news for Stair Billy-bob. I just blended in with his attack and then applied the technique called kotegaeshi. This technique is mainly used in Ju-Jutsu and Aikido. Saying that it's such an effective technique that many other martial arts also use it. Kotegaeshi translates out as, small wrist turn. And that is exactly what you do with devastating results. For safety in practice, the attacker has to completely flip themselves over to relieve the immense pressure applied to the wrist. Now stair Billy-bob was more a practitioner of downing several pints of larger and had no martial art experience. Needless to say, with one hell of a loud crack, I broke his wrist.

Within a Nanosecond, the pain receptors in Stair Billy-bob's brain and wrist kicked in and he began screaming in pain. His fellow clan members seemed to be frozen on the spot as they looked at his limp hand that was facing the complete opposite way. One said in what I think was a deep black country accent;

"Fucking hell Baz, that looks fucking bad!

Before anyone could say or do anymore, Carlos stood in a fighting stance with his guard up and said;

"Three down, now who wants to be next? If you are smart you can put down your weapons and walk out of here. However, if you don't me and friend Bruce Lee are going kick the crap out of you."

Sadly, smart is not what a Billy-bob is about. The three Billy-bobs left were all carrying weapons and we had nothing. Psychologically to them, that gave them the upper hand. Add to that, a high dose of adrenaline, booze, a few illegal substances, and anger, and what you have is an illogical nutter.

With a lot of bravadoes, each one rushed in screaming and waving their weapons in the air. Carlos and I stood steady and just as we were about to take these crazed idiots on, I then heard the distinctive sound of gunfire. Within the blink of an eye, all three collapsed wounded or dead on the floor. Shocked by this, my first thoughts were that the police or UN troops had arrived. However, as I looked around and could see several gunmen and they were civilians.

Carlos looked at me with a serious face and in a half-whisper said;

"Don't move, just stay calm and let me handle this."

He didn't wait for my acknowledgment. Calmly he then walked over to the gunmen and in Spanish, he greeted them and spoke for a few minutes. Then he and the gunmen approach me. A tall grey-haired man armed with a machine gun greeted me saying;

"Hola Senor Jameson, please do not be alarmed. We are not here to hurt any of the hotel guests. This load of scum gang-raped the fourteen-year-old daughter of Diego, the man standing next to you. As law and order have broken down, we are here to administer justice.

What this man told me turned my stomach over. It is beyond comprehension to understand how could they do this. I looked around at the dead, dying, and injured Billy-bob clan and in disgust I said;

"Senor, had I have known about this awful rape, I would not have taken it so easy on these scum balls."

The man acknowledged with a nod and then in a sympathetic tone said;

"Senor, I have also heard of the tragic death of your wife. Please accept my and the condolences of the people of Tenerife. This Sunday we will light a candle and says prayers for her at our local church.

Oh, one other thing. I hope you and Carlos understand that what just happened and is going to happen to these thugs, never happened. Also, once we are done a clean-up crew will dispose of the bodies."

Before I or Carlos could say anything, he and his men then turned, and their attention to the surviving Billy-bobs and unmercifully began administering justice. I have to say things then got gruesome.

King Billy-bob had managed to crawl a feet meters from the toppled chair when one of the gunmen shot him in the back of his leg. King Billy-bob screamed in pain and slump face down on the floor. It was then Diego's turn. He picked up the knife that had been used to attack me and while two other Spaniards pulled down King Billy-bob's jugging bottoms. Diego hacked off King Billy-bob's cock and balls and then shot him in the back of the head!

Seeing this, stair Billy-bob tried to make a run for it. A single bullet in the centre of his back stopped him dead in his tracks and he crashed to the floor. However, unluckily for him, he was still alive. And with the look of an aggrieved father, Diego's armed with the now bloodied knife took his revenge.

The only Billy-bob left was the one that Carlos had caught with the spinning roundhouse kick. He had been unconscious for a while and as he resumed consciousness, he was in for the surprise of his life or his death. His trousers had been removed and Diego was standing over him. He looked around and could see all his Billy-bob clan dead and mutilated. Then terror set in and he began to scream;

"Jesus, Jesus help me!"

Diego made short work of the removal of his manly parts and then to my surprise Diego began interrogating the ball-less man. In broken English and anger in his voice, he asked.

"Violador, where are the other two?"

Scared shitless, the sobbing Billy-bob answered;

"Second floor, room 210."

Diego then shot the Billy-bob at point-blank range in the face and except for a tall grey-haired man armed with a machine gun, they all rushed towards the stairs. Carlos pulled on my sleeve and said;

"Come B.J, it is time to leave."

Before we could move, the tall grey-haired man armed with a machine gun said;

"The streets are not safe, for yours and Senor Jameson's safety, let my driver will take you down to the marina. Also, take these. You might need them. Dispose of them in some deep-sea when you have finished with them."

He handed Carlos his machine gun and a handgun that he had tucked into the back of his trousers. Carlos thanked him in Spanish and we made our exit towards our ride. As we walked out in low voice I said to Carlos;

"Who the hell are those guys?

Looking straight ahead, Carlos replied;

"They my friend, are known as the Islas Canarias Mafia. Or in English, the Canary Island Mafia. Many years ago, these men were the local fisherman. However, following the crippling of the Islands' fishing industry, the local fishermen began smuggling tobacco and alcohol to keep their business alive. The success of these tobacco and alcohol smuggling activities led to the creation of a clan-based group who make their entire living off smuggling.

B.J, now that business has extended not only into the drug world but anything your bank balance can afford. The gentleman who gave us the guns is Alejandro García the Mafia Boss on Tenerife."

In my time I had met quite a few people who operate on the other side of the law, so what Carlos just told me didn't surprise me. As we sat in the back of Alejandro García's white Mercedes, I asked Carlos a question that I wasn't sure he would answer. So, choosing my words carefully I inquired;

"I noticed that you seem to know this Alejandro García and his men well. How is that?"

Carlos looked at me and laughed. He then answered;

"If you want to open a new business on Tenerife you have to get approval from the local government. With that approval, you can negotiate your local tax with the man we just met. So, I pay my local taxes for my parascending business to the Islas Canarias Mafia.

For paying my taxes, I get to be the only parascending business on this beach. I and my brother-in-law make a good living out of this. So, everyone is happy."

I gave Carlos a nod and a knowing smile. Then suddenly we heard some loud, manly cries. Cringing, I suspected the cries were from the other two Billy-bobs. To my horror, my apprehension was confirmed. From our car window, we witnessed two males being thrown headfirst from a second-floor balcony. Within seconds, each hit the concrete ground with a bone-breaking thud followed by a hail of bullets. Although I was genuinely shocked, I couldn't help but look. The bodies lay bloodied, broken, and twisted. However, it was obvious that before being thrown to their deaths and repeatedly shot, both men had been de-bagged and their genitals cut off.

Without batting an eyelid our driver got out of the car, pulled out a handgun, and fired several rounds at the corpses. He then got back in the car and waved to an approaching refuged collection trunk. Carlos nudged me and, in a whisper, he said;

"I guess the clean-up team has arrived."

Chapter Seven, They all speak

It took about a fifteen-minute drive to arrive at the marina Puerto Colon. However, that fifteen minutes was extremely daunting. I could see fires raging through large hotels and adjoining buildings. Numerous shops had been looted and cars set alight. What disturbed me more was, the sound of sporadic gunfire. I was not sure if this was the local police, army, or island mafia trying to enforce control. Or even scarier, the thought that tourists had been able to get a hold of guns and were on the rampage.

I was therefore extremely relieved to see that the front of the marina was now barricaded and guarded at all angles by heavily armed Islas Canarias Mafia. As soon as they got sight of their Boss's Mercedes car, they opened the fortified barrier and our driver dropped us off in the main car park. We then headed along the jetties to Carlos's boat.

With one of his best toothy smiles, Carlos pointed to a stunning looking boat and enthusiastically said;

"This my friend is Isabella. She is fifteen-point nine-meter-long and almost five meters wide. Although she was built in nineteen ninety-two, she was refitted a few years ago for thirty thousand English pounds to a very high standard. While moored in the marina, the Isabella has a hook up for the electricity and I can connect to the marina's WIFI."

Mentally noting that Carlos had named his boat after his late wife, I could see this boat meant a lot to Carlos. So, I politely asked for permission to come on board and with an even bigger smile, Carlos saluted and welcomed me onboard. As we walked through the flybridge and went below, Carlos explained that this fine vessel was a four-eight-five president yacht, that has a master stateroom, large flybridge, and can comfortably sleep four. Looking around, I could see he wasn't joking when he said it was fitted to a very high standard. The master stateroom was fitted with dove white leather seating. A highly polished bar area with a beautiful matching dining table and six chairs, desk, and wooden flooring that you could see your face in. And to top it all, he had a man-sized flat-screen television with a state-of-the-art built-in sound system. I had to say it;

"Wow this is some boat, you live in luxury."

Carlos nodded and looking around he replied;

"Yes, my friend it is nice, but this was not what I and my wife had planned."

He paused for a moment and then continued;

"Just outside Los Cristianos, we had a nice large modern villa. This was going to be the home we were going to raise our children in. Then the tragedy happened and my heart was broken. I could not face seeing the villa again, so I lived with my brother-in-law for a while. In the end, I drew up some courage, put it on the market, and sold the villa.

Being a local, I heard the British couple who owned this boat did not want to return to the island due to worries about the covid pandemic. It worked to my advantage as they were desperate to sell. So, with a little help in the negotiations from Alejandro García, I bought it two years ago. That's when I began to re-sort my life out and started the parascending business."

After listening to what Carlos just said, I took a moment to reflect on my situation. My wife had just been killed and I too had to face life without her. I took another look around the luxurious master stateroom and holding back my tears I said;

"Luxury can't replace a loving wife."

Carlos's smile had faded. He let out a deep breath and in a low voice he muttered;

"Nothing on this earth will ever replace my Isabella or our unborn baby. I know it will be the same for your wife Shelia."

Nodding in agreement, I asked;

"You told me you once taught physics at college. I hope this question doesn't offend you, but here goes. Did you stop teaching because of the death of your wife and baby?"

Carlos let out a long sigh and answered;

"Si, your right, from the day of my wife's death, I never went back to college. Simply, I just could not look at all the young students and not think that one day one of these bright youngsters could have been one of my children."

We both slumped into a soft leather chair and sat in silence for a while. I guess my body and mind were completely fatigued. With the gentle swaying of the boat, I fell into a deep sleep. I must have slept for a few hours because when I woke up it was dark outside. Carlos was sitting at his desk and from his body language, whatever he was looking at on his laptop it was disturbing him. I stood up and walked over to where he was sitting and glanced over his shoulder. To my astonishment, his laptop screen was full of posts on several media sites. Each site had been translated into English with mainly Spanish locals reporting that their loved ones who had been killed in the recent uprisings were talking to them!

Carlos looked back at me and pointing the screen he said;

"Oh my god BJ, what happened with you and your wife has been happening to lots of people all over the island. It also appears that for the last few hours no one has had any communication with their dead loved ones. When was Shelia last in touch with you?"

I had to take a few breaths to calm myself down, this news had thrown my mind was in a turmoil. After a few moments, I answered Carlos saying;

"I think it was when Shelia told me that my daughters should not get on the flight to Tenerife. I have to say, I'm finding it hard to know what day it is. But it could have been just after breakfast time two days ago."

Instantly Carlos turned his attention to his laptop and scanned through each post. After what seems like an eternity. Carlos swivelled around, shook his head from side to side, and informed me that there was no conclusive time scale for others who had last had contact with their deceased loved one. All he could confirm was they had now stopped communicating.

I thought about this for a moment and then remembered that we had a second massive storm. Although I was grasping at straws. I then tried to gauge if this had any relevance to not hearing from Shelia and the others not hearing from their loved ones. However, this was well beyond my mental comprehension. So, I told the physics teacher about this and asked if he thought there was a possible link.

Carlos burst out laughing and through his laughter replied;

"Whatever this is, it's not in the realms of any physics I know of. All of this is absolute craziness. The laws of physics have certain rules and my friend whatever is happening isn't playing by the rules.

Tapping his stomach with both hands, he continued;

"Look B.J, I am staving. Let's have some supper and chill out for a while. The world outside will still be crazy in an hour or two's time, but you and I need to eat."

You know it's funny, I hadn't thought about food all day. But the mere mention of it sent pangs of hunger through my stomach. So, we both went to the galley, found some ready meals in the freezer, and devoured them within minutes. After our fast food meal, I asked Carlos if I could browse through the posts on these other people who had had contact with their dead loved ones. Smiling he said;

"By all means, knock yourself out. With food in my stomach, I feel heavy-eyed, so I'm off to bed. Your cabin is just down the corridor and the bed is made up for you. B.J, try not to stay up too long"

As he walked away, I wished him a good night and then went to do some internet surfing. It was heart-breaking to read each post. All of these people had just lost a loved one by acts of extreme violence. Now that alone is hard enough. But then those just passed start talking to you, and only you, their loved one is the only person who can hear them. They like me, must feel as if they are going crazy.

As I scanned through each post, I realized that what these people received was just words, no actual sentences. It was also reported that the words were extremely jumbled up. This surprised me as Shelia's messages were extremely coherent. As I looked further, I came across a name in a post I immediately recognised, it was Pedro Iglesias. My blood ran cold. This was the manager of the hotel I had witnessed being killed. His grief-stricken wife Maria had posted that he has spoken several garbled words. However, she also wrote a few things s believed he kept repeating. They were, "To Amo." That means, love you in Spanish. Bugger, those two words got to me. I had to compose myself for a while and then continued.

My next line of browsing was to do a google search and see if there had been similar events recorded. That ran up a complete blank. However, the search engine brought up several sites related to talking to the dead. I have always been a sceptic of paranormal activity. However now, I like all those others who have lost loved ones we all needed some answers. So, keeping my cynic head-on, I continued looking for conceivable answers.

One site I came across caught my attention. It gave instructions on how to speak with the dead by talking through the power of your mind. It stated, some paranormal experts believe that the ability to talk to the dead is not limited to professional mediums, but that the capability lies within anyone who can heighten his or her spiritual awareness. It may take time and practice before you can connect to a dead loved one, but it is possible according to this theory. The theory is; to quiet yourself and clear your mind as though you are preparing to meditate. Sit in a location that is silent and free from distraction. Close your eyes and empty your mind of anxiety and thought. Ask basic yes-or-no questions, and request a specific method of answering. The most common two methods of reply are knocking and flashlights.

In my martial arts training, I had done ancient meditation techniques. So, this was something I was familiar with and could do. I also believed that we had all gone well beyond the replies with knocking or flashlights. So, I relaxed in my chair, closed my eyes, and set about clearing my mind. Gradually brought my senses into "soft focus," or a state of being in which I am less aware of the physical details around me. I then tried to feel any presence, but I felt nothing. Just saying her name, mentally, I called out to Shelia, but nothing happened. Then I repeated the process several times and each time absolutely nothing happened.

Frustration soon set in and my inner calmness turned to rage, followed by lots of profanities. This wasn't working for me. Nevertheless, I wasn't going to give in. I had also read that Mediums are well versed in connecting with spirits of the dead. So, I decided to wait until morning and ask Carlos if he or any of his island contacts knew someone who was a Spiritual Medium. If he did, we could use this person to try to contact Shelia or any of the other dead victims. Then we might get some answers to all this madness.

Looking at my watch, it was now well after two in the morning. How time had flown by. I couldn't believe that I had been browsing and attempting to meditate for over three hours. Enough was enough, it was time to turn in. I had a quick wash, brushed my teeth, and as my head hit the pillow, I fell asleep.

It was the smell of bacon cooking that woke me up. Wow, I thought that smelled good. I quickly got up and went to the galley and was greeted by Carlos; With a big smile he said;

"Buenos Dias Senor Jameson. I hope you slept well. I am just cooking breakfast. I have fresh bread and eggs courtesy of Alejandro García and some bacon from the freezer. Would you like some?"

With my mouth watering, I nodded and as we ate, I told Carlos about my internet browsing and my thoughts on trying to contact a legitimate spiritual medium. He thought about this for a few moments and said being a man of science he had always dismissed such things. However, he added given the extraordinary circumstances anything was worth a shot. While I went and had a much-needed shower, Carlos made a few phone calls, and just as I was dressing, he called me and said;

"Amigo, it looks like we are going to have a visitor. It's Alejandro García and he is bringing someone with him. Now before he comes, there are a few things I need to ask you. First, do you believe in God, and second what religious faith are you?"

From Carlos's questions, I guessed the person that Alejandro García was bringing had something to do with the church. I didn't want to blow this but, in this case, I had to be honest. I walked up to where Carlos was sitting in the master stateroom, looked straight into his eyes, and told him I was a non-believer and had no religious beliefs. Carlos grinned at me and informed me he too was a non-believer. That left the question why did he ask this in the first place? However, he was already on this and proceeded to explain;

"B.J, Alejandro García is a deeply religious man. He financially supports the local catholic church and he is a very active practitioner throughout Tenerife. If we want his help, it's probably best not to mention our own disbeliefs."

I told Carlos that throughout my life I have always respected other people's religious beliefs. So, I didn't have any problem with Senor Alejandro García being a devout catholic. My answer seemed to please Carlos. Then a few minutes later an armed entourage turned up with Alejandro García. By his side was a small very attractive woman. Her clothing was elegant and I would say extremely expensive. Carlos went and greeted them and brought them into the master stateroom where I was formally introduced to Senor Alejandro García and his sister, Senora Valentina García.

We all sat down and Senor Alejandro García opened our discussion with;

"Gentlemen, since a child my sister, Valentina has had a gift of communicating with those who have passed to the spirit world. The Catholic Church, through the Holy Office, has declared it is not lawful to take part in spiritualistic communications or manifestations of any kind. Whether through a so-called medium or without one, whether hypnotism is used or not, even with the best of intentions among the participants, whether for the purpose of interrogating the souls of the departed or spiritual beings. Whether by listening to their responses or even in idle curiosity, even with the implicit or express protestation of not having anything to do with the evil spirits. All of that being said, my sister is not a heretic. Far from it, she has helped many in both the mortal and spirit world."

Valentina had dropped her head a little. Her cheeks had flushed red and I could see she was a little embarrassed at the speech her brother had just made. Raising her head, she looked at her brother and requested that she be able to talk to us. Alejandro García laughed out loud and answered;

"Little sister, when have I ever been able to keep you quiet. Pray, continue. Valentina gave a small polite smile and looking directly at me she said;

"Senor Jameson, please accept my sincere condolences on the tragic death of your wife Sheila. The passing of a loved one is heart-breaking, but I have some news for you. Please brace yourself for what I am about to tell you. Shelia and many others who died over the past few days have been in touch with me."

Well, that was one hell of a bit of news. To say the least, I was gobsmacked. However, before I could reply. Senora Valentina put her hand up to stop me and continued;

"I can see from the look on your face that this was something you were not expecting. However, Senor Jameson, brace yourself again as I need to tell you more. Shelia and many others are not in the spirit world. They all seem to be held in some energy field or plane of existence that I have no knowledge of."

Once again, Senora Valentina gave a polite smile and invited Carlos and me to ask some questions. I jumped in first asking;

"Senora Valentina, I have a few questions. The first is what exactly did Shelia say to you? Second, could you also re-count what the others are saying? And finally, you say they are not in the spirit world. I have no understanding of what the spirit world would be like. So, could you explain how you know that they are somewhere else?"

Without hesitation Senora Valentina replied;

"These are all the questions I would ask. Therefore, I will answer them in the order you asked them in. Your wife told me when she first passed over, she was alone in a vast space. Then others came and now she feels crowded. Senor Jameson, Shelia keeps trying to contact you, but she says there are too many.

When we talk of others who have passed away through the violence in Tenerife, we are talking about a few thousand. They are all trapped and confused. So, the messages I get from them are no more than a few words. All they want is to do at this stage is to contact their loved ones and tell them that they love them.

As to explaining the spirit world from our own existence. Since I was a child, it is all I have known. What is commonly called death does not destroy the body. It only causes a separation of spirit and body. The principle of life, inherent in the native elements, of which the body is composed, still continues.

In the spirit world, people still have bodies. These bodies are not biological like ours, they are made of their inner spirit. Or another way of looking at it is, their new bodies are made from their previous existence energy. Their lives have structure and they enjoy community life. Also, they are surrounded by landscapes that are like those on Earth. However, things work very differently in spiritual reality. Everything there is vivid and much more alive. What they see responds to what they are thinking.

When I am in contact with the spirit world, I see them as real people with all of the same features as a living breathing person, but they have passed on. From my experience, their appearance never changes. It's as if they are frozen in everlasting time. Simply, those in the spirit world are just normal people that have moved onto another realm of existence."

Chapter Eight, S.T.O.P

After Senora Valentina finished her explanations on the spirit world, she invited Carlos to ask some questions. However, he surprised all of us by graciously declining this. He said he had noted all that had been said and had a few thoughts of his own that he would like to share with us. We sat in silence as Carlos spoke;

"I think we can all agree that what has happened on Tenerife is something we as yet have no explanation of. I do however have a few theories that I would like to share with you and ask that what I am about to say is received with an open mind. Also, these theories will take some time to explain, therefore I would ask for your patience while I talk you through them."

Carlos waited until we all approve and then continued;

"I have to say, the events that have transpired over the last week or so have been extraordinary. We could discount the freak storms as just an anomaly that mother nature throws up every so often. However, governmental and commercial weather manipulation had been taking place globally for well over half a century.

One method is cloud seeding. Cloud seeding started in 1946 by Doctor Vincent J. Schaefer. The method commonly used sprays clouds with chemicals. The most common chemicals used for cloud seeding include silver iodide, potassium iodide, and dry ice (solid carbon dioxide). Liquid propane has also been used, which expands into a gas. They all work to promote rainfall by inducing nucleation – what little water

is in the air condenses around the newly introduced particles
and crystallises to form ice

Problems with these seeding methods have been reported as
early as the nineteen fifties when the British government set up
Project Cumulus initiative to investigate weather manipulation,
in particular through cloud seeding experiments. In August
nineteen fifty-two a severe flood occurred in the town of
Lynmouth in North Devon, England. Nine inches (two hundred
and twenty-nine millimetres) of rain fell within twenty-four
hours. Ninety million tonnes of water swept down the narrow
valley into Lynmouth and the East Lyn River rose rapidly and
burst its banks. If I recall correctly, thirty-five people died and
numerous buildings and bridges were seriously damaged.

Then there are concerns about altering the weather. Through
the process of cloud seeding, moisture is taken from the air,
therefore, removing potential rain that would have fallen in
another region. While some areas can be relieved of drought
others can be deprived of the much-needed rainfall.

We also have some serious worries about how cloud seeding
affects the environment. To try to alleviate these fears, the US
Public Health Service claims there is a negligible environmental
impact of cloud seeding. That said, silver iodide, when studied
in labs, is a different story altogether and is indeed toxic and
dangerous. This same study says that silver is not known to be
carcinogenic to humans.

Weather control can also be used in warfare. Before the
Environmental Modification Convention signed in Geneva
in nineteen ninety-seven, the United States used weather
warfare in the Vietnam War. Under the auspices of the Air
Weather Service, the United States' Operation Popeye used
cloud seeding over the Ho Chi Minh trail, increasing rainfall
by an estimated thirty percent during nineteen sixty-seven and
nineteen sixty-eight. It was hoped that the increased rainfall
would reduce the rate of infiltration down the trail.

It is also interesting to note that the USSR was also claimed to have flown cloud seeding missions in an attempt to create rain clouds to protect Moscow from radioactive fallout from the Chernobyl nuclear disaster. More recently, the Russian Air force has also been reported to have used bags of cement to seed clouds. In China before the two thousand and eight Olympic Games in Beijing, the Chinese authorities used aircraft and rockets to release chemicals into the atmosphere. Other countries have been reported to be experimenting with cloud seeding to prevent flooding or smog.

While I have painted a bad picture of cloud seeding, it can also be argued that this weather altering is a good thing. In Colorado America, they want to increase snowmelt into the Colorado River. This river sustains over 30 million people across the Southwest. Currently, most of the river basin is experiencing a drought. To combat this, more than a hundred cloud seeding machines are set up in mountainside backyards, fields, and meadows. The U.A.E has a cloud seeding program that according to reports has been very successful. They have had a marginal yield of more water for crops. A boost to water wells. And another advantage is that seeding is significantly cheaper than desalination, I believe it's about 60 times cheaper.

I now want to familiarise you with another form of atmospheric control technology that has been around since before the nineteen nineties. It is called, High-Frequency Active Auroral Research Program or HAARP. The HAARP research program is jointly funded by the U.S Air Force, the U.S Navy, the University of Alaska Fairbanks, and the Defence Advanced Research Projects Agency (DARPA). I also believe funding has come in from several other sources.

The HAARP project directs a 3.6 MW signal, in the 2.8– 10 MHz region of the HF (high-frequency) band, into the ionosphere. The signal may be pulsed or continuous.

Effects of the transmission and any recovery period can be examined using associated instrumentation, including VHF and UHF radars, HF receivers, and optical cameras. This will advance the study of basic natural processes that occur in the ionosphere under the natural but much stronger influence of solar interaction. HAARP also enables studies of how the natural ionosphere affects radio signals.

HAARP is the subject of numerous conspiracy theories. Various individuals have speculated about the hidden motivations and capabilities of the project. For example, the deployment of HAARP as a military Electromagnetic weapon that packs an invisible wallop hundreds of times more powerful than the electrical current in a lightning bolt.

I have also read conspiracy theories that HAARP has the capability of triggering floods, hurricanes, droughts, and earthquakes. Over time, HAARP has been blamed for generating such catastrophes as well as, thunderstorms in Iran, Pakistan, Haiti, Turkey, Greece, and the Philippines. HAARP has also been blamed for major power outages and the downing of TWA Flight 800.

Nowadays, the U.S is not the only country to have HAARP technology. All the big players Russia, China, the U.K, India, Japan and so on all have some kind of HAARP technology. Modern technology allows us to geo-engineer different aspects of the environment. They are now looking at building an artificial mountain in Dubai to promote rain. New weather control technology includes space satellites, microwaves, and lasers technology. The technique of using lasers works is based on ultra-fast, ultra-short laser pulses, which generate intense lasers that are low-energy as the pulse is very short. This results in cooling things down rather than heating them. The process forms clouds and can even trigger lightning."

As soon as the last few words left Carlos's mouth, he instantly knew that this struck a very soar nerve with me. He immediately paused and looking at me said;

"I'm so sorry my friend, I got a little carried away with all my data. It was insensitive of me to remark on the lightning. Please accept my apologies."

Taking a deep breath, I replied;

"Carlos, thank you for your concern, but please do not pull any punches on my behalf. I, Shelia, and all those killed and their loved ones want, no need answers to this madness. So, when you are ready, please continue."

Carlos, being Carlos stood up, came over and hugged me. Now standing, he looked at each of us, sighed, and continued;

"For my theory to have any logical foundation, we have to look at the facts. The storms that hit our island are unparalleled to others we have historically had. They were so powerful that they took out the power of the whole island and disrupted all of the mobile phone networks. Lightning struck and killed Mrs. Jameson. Tourists for no apparent reason began attacking and killing hotel staff. Anarchy is now widespread on the island and a state of emergency has been declared.

All of this is not a coincidence. My theory is that we are part of some governmental, terrorist, or criminal intricate test program. This test program is to see how easy it is to completely destabilize a large populated area and Tenerife was its first candidate.

I would also like to stress that advanced weather control technology is not the only weapon technology being used. Looking at all the killings that have taken place all over Tenerife, I believe another kind of weapon technology has also developed, possibly a HAARP weapon. This high-tech weapon somehow works in conjunction with the storms. What is terrifying is, this weapon targets the human brain. Although I don't have all the data and therefore am speculating. I think, through the storm's electromagnetic activity, the human brain's neurological pathways are being temporally disrupted. The neurological disruption manipulates the victim's brain in such a way that they can be made to attack a particular race, group, or even workforce. In this case, it was the Spanish hotel staff.

Now, as to the dead talking and being trapped in an unknown place. For some reason, their life's energy seems to have been captured and stored. The technology to do this is beyond anything I know of. As to the purpose of this, again I do not know. Saying that I would guess that HAARP, weather control, storms, lightning, neural pathway manipulation, and spirit capturing are all tied together.

At that, Carlos did a small martial art type bow, sat down, and invited us to either ask questions or discuss his theories.

It was Senor Alejandro García, who kicked things off by first blessing himself and then addressing Carlos;

"You are a well-educated man and I thank you for what you have just spoken about. It has given this small gathering a better technical understanding of what could have possibly have happened on Tenerife. This new chaos we see around us now will take a long time to sort out, possibly longer than the Covid pandemic. I Alejandro García, will help wherever I can to protect our local people. As the future of our tourist trade, well it is hardly back on its feet, but with this now, it's devastating. I believe it could be talking many, many years before that picks up again.

Now, looking at a much bigger picture, I shudder to think of the mayhem this would have if big countries like Spain,

England, or the United States of America were targeted with this technology. While Tenerife has lost several thousand lives, on a bigger scale, we could be talking millions if not billions. Adolf Hitler killed around two-thirds of the Jewish population of Europe. Just imagine what he could have done if he had had this technology?"

Alejandro García then paused and took out his mobile phone. He pointed it at each of us and commented;

"What you now see is a modern communications device. It has many remarkable features. As well as a telephone and link to the internet. This small device is a camera, video and sound recorder, radio, sat-nav, and storage device for your contacts, files, photos, films, games, and books. All of these are very useful for modern-day mankind. Disrupting mother nature's weather, using weapons to alter brain patterns, and killing thousands of innocent people is the complete opposite. It goes against any humanitarian ideology or religious belief.

However, Carlos did miss a few things globally that may have some relevance to HAARP and storm activity. Russia has recently been invaded by a plague of insects dubbed as a mosquito Apocalypse. Roads in the port city of Taganrog on the Azov Sea were covered an inch deep by the creatures.

Also, it has been reported that in numerous places around the planet that large flocks of birds have fallen dead from the sky unexplainably. Some scientists and ornithological specialists theorize that a turbulent thunderstorm may have been the source, flinging the birds into the air, disorienting them, and then chilling them enough to cause the birds to expire.

Although I am a religious man, I am not swayed by other's who strongly believe that all that is happening is a sign of what Jesus said in Luke 21:10,11. I quote; "Then said he unto them, Nation shall rise against nation, and kingdom against kingdom: And great earthquakes shall be in diverse places, and famines, and pestilences; and fearful sights great signs shall there be from heaven."

What's happening now is not the will of God. It is the will of evil men and women. You could even say it is the work of the devil. However, we look at it, it has to be stopped. I have wealth, resources, and influence and will put these at your deposal. I would ask if you will join me in a quest to defeat this evil."

Inwardly, I had to laugh to myself. If I were not sitting here amid unexplainable chaos with a dead wife, I would swear this was the plot and script for an elaborate disaster movie. Looking at Alejandro García I said;

"Senor Alejandro García, our army is only four, how can we fight against an unknown force with unknown resources.?"

It was the first time I had seen Senor Alejandro García smile. He replied;

"Senor Jameson, the fight against this has already begun. The eyes of every government around the world are looking at Tenerife. They will have already begun to analyse what has happened and realize that an act of terrorism like this could soon be targeted at them.

However, knowing that they were involved in certain aspects of this, like HAARP weather and mind control research. They will also do their utmost to conceal the truth not just from us, but also from other governments. Now, taking this to the extreme. Imagine that Spain found out that Russia, China, or the U.S technology was used in this attack on Tenerife. Realistically this could lead to world war three and that is not good for any species on this planet.

What is needed is good solid information to pressurize these governments into being transparent and to act in the interests of the populace now. And that is where we come in. Our army will be vast, millions if not billions will enlist. All we have to do is recruit them. And I have some ideas on how to do this. First, we need to set up a website. Next, we open YouTube, Facebook, Tik Tok, Twitter accounts, and any other social networking accounts that get us noticed. After that, we collate trustworthy information and then post it. The next step will be contacting the world press and media for an exposé. All of this needs to be done quickly so, the time scale I am putting on all this is only days, not weeks, months, or years."

Wow, that gave us a lot to think about, or that's what I thought. I was going to suggest that we have a coffee break to reflect on all that had been said. However, what Senor Alejandro García had said certainly fired Carlos up. Within a few seconds was back on his feet and then he began to build on Senor Alejandro García plans by adding;

"Yes, yes, all of this could work. The creation of a website is easy and so is opening many social networking accounts. YouTube now has lots of competition from sites like Vimeo, Metacafe, Veoh, The Internet Archive, Crackle, Screen Junkies, Myspace, The Open Video Project, and many more. For maximum exposure, I think we should target them all.

Next, our campaign needs a name that will immediately identify us and our objectives. How does S.T.O.P sound? It stands for, Stop Terrorising Our Planet."

Well that brought a smile to all our faces and we had to agree, the small punchy name S.T.O.P was very fitting. By now, Carlos was on a roll and he had us designing a logo and composing a mission statement for S.T.O.P. So, without any votes and just by sheer enthusiasm, our army of four was borne and our S.T.O.P. battle began.

Chapter Nine, Red Flag

Within a few hours of some heavy keyboard bashing, Carlos had set up a rather nice-looking website. To complement this, he had added links to our YouTube, Facebook, and Twitter accounts and several other social networking sites. Senor Alejandro García had been busy too. His men were spread-out all-around Tenerife and he got them to send videos of the mayhem that was happening all around the island.

Thanks to Senor Alejandro García, Carlos was able to download some rather expensive video editing software. After familiarising himself with it, he began the task of editing all the video footage. However, the most difficult part was editing out any scenes where "local mafia justice" was been applied. For narration, Carlos used Senora Valentina's voice.

While all of this was going on, I had time to contact the British Embassy Helpline. That task alone was infuriating. Twice, I was put on hold for over three-quarters of an hour and then without warning completely cut off! On the third occasion and after only another half-hours wait, I finely spoke with someone, who in turn passed me on to another person. The person introduced herself as Theresa Tarragon-Jones and said she was an attaché for the British Embassy. Ms. Jones informed me that the Embassy had already got all the details of my wife's death and could do nothing until the airports were re-opened and martial law had been lifted. She then added that my travel company or airline would then possibly be the first to contact me. When I asked for a time scale for this, she told me that it could be anything from a few days to several weeks.

When I asked what I should do in-between time, laughingly Ms. Theresa Tarragon-Jones just told me to keep my passport safe, stay at the hotel and someone would get in touch with me. With a little sarcasm in my voice, I asked her if she was aware that hundreds of hotels had been set on fire and were un-habitable. Others I stated are now being controlled by British, European tourist thugs. There is no food or water and rape, robbery, and pillaging are widespread. Calmly and I guess from the comfort of her office in Westminster she said; "Mr. Jameson you are not the only British person who is stranded on the holiday island of Tenerife. As I said before, stay in your hotel and you will be contacted." At that, she hung up the phone!

I was fuming, I tried to visualize what Ms. Theresa Tarragon-Jones would be doing right now if she was in any of the Brit's situations on Tenerife. I bloody know she or anyone else just would not be sitting calmly in their hotel room. Because of the fires at the hotels, thousands of families were now forced to live on the streets without any food, water, or sanitation. And as for those who were lucky to still have a roof over their heads, they would be under constant attack from the hotel bullies and the now desperate homeless who needed shelter.

My irritation turned to anger and I thought about the blasé way Ms. Theresa Tarragon-Jones said it could be a few days or it could be several weeks before we could be contacted. When a disaster or famine happens anywhere else in the world the British government spends millions in aid. The Red Cross and relief aid workers are mobilized immediately. So, what the fuck has happened now? British people need emergency rations and shelters now. By now, my blood was now at boiling point.

Then I felt a gentle hand on my shoulder, it was Senora Valentina. She inquired;

"Senor Jameson you seem a little agitated, are you OK?"

Shaking my head, I answered;

"Not really. I have just been in contact with the British Embassy and they were no help. I have no idea when I can take my wife home to bury her."

To my surprise, her eyes filled with tears and she said;

"Yes, I can feel your anguish. Shelia says she is sad too. Senor Jameson, she is only sad because you are sad. She wants you to know that burying her body is not that important. What is important to her is that you and your family love her. She also says she wants you B.J to find a way to free her and the others trapped in this strange place."

For some odd reason, I did not find it strange to hear Shelia talking through Senora Valentina. Trying my best to hide my emotions, I asked her;

"Would you let Shelia know that I love her with all my heart? And the girls love her and miss her terribly. Please also tell her that I will do everything within my power to help get her free from where she and the others are."

Smiling, Senora Valentina nodded and said that my words had made Shelia happy. She then added;

"Come BJ, it's time to eat and my brother has got a local restaurant to cook us some good Indian food. They will be delivering it in a few minutes."

Wow, that was a surprise, I love Indian food. My new Mafia friend was full of surprises. I would have put him down as a traditional Paella guy, but a hearty curry was just what I needed.

It was kind of funny to see a take away being delivered by an armed guard. However, the Indian meal was fantastic and so was the company. We chatted and laughed as if there was nothing wrong outside. When we finished our meal, except Carlos, we all helped clear the dishes away. Carlos had headed for his computer to see if any traffic had come our way and oh boy was, he in for a surprise. Each social media channel had gone berserk, we had, had thousands of hits, comments, and friend requests. However, one had red-flagged him and he called us all over to see what had been sent. The information had been sent by Anonymous and read:

Because of what you want to achieve. The following is information is something you might want to add to your website and social media sites.

Sea-Based X Band Radar-1 or SBX-1 as it is known is the U.S. Government naval vessel, that is capable of traveling 8 knots under its own power. This naval vessel measures 240 feet wide, 390 feet long, and 280 feet high from its keel to the top of the radar dome. According to the U.S government, its prime purpose is for communications and radar missile defence. Its GPS satellites can detect actual missile launches. This, however, is not the true nature of this vessel. It has the capability of introducing earthquakes, weather warfare, and Psychotronic and Electromagnetic Weapons.

Earthquakes.

The earthquake in China on May 12, 2010, devastated the surrounding property and killed more than 90,000 people. The Chinese government blamed the American HAARP program for the earthquake but so far has not taken any retaliatory steps against the U.S. There have been discussions between Russia and China about what to do against such a weapon for which at that time, they had no defence. Now, they too, and many other countries have their own land, sea, air, and orbiting satellite HAARP and electromagnetic weapons program.

Although it has been denied, it is possible that the earthquake in Haiti in January two thousand and ten, the earthquakes in Chile February and March two thousand and ten, the March two thousand and ten earthquake in Taiwan, and the February two thousand and eleven earthquakes in New Zealand were also caused by HAARP.

HAARP has also been associated with the two thousand and eleven earthquakes off the Pacific coast of Tōhoku and the following tsunami. The earthquake and tsunami caused extensive and severe structural damage in north-eastern Japan. The most extensive being, the level 7 meltdowns at three reactors in the Fukushima Daiichi Nuclear Power Plant complex, and the associated evacuation zones affecting hundreds of thousands of residents. Many electrical generators were taken down, and at least three nuclear reactors suffered explosions due to hydrogen gas that had built up within their outer containment buildings after cooling system failure resulting from the loss of electrical power.

In January two thousand and seventeen the SBX-1 was deployed into the Pacific during North Korean threats of ICBM and nuclear attacks on other nations. Since that time, North Korea has entered into talks to discontinue its nuclear program.

Indonesia has spent millions on disaster preparedness since a massive earthquake and tsunami in December two thousand and four. However, all of this failed. On September twenty-eighth, two thousand and eighteen after six p.m. with a magnitude seven-point five slip-strike quake-hit Palu, Indonesia, and its surrounding islands followed by a tsunami with waves as high as twenty feet. Strangely, dozens of buoys in the Java Sea were broken, damaged, or stolen. Others that functioned were not at the right spot and estimated the tsunami risk inaccurately.

Psychotronic and Electromagnetic Weapons.

The electromagnetic weapons target the mind waves creating messages for the application of thought control at a double input of 3k-4k hertz along with with15k hertz frequencies; as well the promulgation of tinnitus thus disturbing the eardrum using frequencies between (100 Hz– 11000 Hz) as a stressor.

Electronic warfare is defined as any military action involving the use of electromagnetic and directed energy to control the electromagnetic spectrum to attack the enemy. The Navy calls this "electromagnetic battle management". Who would that enemy combatant be; a person or persons that is seen as so seemingly dangerous or threatening to the power structure? That enemy would be you and I.

This classified technology has been created by governments and the military and used on its own citizens. Helpless citizens who have been victimized by **billion-dollar** government-funded technology designed for quiet wars, to create harm. What the powers that be are looking for are responses, which they can track, measure, and log. This in effect, is an omnipresent electromagnetic gulag in the privacy of your own home, workplace, or streets.

Psychotronic weapons can cause a person to hear words in their head, cause mental and physical illness, or even end his or her life.

Ultra-sonic weapons.

There are two ways of weaponizing ultrasonic sound waves. The first involves heating up cells in the body, causing damage, while the second is via a process known as cavitation, whereby bubbles form in the body, much like a deep-sea diver experiences when he returns to the surface too rapidly and suffers the bends. In two thousand and eighteen reports of ultra-sonic attacks were made on senior officials in China, and previously in Cuba.

I will post more soon. Good luck in your quest. Anonymous.

At that, the post ended. The first question that came into my mind was, is this just some crazy conspiracy theorist who has joined some dots together to paint his or her own doom and gloom picture. Well with all that had happened on Tenerife, I for one was on the side of believing this.

Carlos stated that this was good additional information and with our agreement, would add it to all our internet sites. With the normal nod of our heads, we all happily consented to this. However, Senor Alejandro García did not look happy. It was apparent he had something to say and it was his sister who invited him to speak up. Holding his hands together as if to pray he began;

> "I have a confession to make to you. Since I was a young child, I have lived my life in a nice safe bubble. Year in year out, I hear of these global disasters on the news and my heart goes out to all those poor people. But other than lighting a few candles and saying a few prayers, I have done absolutely nothing. How could I have been so naïve not to have noticed that HAARP and all of the other terrible things had been going on?

Senor Alejandro García was, of course, right, but he wasn't the only one who had been we had naïve. With a few exceptions, I think most common folk on this planet had also been extremely naïve and deliberately deceived by the powers to be.

We then began a discussion on the mobility of a HAARP-type weapon and wondered if their massive sizes could be reduced to make them portable in smaller sailing vessels, vehicles, trains, or airplanes? We knew of Airborne Warning and Control System, a mobile, long-range radar surveillance and control centre for air defence. But, could it be used as a mini HAARP? The only problem we could see was they and all the HAARP devices needed enormous amounts of power. However, we did note that all the power went out on Tenerife when we had the storm and wondered if this was connected? That certainly gave us something to think about.

The discussion then moved on to electromagnetic weapons and other mind control weaponry. Our main concern was on the hotel staff are the prime target. We as laymen could only speculate on how this was done. So, we guessed that each tourist's brain's synaptic pathway must have been hit with mind waves creating a message that drove them into a frenzied attack. I restated that this attack could have just a trial and now it had been proven, more attacks were likely.

As I looked at Carlos, I could see his thoughts were elsewhere. So, I asked;

"Are you OK, you seem worried?"

Frowning and giving a half-smile. Well perhaps it was a grimace, he replied;

"Oh, with this massive internet response, I am just trying to think how we are going to analyse all the data we get, reply to all these thousands of comments and accept all friend requests. I only have one laptop and it will take us days, if not a few weeks to answer each one."

However, on hearing this, Senor Alejandro García came to the rescue saying;

"That my friend is not a problem, I have a warehouse full of boxed, brand-new state-of-the-art computers, printers, mobile phones, and other office essentials. To compliment all of this, I have some office space and many able-bodied people who will be happy to help. Just let me know what you need and I will get it for you."

Now with a big smile on his face, Carlos thanked him and said he would make a list up. Carlos then added, that given all the chaos that was happening outside the marina, he thought it would be safer for the two of us to continue working from his boat. In light of this, he asked if we could have two laptop computers and a printer. Without hesitation, Senor Alejandro García graciously agreed. We all then spent another hour or so of reading through the internet messages and posts. Finally, with bleary eyes, we all agreed we were feeling exhausted and it was time to call it a day. Senor Alejandro García and his sister said their farewells saying they would be back tomorrow, refreshed and ready to start again.

Chapter Ten, Geo-what?

Soon after the García's left, I and Carlos hit the sack. Although I went to sleep quickly, it wasn't soon before I was wide awake again in a lather of sweat. I'd been having a nightmare about rescuing Shelia. Although I could not recall the whole nightmare. The bits I do remember are being chased by some freakish ghouls down long, endless corridors and hearing Shelia constantly calling for help. After that, it took me a while to go back to sleep, and then bugger me, I had the same bloody nightmare. This happened four times that night. So, at just after six-thirty in the morning, when the extremely cheery Carlos came knocking on my cabin door, calling, wakey, wakey, rise and shine, the García's are coming for breakfast. It wasn't what I wanted to hear.

Now, when I say breakfast, the García's brought their own cook. While we drank fresh ground coffee, unpacked and set up, not just two, but four new laptops. Paula the cook, rustled up a scrumptious breakfast with all kinds of cereals, croissants, eggs cooked any way you wanted them, British sausages, bacon, hash browns, baked beans, tomatoes, and beautiful fresh bread, toasted to perfection and loads of fresh fruit and juice. After this, with my lack of sleep, I was ready for a nap. But overnight our website and social media sites had all gone bonkers. So, with our new laptops all fired up, we began analysing and replying to the thousands of posts.

Although we all thought it, it was Senor Alejandro García who stated;

"Why do you get so many idiots posting absolute rubbish? It is obvious that these people have never been affected by a disaster. Are their lives so dull that all they do is write garbage?"

Well, I could not tell how many stupid irrelevant posts or comments I had had. But, for every one bad one I had, I then nine or ten more than either gave support, information, or told their own sad, sad disaster experience and then shared their thoughts on Mind, Storm, and earthquake manipulation.

Some of our posties attached files, links to other sites, and lots of photographs. While each one had some relevance, a pattern was beginning to emerge in some of the photographs. They were all showing the sky with what looked like lots of grid-like airplane vapor trails in them. A little further investigation told me these were Chemtrails (short for "chemical trails"). My investigations then lead me to several sky-watch internet sites and Oh boy, I had just found another form of geoengineering that had possible links in with HAARP technology.

Reading further into this revealed that Chemtrails are used officially used to help with global warming. However, it was the "unofficial version" that I was interested in. In this form, they are used to enhance the atmosphere by spraying chemicals that create an atmosphere that will support electromagnetic waves, ground-based, electromagnetic field oscillators called gyrotrons, and ionospheric heaters. Particulates make directed energy weapons work better. It has to do with "steady state" and particle density for plasma beam propagation.

Now, I have to admit, while I grasped the basic idea behind this, the science was too much for me. So, I thought this should be handled by Carlos. He smiled and told me that he had already heard of chemtrails. But he admitted that this link to making energy weapons work better was new to him. While we were discussing this, the García's joined in and they raised three valid, but complicated questions. The first was, irrespective of what they are being used for, what chemicals were being used? Secondly, are these chemicals harmful to humans, birds, insects, and livestock. And finally, as they fall to the ground in rain, did these chemicals contaminate the ground and water?

It didn't take much digging to find the answer to question number one. Our jaws dropped when we read the following toxic list; Aluminium, Barium, cadmium, nickel, mold spores, yellow fungal mycotoxins, viruses, strontium 90, Chaff, that is Mylar fibres (like in fiberglass) coated with aluminium, desiccated blood cells, plastic, and paper. And the best — radioactive thorium. However, the one chemical that is being used the most is aluminium. To chemtrail, the sky's a spray system is used from Boeing C-17 Globemaster aircraft and specially modified Boeing 707 aircraft. We guessed that other aircraft could also be specially modified and used. And we did not rule out the use of high-tech drones.

As to the health risks, what goes up, must come down and it looks as if we're being bombarded daily with all kinds of nasty chemicals and radioactive fallout. It also seems that certain chemicals produce comparable symptoms. Common symptoms of barium and other chemical poisoning include Muscle weakness and tremors, difficulty in breathing, stomach irritations, anxiety, cardiac irregularities, and paralysis.

Aluminium can also cause all sorts of undesirable health problems. This chemical primarily attacks the central nervous system and can cause everything from disturbed sleep, nervousness, memory loss, headaches, and emotional instability. Now if you throw in some fungal forms, things get nasty. According to Polymer research chemists who have studied atmospheric polymers for years. They have identified microscopic polymers comprised of genetically-engineered fungal forms mutated with viruses, which are now part of the air we breathe. Now according to my philosophy, the only thing we should be having in our lungs is good fresh air. So, genetically-engineered fungal forms mutated with viruses don't sound good.

Now things get really serious with radioactive Thorium. This can be stored in our bones. Because of these facts, it can cause bone cancer many years after the exposure has taken place. Breathing in massive amounts of thorium may be lethal. People will often die of metal poisoning when massive exposure takes place.

We then read the effects chemtrails have on the environment. And things just did not get any better. From what we could see, most major countries around the world had some sort of chemtrail program. This alone had led to major complaints about reduced or dangerous air quality. Complaint lobbyists also attributed the deaths of thousands of birds who globally just fall from the skies after flying through dense chemtrails.

In many remote areas, wildlife biologists and water specialists have reported elevated levels of aluminium, barium, and strontium in the mountain's snow, polluting drinking water, rivers, and soil. Now, all of this can't be good for humans, fish, livestock, crops, tree's, plants, or living thing on our planet. However, to our surprise, we could not find any large-scale environmental studies done on chemtrails in densely populated areas. Perhaps this was because, in heavily populated areas like those close to cities or airports, chemtrails are thought to be just airplane vapor trails?

We had now spent well over two hours investigating the environmental issues of chemtrails and Carlos thought that we should get back on track looking at chemtrails as a weapon support system. To be true it was a fair point. So, as a group, we decided to try to get a hold of any pictures of the sky over Tenerife. Our priority was just before the storm that killed my wife but, we also wanted any that were taken before the storm where Tenerife erupted into a massive killing field.

It was only a second after this, that I remembered I had taken loads of pictures and some video of Shelia when she was parascending. That instantly brought me out in a cold sweat. However, I dug in and told the others what I had. Seeing that this was upsetting for me, Senora Valentina suggested that I give the camera to Carlos, who could upload the pictures and video. After that, she recommended I go for a walk while they reviewed them.

Senora Valentina had offered some good advice. As I walked up and down the marinas labyrinth of jetties. I tried to focus my mind on all the fine sailing vessels moored in the marina. However, it was proving to be difficult. I had a detail of four armed guards with me and as I looked inland, I could see several plumes of smoke from burning buildings. My gaze took me upward to the sky. The mid-morning sky was a beautiful turquoise blue with no cloud's insight. Mentally, that triggered my photographs and video of Shelia parascending. I then began to wonder if not seeing them was the right thing for me. Gritting my teeth, I decided I needed to see them and with a quickening in my pace, I headed back to Carlos's boat.

On entering the master stateroom, I was taken by surprise. With tears in her eyes, Senora Valentina ran over to me, threw her arms around me, and emotionally said;

"B.J, your wife was beautiful with a loving, kind heart. Now, seeing her photographs and video, I can understand how much you miss her."

Now, if that didn't get the tears rolling down my face, one look at Carlos crying his eyes out, did. And, the sea of tears didn't end there. Even Senor Alejandro García had his handkerchief and was drying his eyes. My photos and video had touched their hearts. It took several minutes for us to gain composure and then I asked to see the photos for myself. Carlos had cast them from his laptop to his smart TV. And there she was, my beautiful wife, all in harnessed in, smiling and about to take the skies. The next photo was of her parascending and just gaining altitude. I was quite surprised by how many photos I had taken, but I remembered that I had turned on the camera's sport mode, so there were over twenty.

Although the photographs were all taken pointing away from land. We could all see in the distance on the better sky shots, the grid pattern of what looked like a chemtrail. Senor Alejandro García spoke, saying;

"Before we jump to conclusions, we have to be realistic about this. Every day on the Island of Tenerife, hundreds of flights land and take off. Then, there is the air traffic to many other destinations. What we are looking at could be just vapor trails on a busy day."

We all agreed it was a valid point and would have to keep an open mind. Carlos then played the video clip of Shelia parascending. At this stage, Shelia was airborne, and looking at the start of the footage, she was enjoying her experience. Once again, the sky was clear, but in the distant sky, we could see the grid shape of a possible chemtrail. Suddenly, we heard some very loud crashes and realised that this was the storm moving in. Within seconds, the sky had blackened and the camera was struggling to focus. We then got an explosion of white light and it was at that point we knew Shelia had been hit by lightning. After that, the camera screen went blank. I guess that's when I dropped the camera and dived into the sea.

Seeing all this got to me again, as hard as I tried not to, my lips trembled and then a bucket load of tears followed. That, needless to say, got everyone else going. For several minutes we sat in silence and, it was me who tried to get us focused again by asking Carlos if any other relevant photographs had been posted. He told us there were a few, but they were similar to my ones. However, he had some interesting one's overland of the storm clouds.

Gathering around his lap to view these, we all agreed that something stood out like a sore thumb. In each photo, you could see a section of the sky well above the dark black storm clouds that were an upside-down funnel-shaped, glowing red to orange. This just didn't make sense as the sun was to the west over the beach and this large glow was above in the north?

Our science buff Carlos came up with a theory that the funnel shape could be HAARP using the Ionospheric Research Instrument (IRI). He explained that the IRI is used to temporarily excite a limited area of the ionosphere. he then added;

"I'm only guessing that the upside-down funnel we are looking at is the downforce created by the IRI when it hits the ionosphere. To take this further, once the clouds have been seeded and are of a storm density, that IRI funnel could be used to enhance the storm magnitude. I would also say that the IRI could with the aid of space-based lasers manipulate the direction of the storm."

In all, it was an interesting theory. So, without delay, we then expanded our internet word search wider. Within a very short period, we found Carlos wasn't the only one who had come up with the same or a similar concept. However, that's all it was, a notion. Sadly, we the same as all those who had taken a good hard look at this had no actual evidence. I think we had hoped we had stumbled on the answer and were a little disappointed. Senor Alejandro García said it was time for a coffee break and he needed to make a few telephone calls. So, while Paula served up some freshly brewed coffee and a few nibbles, Senor Alejandro García walked outside to make his calls.

After about twenty minutes, he returned and asked us all to sit down as he had some news to share. Clearing his throat, he began;

"As you are aware, the Spanish Government has declared a state of emergency in Tenerife. With the killing of thousands of hotel staff, it has been deemed necessary to detain all tourists on the island for questioning. To do this, all tourists are to go to designated collection points with their passports and belongings. From the collection points, they will be transported to a holding centre for questioning. As I understand it, each tourist must contact their embassy where they will be told where their designated collection point is and what holding centre, they will be interviewed at. Complying with this is mandatory. If for any reason a tourist does not conform to this, they will, when found, be arrested and imprisoned in a Spanish military compound.

I have also been told that the detention of all tourists has been approved by the U.N and that they will be overseeing tourist transportation and the facilities, accommodation, and security at each holding centre. Great Briton, Germany, France, and other EU members are sending over senior police officers and investigators to assist with the interviews. As to how long this process will take, no one is certain. But, given the complexity and scale of all the interviews, with the following investigations, subsequent charges, and prosecutions. They are initially talking of anything from one to three months. However, that time scale will be reviewed and extended if necessary.

As to you Senor Jameson, the Spanish authorities now understand that you are on this island as my guest. Therefore, you only have to stay here until the airport is open again. Once it is open, I will arrange private air transport so that you can take your wife back home. I, therefore, suggest that you contact your family and begin to make the necessary funeral arrangements. I would also respectfully ask if you would allow me, my sister, and Carlos to attend your wife's funeral."

I just could not believe my emotions, by now, I would have thought that there were no more tears left. But, on hearing that I could soon take Shelia home, I brought on another massive flood. And yes, that got everyone else going. Through the sobs and passing around a box of hankies. I thanked Senor Alejandro García for his hospitality and kindness. I then stood up, shook his hand, and said it would be an honour to have him, his sister, and my friend Carlos at her funeral.

Smiling, Senor Alejandro García thank me and said he would now like to brief us on the progress he has made in setting up an office for S.T.O.P. Still smiling he continued;

"Well on that front, I have good news. We are taking some office space in the Club Nautico's clubhouse. In about an hour, a delivery will arrive with the new computers, mobile phones and plenty of office equipment. Around the same time, six new office staff members should arrive. These people are Spanish ex-hotel staff who survived the attacks and are now out of work. Each has been briefed in what we are doing and with all that had gone on have the same mindset as us. At times, I will be busy looking after business so I would like to suggest that they report directly to you Carlos, and also to you Senor Jameson."

I have to admit; this guy was really on the ball. Those sentiments were also shared by Carlos and Senora Valentina. In a spontaneous action, we all gave Senor Alejandro García a round of applause.

Chapter Eleven, Get organized

With the news that I would be soon bringing my wife's body back home, I knew it was time to face-time my daughters. After briefly telling them about what had been happening on Tenerife, and I do mean briefly. I asked them to contact the Co-op funeral service that we had a pre-paid plan with and begin the arrangements. The kids already knew it was their mom's wish to be cremated, so I left the choice of coffin up to them and we agreed that we would have no flowers, but ask for donations to the Tenerife disaster fund. We also decided that given Shelia's martial arts training, it would be appropriate to hold a gathering after the funeral at my largest martial arts centres. After that, we chatted, reminisced, and cried about what a fabulous mom Shelia had been.

After I finished my face-time call, we had a late, but extremely delicious lunch of Paula's mixed meat paella. That was followed by, homemade Tarta de Santiago. Bloated, we then, with our armed guards headed over to the marina's clubhouse to meet our new team. However, to say I was shocked, upset, and amazed all in one, was an understatement. Each team member was heavily bruised and swathed in all manor or bandages. In truth, they looked like they had gone through hell and hadn't come back.

Juan José was in a wheelchair, this courageous young man had, had both legs broken and he had been beaten badly. Santino, a waiter, had been kicked and punched and when he fell to the floor he was repeatedly stabbed with knives and forks from the restaurant. Lorenzo's story was equally horrendous, he too had been beaten, but then, someone using lighter fuel had set fire to his back. Ricardo's tale was even more bizarre; he was the hotel's indoor spa and pool manager. After beating him senseless with heavy wooden deck chairs and loungers, he was assumed dead and thrown into the pool.

The two ladies in our team hadn't fared well either. Nicole a cleaner, nose, jaw, and several teeth were broken. On top of that, her arms and legs were just one mass of bloodied bruises. This poor woman had been dragged by her ankles face first, down several flights of stairs. Luckily, she was saved by Senor Alejandro García men, who shot dead her all males attackers. And then there was Melanie, who worked as a hotel hairdresser. Her attack began with several women, who tore out most of Melanie's head hair. Holding her down, they then forced her to drink various hair chemicals, before stabbing her repeatedly with the salon scissors. According to Melanie, the only thing that saved her was she lost consciousness and her attackers must have thought she was dead.

It wasn't until after meeting these six courageous people, that I grasped that while thousands had been killed. thousands more had been beaten to a hair's breadth of their lives and had, miraculously survived. This is where I have to give our new team the utmost respect. You would think that these poor battered and broken people would want their attackers apprehended and given the appropriate punishment. However, this was not the case. They knew that deep down that what had happened was beyond their attackers' psychological control. What they truly wanted was, to find out what had caused these tourists to react in such a terrible way. And once that was established, they wanted their government to act through the criminal justice system or if necessary, armed forces to punish those responsible for this atrocity.

While we were all chatting and setting up our new computers, printers, and mobile phones. I briefly caught the backend of a conversation between. Ricardo and Carlos. Ricardo was offering his condolences to Carlos and instantly I thought Ricardo was on about Carlos's wife. But then I heard the name Salvador? I instantly recalled that Salvador was Carlos's brother-in-law. Hearing the name puzzled me, were they talking about the same Salvador who was the best speed boat 'Capitan' in all of Tenerife? I waited until Carlos was on his own and trying to be tactful, I inquired on how Salvador was doing? Well, my smiley friend's face dropped. Within a Nanosecond Carlos's eyes filled with tears and looking at the ground he answered;

"B.J, I didn't want you to know this, but Salvador is dead."

He then just left those words hanging in the air and began to sob. I gently placed my hand on his shoulder and told him that I was so sorry to hear this and inquired on how he had died? Carlos then looked up at me, sighed and moved his head from side to side, and said;

"I know if I tell you it will upset you and you have gone through too much. So, it's probably best that we don't talk about this. Let's just leave this alone, OK."

Well, after what Carlos had said, I wanted to hear more. Nevertheless, seeing the distress in my friend's face and heart, I knew it would be cruel to pursue this. Talking in a soft tone, I told him;

"Carlos, you are a very kind, considerate man. Once again please accept my condolences on the passing of Salvador. I am truly sorry for upsetting you. I will respect your wishes and will not bring this up again."

Still looking at the floor, Carlos nodded in agreement and said "OK". Drying his eyes, he then suggested that we go see how our team is doing on the computers.

Senora Valentina had organized our team, so each person could gather information on specific areas of interest. Like telephone calls, emails, posts, pictures, videos, and information came in, Juan José sorted these into their applicable zones and sent them to the appropriate team member. They, in turn, answer the relevant telephone calls, review, red flag, or file any documents and reply to the emails or postings. All the calls, posts, emails, or documents that were red-flagged would then be dealt with by myself, Carlos, and the García's.

One area that we were inundated with were cases of dead loved ones contacting the living. To our amazement, almost every person that had been killed on Tenerife had tried to contact their loved ones. Although the workload was heavy, Senora Valentina said she would individually handle each case. She began by setting up a simple question and answer template that was emailed to the person. Upon completion of this, she would then directly contact the grieving individuals and see if she could contact their dead loved ones.

Because of all the internet buzz about the 'the talking dead on Tenerife.' The press, media, and television soon got a hold of this wanted to interview S.T.O.P's spiritualist, Senora Valentina. As a group, we talked about this and decided that although we had no real information to offer, it would be a good platform to speak about S.T.O.P's objectives. So, Senora Valentina agreed to the holding various interviews and as this was a hot story, within an hour, the B.B.C, C.N.N, and other world-wide TV news teams rolled up at our marina headquarters.

For the TV interviews, Senora Valentina dressed in an extremely smart dark blue Armani two-piece suit. To complement this, she wore a white silk shirt and a delicate string of white pearls. As always, her hair and make-up were immaculate and in front of the camera's she looked fantastic. The interview began by introducing her as one of the leading Spiritualists in Spain to which Senora Valentina corrected them by saying;

> "Please let me stop you there, I am not the leading Spiritualists in Spain. That honour and title should go to others. I am just a simple born and bred Tenerife girl. Since I was a child, I have had the gift of being able to communicate with those who have passed over to the spirit world."

With that out of the way, the questions turned to 'the talking dead on Tenerife.' Senora Valentina explained that those who had died had not gone to the spirit world, but some other shadowy realm or dimension that she was not familiar with. She then added;

"The first encounter I had was with a lady known as Shelia Jameson's. This lady was the woman, who you might recall, was killed a few days ago by lightning in a freak storm. At that stage, Shelia informed me she was alone in a strange place. Since then, we had a second but much larger storm over Tenerife. Sadly, that prompted a spree of violence that resulted in thousands of hotel workers being killed. As soon as these people passed over, they immediately joined Shelia in this mysterious realm. Since then I have been in contact with hundreds of these poor, lost souls who cannot pass to the spirit world."

For a few moments, silence fell in the interview room, then a man from C.N.N asked;

"Are you implying that the storms over Tenerife were somehow manufactured and they, in turn, have created a shadowy realm that has captured thousands of souls in it? To me Senora, this sounds like something out of a Harry Potter movie."

That brought a roar of laughter around the room. Even Senora Valentina gave a small courteous smile. However, she was not fazed by this and answered;

"Sir, I am sure your anecdote meant no offense to The Jameson family or all the families of those who were tragically killed on our beautiful island of Tenerife. However, they like S.T.O.P want clear answers on how all of this happened. Furthermore, globally we do not want this to ever happen again."

Senora Valentina then asked the C.N.N reporter to stand up. With a few prods and words of encouragement from his fellow reporters, he reluctantly stood and Senora Valentina continued;

"I see from your C.N.N reporter's tag you are an American with the name, Neil Armitage."

Neil just nodded. With her polite smile Senora Valentina and to the astonishment of everyone she said;

"Senor Armitage, both your parents passed away in a car accident when you were only seven. Their Christian names were not Armitage. Am I correct?"

Neil looked stunned, he was struggling for words and just nodded in agreement. Looking sad Senora Valentina then added;

"Before I continue, I want to apologize to you, Senor Armitage. The next thing I say will cause you distress, But I hope you understand that it is important to show everyone that I represent S.T.O.P and we are a credible organization.

Five years ago, you lost your daughter Anne to an overdose of drugs. She says, she loves you and Mommy dearly and regrets the heartache she caused you."

All the cameras immediately swung around and zoomed in on Neil Armitage's face. The poor man slumped into his chair, put his hand over his face, and broke down.

While the room was still stunned, Senora Valentina spoke again;

"Ladies and Gentlemen, I would now like to continue and let you know that over the past few days, I have spoken with many who died on Tenerife and they are very scared and confused. Even when I visit this strange realm, I sense constant fear and it frightens me.

I can assure you as a spiritualist, this is not normal. Those who have passed on to the spirit world are normally in a happy, safe place. The only sadness generally felt is, they miss their living loved ones.

As you are aware, my main role at S.T.O.P is the spiritual liaison. But, S.T.O.P was set up to investigate and help stop what has happened on Tenerife from ever happening again. To date, our investigations have led us to areas that does indeed sound like something out of a Harry Potter movie. That is, the dead talking, mind control, and something that we feel is strongly associated with all of these, weaponized weather manipulation.

Now before you think that S.T.O.P is just another crazy conspiracy group. Let's take a few moments to look historically at the supporting evidence we have gathered. In eighteen, eighty-six, Nikola Tesla invented a system of Alternating Current power source and transmission system. He also created the "Tesla coil," which is still used in radio technology. Cloud seeding started in nineteen forty-six by Doctor Vincent J. Schaefer and the technology for this has advanced immensely since then. Then in nineteen sixty-one, a scientist proposed to light up the night sky by electron gyrotron heating from a powerful transmitter.

Next, we have the invention of the Ionospheric Research Instrument or simply, the IRI. The IRI is designed to temporarily modify thirty-mile diameter patches of the upper atmosphere by exciting, or "heating," their constituent electrons and ions with focused beams of powerful, high-frequency radio energy. A household analogy would be a microwave oven, which heats dinner by exciting the food's water molecules with microwave energy. Some scientists state that purposefully disturbing this sensitive layer could have major and even disastrous consequences.

Now if that's not scary enough, we have HAARP (High-Frequency Active Auroral Research Program). Work on

HAARP began in nineteen ninety-three, it uses a massive IRI covering 13 hectares. In January of nineteen ninety-nine, the European Union called the HAARP project a global concern and passed a resolution calling for more information on its health and environmental risks. It is believed that major aspects of the program are kept secret for alleged reasons of "national security." Yet there is no doubt that HAARP and electromagnetic weapons capable of being used in warfare do exist.

In nineteen sixty-three an eminent doctor explored the effects of external magnetic-fields on brainwaves showing a relationship between psychiatric admissions and solar magnetic storms. He exposed volunteers to pulsed magnetic fields similar to magnetic-storms and found a similar response. US 60 Hz electric-power ELF waves vibrate at the same frequency as the human brain. UK 50 Hz electricity emissions depress the thyroid gland. Three years later, Moscow scientists tell the West that Soviets pinpointed which pulsed magnetic field frequencies help mental & physiological functions and which do harm.

Although HAARP is licensed to transmit at a frequency in the range of 2.7 to 10 MHz we have to take into consideration, technology has advanced greatly since nineteen sixty-three. Therefore, there is nothing to stop unscrupulous groups from obtaining this technology and abusing this frequency range for the purpose of mind manipulation.

Now let's jump forward in time. Some respected researchers allege that secret electromagnetic warfare capabilities of HAARP are designed to forward the US military's stated goal of achieving full-spectrum dominance by the year 2030. Others go so far as to claim that HAARP can and has been used for weather modification, to cause earthquakes and tsunamis, to disrupt global communications systems, and more.

I would like to point out the U.S is not the only country involved in a HAARP project. Great British has a facility at Menwith Hill near Harrogate, and there are five other countries involved in the development of this weapon.

Ladies and Gentlemen, as you can see historically, we have a long history of inventions and technological equipment that can be used for the greater good of mankind. However, that same technological equipment could also be used individually or in an amalgamation, as a horrific weapon. I, therefore, put it to you that unless someone can conclusively prove otherwise. I and S.T.O.P believe that such a weapon has been used on Tenerife and that this was just a testing ground."

Senora Valentina then paused and invited questions. However, everyone in the room was temporally stunned at what they had just been told. Breaking this silence, CNN's Neil Armitage then stood up, thanked Senora Valentina for her insights, and said she had given everyone a lot to think about. The only one who had a question was Gillian Townsend from BBC worldwide news.

"Senora Valentina you have detailed that mind control and weaponized weather manipulation were high on the list of enquires into the disaster here on Tenerife. Do you at this stage of your investigation have any personal theories on why those who were killed are in a different realm or dimension to those in the spirit world."

Looking serious at the camera's, in a concerned tone, Senora Valentina answered;

"Gillian, you must understand that the relatives of those who have been killed are grieving for their loved ones. Their hearts are already breaking from their violent deaths. On top of that, they are trying to deal with hearing their voices from an unknown place. Any irrational speculation about this on my behalf will only cause them more grief. Therefore, until I know more, I must decline to answer that question."

At that, and without any further questions, the T.V news channels reporters and their camera teams packed up their equipment and left.

Senora Valentina was still sitting in her interview chair motionless. As I, Carlos, and Senor García approached her, she looked at us and began to shake and then cry. Seeing this, we rushed forward and gave her a big group hug. I guessed that while she had been interviewed, she had been on an adrenaline high, and now she was experiencing the low. As she began to calm down, we began to discuss the interview. We laughed and joked, saying she should get a job on as a newsreader, as she looked stunning and handled things with an air of professionalism. It was I who stated that what she said was brilliant and asked how on earth did she remember all those facts. By now she was back to her old self and with some jubilance in her voice, she answered;

"My brilliance does not just stop at being the world's best spiritualist, stunning looker, and T.V presenter. I also have a photographic memory, believe it or not, I only read some of those details an hour or so before the interview. However, just in case I had a memory relapse, I got Juan José to set a micro Bluetooth earpiece for me and he was on standby in the computer room with all the information."

Well, on hearing this, we all just howled with laughter. After that, Paula brought in some much-needed coffee and we continued to discuss the T.V interview and what impact it would have on S.T.O.P. To gauge this better, we all headed on over to our main computer room, where we were greeted by Juan José. He and the rest of the team applauded Senora Valentina for her brilliant T.V interview. And then, excitedly, he told us that as soon as the T.V interview finished, the hits on our web and social media sites had gone crazy. He then added that several prominent newspapers, dozens of radio stations, and podcasts had been in contact would like to interview Senora Valentina as soon as possible.

While this was still a hot 'news' story and to maximize S.T.O. P's exposure, Senora Valentina agreed to every single interview. Now, that was a very tall order. So, to help with this, Juan José took on the role of her assistant. Within a few minutes, he set up a computerized minute by minute dairy, therefore restricting the interviewees to exact time slots.

Before the television interview, Senora Valentina had had a few fellow spiritualists contact her saying they too had been in touch with those who had been killed on Tenerife. To Senora Valentina's mind, most of these spiritualists seemed genuine people, and they too were mystified as to where on a spiritual plan these lost souls had gone. Needless to say, that all changed within minutes of the interview going live. She was inundated with all kinds of spiritualists and religious people from various beliefs who offered us help and where needed, spiritual guidance. However, she also got loads more, which she could only describe as absolute fruit cakes.

Our interview also got the attention of several online, YouTube, and similar channels that investigate alien U.F.O's, space anomalies, and possible alien visitations. Each ufologist put forward various hypothesizes that alien technology and indeed aliens could be involved in the Tenerife incident. They even suggested that this could be the prelude to something much bigger. Although the consensus on this was, let's keep an open mind and see if any evidence pops up to substantiate these theories, Senor Alejandro García thought it was a load of rubbish.

Carlos tried putting the things into perspective, by saying;

"Senor García, any investigation that has so many variables as the one we have, needs to be examined broadly. If that spectrum takes us to look at things, not of this world, or indeed things that are influenced by extra-terrestrial beings, then we cannot ignore it."

We all could see that with his religious convictions, this was difficult for Senor Alejandro García. But in the end, he agreed that yes, if something of significance came up, we should look into it. However, we knew he was very sceptical of alien involvement.

Chapter Twelve, Recruitment

After a really busy day, we, that was everyone in the team, we're all mentally exhausted. So, Senor García congratulated the team on how hard they had worked on their first day told and sent everyone home. After saying goodnight, the García's headed home and I and Carlos went to the boat. No sooner than I put my foot on the gangplank, I got a call from the British Embassy. It was Theresa Tarragon-Jones and she sounded pissed off. In her best British accent, she inquired;

"Mr. Jameson. where the bloody hell have you been all day? The home office has been trying to contact you!"

Before replying, I quickly looked at my call log and I had had seventeen missed calls. To make things worse, somehow, in one of that magic, the phone has a mind all of its self, my phone was set on silent? Now try explaining that a pissed off attaché from the British embassy. So, I choose to ignore her sarcastic tone and keeping it unpretentious, I replied;

"Ms. Tarragon-Jones, so sorry, been rushed off my feet today. How can I help you?

You know when someone is cross, you hear them sucking air through their teeth. Well, that's what Ms. Tarragon-Jones did before she answered;

"The British home office has sent me to talk with you. I have now been standing at the gates of this bloody marina a few several hours and the local thugs won't let me in."

Inwardly, I couldn't help but laugh. After our last telephone conversation, I felt like throttling her. So, the thought of this super-bitch having to hang around for a few hours in thirty degrees of heat, pleased me. However, I was also curious as to why she had been sent from the U.K to see me and how she got here? I told her I would come down to the gates in a few minutes and before I left, I quickly briefed Carlos on my phone conversation. He was as baffled as I was and thought it wise to notify Senor García on this new development. With that done, I and my armed guards headed on down to the marina's gates.

It's funny how from a telephone conversation you form a mental image of the person you are chatting with. I had got Ms. Tarragon-Jones as a short, duppy middle-aged spinster. Well, I was way out on that. She was red-headed, tall and slender, smartly dressed, and about thirty years old and she wasn't alone. She had two plainclothes, big, broad-shouldered blokes with her, who I guessed were her protection detail.

I walked over, said "Hello" and introduced myself. Ms. Tarragon-Jones was her normal abrupt self and said;

"Yes, Mr. Jameson, I know who you are. Now, tell these thugs to allow us in."

Before we went any further, I apologized to Senor García men at the gate for this lady's rudeness. I then told Ms. Tarragon-Jones that while the murders, riots, arson attacks, rapes, and acts of extreme violence have been going on, these brave men have been trying to maintain law and order. However, my little speech fell on deaf ears. Once again in her curt way she answered;

"The British government does not condone any acts from local Spanish militia. The Spanish government has requested that the U.N oversee the restoration of law and order."

The gate gauds could all speak perfect English, but as the one man raised the barrier, I heard him say in Spanish;

"Ella es una fucking idiota. (She is a fucking idiot)"

At that, all of Senor García's men began to laugh and even I had to smile. Nonetheless, keeping a stiff upper lip and with her attaché case in hand, MS Tarragon-Jones strolled through the gates as if she owned the marina. Then, as she walked past Senor García men, in a good Spanish accent she replied;

"El imperio Britanico gana de nuevo. (The British Empire wins again)"

I looked at the two protection officers and said;

"Looks like you've got your work cut out their lads."

Keeping a professional decorum, they both just nodded and we proceeded to Carlos's boat. As we approached the boat, Carlos greeted us on the gangplank and welcome everyone onboard. To my surprise, Ms. Tarragon-Jones dropped her arrogant attitude, kissed Carlos on the cheek, and thanked him. Carlos then guided everyone into the master stateroom and served us some cool refreshments. As we sipped our drinks, Ms. Tarragon-Jones got straight down to business. First and this made me smile, she asked Carlos to find something to do in the galley. With Carlos gone, she opened her attaché case and pulled out some documents. Looking at me she opened the one file and said;

"Mr. Jameson, since the death of your wife, the British government has been following your activities closely. We feel that as a British subject, your involvement with S.T.O.P could be of some service to your country; therefore, we would like to offer you a position in our diplomatic core.

Your duties should you choose to accept this role, would be to disclose any relevant information to us, before you put it in the public domain. In turn, you would also be privy to otherwise confidential information that would be yours to disclose as you and your S.T.O.P team see fit. Now Mr. Jameson, before I proceed further, do you have any questions you would like to ask?"

With all of this just thrown at me, I couldn't help be suspicious. Why would the British government want any involvements with me, S.T.O.P, and Senor Alejandro García, who they must know is the mafia boss for Tenerife? As I was pondering this, I could see Ms. Tarragon-Jones was monitoring my reaction. She then put her hand up to stop me from asking any questions and said;

"Yes Mr. Jameson, you are right to be apprehensive. We do know all about you and your associates. However, when it comes to the protection of British citizens and indeed the national security of Great Britain, we must use all resources available.

Mr. Jameson, you seem an astute fellow and must have deduced from what I have just said that there is more going on than what I have so far revealed. That deduction would be correct. However, in the interests of National security, you and S.T.O.P will only be given information on a need to know basis.

What I can tell you is, The British Government is on 'Red Alert Status.' I can also assure you that we had nothing to do with what has happened in Tenerife. Now, what we do believe is, what happened on Tenerife was just a test run and the UK could be a potential target. To prevent this from happening, at this point we are gathering as much intelligence as we can.

Now, this is where you and S.T.O.P come in. You have the ear and trust of the media and internet community globally. All we ask is that filter through any sensitive information to us first. We can then analyse this information and act accordingly. Oh, and if you think you might have a conflict of interest with Senor García and the Spanish government, don't worry. On issues related to the Tenerife disaster, we have a joint agreement with the Spanish government to share all relevant intelligence."

I have to say I was still uneasy with Ms. Tarragon-Jone's motives. Saying that throwing in the UK could be a potential target did raise the stakes. It was now my turn to ask some questions, so I fired my first one in;

"Why do I need to be a member of the diplomatic core? Surely S.T.O.P could work with the British and Spanish government without all this cloak and dagger stuff?"

Without flinching and with a hint of sarcasm in her voice, Ms. Tarragon-Jones answered;

"Try not to be so naïve, Tenerife is now under martial law, if thing escalates, this may be extended to the UK other European countries. As a diplomate, you would be able to communicate with our embassy through our official channels. Also consider travel, up to now the airports are closed on Tenerife, so the R.A.F brought me over in a transporter. I know you plan on bringing your wife home in a private plane. What are you going to do if British or European air space is closed? We could arrange transport and should you by then have acquired any documents, you could bring these in a diplomatic pouch."

Despite being shot down in flames, I tried to bounce back and hit her with my next line of questions;

"You mentioned that the British government would be willing to share information with S.T.O.P, why? Now assuming that your motives only in the interest of national or global Security, does that sharing also include information from your partners?"

With a nod of her head Ms. Tarragon-Jones replied;

"Mr. Jameson, this is for your ears only. At this stage, with our intelligence gathering, Great Britain, Spain, and numerous other countries are grasping at straws. However, we do feel that leaking certain bits of information might open up more pertinent routes of investigation. S.T.O.P is the ideal platform for this. Now, as to your question on sharing information, all of Great Britain's allies are willing to work with S.T.O.P.

You may be also interested to know that the British Government's commitment to this venture is extremely serious. Should you want to proceed with this, Great Britain and her allies are willing to assist with resources and finances."

Under normal circumstances, I'm a pretty calm person, but as Ms. Tarragon-Jones words began to sink in, I could feel my heart racing. She had certainly put forward a compelling augment and I felt that had no option but to enlist. My mind raced as I tried to compose some elaborate acceptance speech, but I just blurted out;

"I'm in."

Keeping her icy exterior, Ms. Tarragon-Jones didn't flinch. She reached into her attaché case and handed me a thick folder. Inside the folder was my new United Kingdom Diplomate passport, documents confirming my appointment as a British diplomatic officer, my British diplomatic officer registration number, gold members debit cards from several banks, car keys and car documents, a robust mobile phone, and to my surprise, an updated firearms certificate that included semi and automatic weapons. As I was reading through the list of arms and firearms I could use, Ms. Tarragon-Jones interrupted me and said;

"Sorry to rush you, but I have an R.A.F transporter on standby and need to get back to the U.K as soon as possible. Most things you have are self-explanatory. To get around, you will need a car. The car keys are to a range rover parked just down the road from the marina gates. To maximize your safety, you will find in the boot is a security box, here's the code. In that box are a secure laptop and some legal firearms. I strongly suggest that you get rid of any dodgy firearms you have.

Oh, and don't worry about the vehicle's safety, until you collect it, I have two protection officers looking after this. The mobile phone is a secure satellite phone that has pre-set numbers stored in it. It can be used to contact me directly or any United Kingdom embassy around the world. Do not use it for anything other than that.

Now that you are fully briefed, it's time for me to go. Please tell Carlos López, it was a pleasure to meet a man of superior intelligence. Please also relay to him, that when he visits the U.K, he can contact me and take me out to dinner."

With that rather forward statement and her expression unchanged, Ms. Tarragon-Jones and her two protection officers got up and left. Well, I have to say that, that lady had done her homework. She seemed to know a lot about Carlos and even knew his last name. Which I hasten to add, was something that I never thought to ask of.

Our guests had barely got their feet off the gangplank when Carlos burst into the master stateroom shouting;

"I never thought I would meet a real live 007 James Bond."

Well that made me laugh, but a thought hit me and with a smile on my face I asked him;

"You weren't eavesdropping, were you?"

Plonking himself into one of the chairs and still laughing, Carlos pointed to a vent in the ceiling and answered;

"We are on a luxury boat that has lots of features, one of those a two-way intercom system from the master stateroom and bridge to the galley. So yes, I was eavesdropping and I have to tell you that am looking forward to dinner with the feisty redhead."

Carlos then informed me that for future protection or denial of what had just happened, he had recorded my conversation. I had to agree that although this was sneaky, it was a wise move and asked that he make copies for me and Senor García. We then briefly discussed my diplomatic recruitment, which inevitably led to numerous James Bond, Miss Moneypenny, and Mata Hari jokes from Carlos. However, we both agreed that this was serious and needed to be fully discussed with the García's present. So, we adjourned this and with the enthusiasm of two schoolboys, we and our guards headed out of the marina to pick up my 007 range rover.

As we approached the car, two big, unshaven and very muscular men approached me, stood to attention, and said;

"Good evening Mr. Jameson. We are the detail that has been keeping your vehicle safe. Can we assume that this duty is now over?

I smiled, shook each one's hand, and replied;

"Gentlemen it's time to go and get a well-earned beer"

I have to admit, this must have been a very dull mission for them, but they were professionals. Without saying anymore, they both saluted me, walked over to a small fiat five hundred, that was parked just in front of my car, and drove off.

Nowadays, you can tell a lot from the key from a car's key fob. Looking at mine, I had already worked out that range rover was a keyless entry. As I approached the car, the driver's door automatically unlocked, the lights came on and the car's footplates extended outward. The footplates had some cool LED lights fitted underneath them that illuminated the ground. As I looked at Carlos, he was grinning from ear to ear, and in his best Spanish come Scottish accent he said;

"Mr. Bond, it looks like Q has sent you a Q-mobile. Where's the rocket launches?"

Laughing, I replied;

"Come on, get in. I want to try out the passenger ejector seat."

While we jumped in the front, our two-armed guards jumped in the back. Carlos then opened the glove box and handed me the extensive user manual. Now, men being men, we choose to completely ignore this and for over twenty minutes, we kept ourselves amused by fiddling and playing with all the controls. Once we got the hang of the seat settings, auto lights, auto wipers, radio/sound system, aircon, satnav, parking sensors, and extensive exterior camera system, auto dash and rear cameras, adaptive cruise control, lane departure warning, and auto park assist settings, we all enthusiastically jumped out, to inspect the goodies in the boot.

Needless to say, on my all singing all dancing vehicle, the tailgate had an auto-open button. I clicked this and as it opened it revealed a large metal box that had been secured to the boots floor. Eagerly, I entered the code, and after a few bleeps, the box opened. Now, this might sound silly, but we all whooped with delight when we got sight of the guns inside. There was a Glock 17 Pistol with a hip holster, a Diemaco C7 Assault Rifle with a nice red eye scope, an L128A1 Combat Shotgun, and a Minimi Light Machine Gun, plus a boatload of ammo and four flash-bangs. The only thing that didn't send our hearts racing was, the chunky looking military laptop.

I did not know what my job as a diplomatic officer entailed, but I knew from all the weapons I had just seen, danger seemed high on the list. This was further endorsed when we opened an extra, extra-large canvas bag that was next to the gun box. As I unzipped this, we were all suspired to find, field binoculars, a spotter scope, an SLR camera with some powerful telephoto lenses, two bulletproof vests, two Kevlar helmets with night vision accessories, two ski masks, combat boots, and a range of day and night combat clothing.

By now Carlos had put on a serious face, he first looked at the content of the bag and then at me and said;

"B.J, I think you will agree that Tenerife's current problems warrant martial law, help from the U.N, and intervention from people like Senor García. That being said, I think your government is going way overboard with all of this James Bond equipment. I also think we must keep a very suspicious mind about your role as a diplomatic officer. You know, with this snazzy car and all the equipment inside it, what we are looking at here goes way beyond passing on internet and media information. Perhaps, my friend, we need to consider some new titles for you like, rogue agent or fall guy. You might also want to think about the words, terrorist and expendable."

I was pleased Carlos and I were on the same page with this and he had a knack for putting his own slant on situations. Rogue agent or fall guy, terrorist and expendable, all were possibilities. However, he did miss something of importance, why were there two of everything. When I put this to him, he grunted and replied;

"It looks like a certain Spaniard named Carlos López is you're accomplish."

Sombrely, we all got into the Range Rover and parked it up inside the marina and then I and Carlos said goodnight to our guards before hitting the sack. Although I was tired, sleep alluded me, my mind kept trying to analyse my role as a diplomatic officer. Out of this sleeplessness, things began to become clear to me that had not been so obvious before, Ms. Tarragon-Jones had been waiting for several hours at the marina gates. She had also travelled from the U.K and all my official documents and debits cards must have been prepared some time before that. Therefore, my acceptance was a forgone conclusion and this had all been arranged well before Senora Valentina's television interview. Before falling into a hazy sleep, I could only conclude that with the British government being on red alert, they must have had some kind of threat issued and they were taking it very seriously.

Chapter Thirteen, High flying

The following morning the García's turned up with their cook, Paula and while she prepared our breakfast, we sat down and I began to explain in every detail Ms. Tarragon-Jones visit. While I did this, Senor García just sat silently and listen, then he broke his silence and said;

"B.J, I have been getting whispers from my Spanish government contacts that something big is about to happen and it could involve one or several countries. To prepare for this, each country is on red alert and are intensifying their efforts to find out who is behind this. To assist with this, I see no problem in S.T.O.P offering any relevant information to both the Spanish and British Governments."

He then burst out laughing and continued;

"Now as to your James Bond 007 role, while we should be cautious about this, you B.J have no option but to play along. You also have to remember that your Miss Moneypenny was only the messenger. Other's in very high government places like M in the Bond movies have sanctioned this. Therefore, Mr. B.J Bond, let's exploit this and see what additional information and resources they provide for S.T.O.P.

Now when we have eaten our breakfast, we are going on our first outdoor information-gathering mission. We will need the Bond mobile and I have brought a few pieces of equipment that I think will help with this."

I don't know what the García's normally eat for breakfast, but Paula did enough food to feed the crew and passengers of a modern cruise liner. However, with all these morning delights, I filled myself to bursting point, then I and the overstuffed Carlos along with the García's headed to the Bond mobile.

Senor García had gotten his men to drop off a crate by the side of the Bond mobile and eagerly he opened it to reveal two brand new Phantom 6 Pro drones with controllers. He looked at us, smiled, and informed us that these are the top of the range and they come with thirty-megapixel cameras that offer great stability with a three-axis gimbal. He then explained that we are going to film and publish our own video footage of the devastation and strife in and around Tenerife.

We all had to admit it was a great idea and for me, it was something I was familiar with. A few years ago, I invested in a drone and had used it several times for filming my martial arts weapon routines outside. However, mine only cost a couple of hundred pounds. In comparison, these Phantoms were mega expansive, but they were the bee's knees with all the latest buttons and bells on them. To make them even more impressive, these new drones had a battery life of over one hour. Senor García had planned this well, he had brought several charged batteries and numerous memory cards, so it looked like we were going to have several hours of material and a whole lot of fun.

Well, before we could take them into the field, we had to do a test flight. Naturally, as a UK registered drone pilot, I volunteered and within a few minutes of tinkering, I had the Phantom drone flying. Carlos, the García's, and our guards all clapped and cheered as I did various aerial maneuverers. However, in truth with its easy to use automatic flying features, such as take-off, landing, follow me, and an auto return home button it was a doddle to fly. After a perfect landing, we then packed the drone back in the crate, loaded the create into the back of the Bond mobile, and headed off to get a bird's eyes view of Tenerife.

Since leaving my hotel for the safety of the marina, this was my first outing and as I looked around the streets of Los Cristianos, all I could see was devastation. Along the way, we encountered several U.N road stops, but as soon as I flashed my diplomatic pass we were waved through. Our first port of call for our aerial filming was the famous Playa de las Américas. I parked up just outside the Monkey beach club and while Carlos and Senor García stood guard, I flew the Phantom so that it filmed inland capturing all the burnt-out coastal shops and hotels.

We thought that about fifteen minutes of video footage was ample, so I hit the retuned to the home button, packed the Phantom away, and headed to our next location, Playa de Torviscas, Costa Adeje. This time, I parked up on the now-empty beach promenade. Other than a few locals who had bravely ventured out to try to salvage some of their stock from their beachside businesses, everywhere was closed and boarded up.

In the distance, we could hear some screams, shouting, and sporadic gunfire. So, I immediately launched the Phantom and flew it towards the commotion. From my on-board monitor, I could see that the local police had come across some looters at the Plaza del Duque pharmacy. From behind their police cars, the police fired tear gas grenades through the broken pharmacy windows. However, they were met with a hail of bullets that pinged off the pavements and ripped into police vehicles. By now we were all huddled around the Phantoms monitor. From there we watched the police returned fire and also shoot several more tear gas canisters into the building. After a minute or so, we could hear some more shouting and five young lads with their hands up, coughing and spluttering from the effects of tear gas, exited the pharmacy.

Within seconds, the young lads were surrounded by armed police, who ordered them to lie face down on the floor. After a thorough search, each one was handcuffed and taken away. By now, we had ample footage, so I brought the drone back to base and we headed to our next destination, a car and van dealership owned by Senor García in San Juan, Santa Cruz de Tenerife.

Some idiots had tried to steal a few vehicles and were caught and detained by some of Senor García's men.

As we arrived, we were greeted by four of Senor García's men. Senor García asked his sister to say to stay in the car. However, I and Carlos weren't so lucky. As part of the 'García family' we were expected to do the manly thing, so we all exited the Bond mobile and followed the four men into the garage workshop at the rear of the car-lot. To the right of the workshop was a hydraulic car ramp where I could see both thieves had been stripped, beaten, and then suspended by their ankles.

Senor García walked over two the two men and said;

"Gentlemen, I understand that you are British holidaymakers who because of the crimes you have committed, are now on the run from the Spanish authorities. Now, you have to understand that we have always welcomed tourists to our island. However, you two have taken advantage of our hospitality. My men tell me you have confessed to committing several murders and numerous robberies. Well, I want to tell you, it would have been better for you to have handed yourselves in the U.N. I am Alejandro García and today it is your misfortune to meet me.

The good people you killed were under my protection. The same applies to those who you stole from. Now to make matter worse, you try to break into a garage owned by me and try to steal some of my cars."

Senor García then turned and spoke to me and Carlos;

"My friends, there is no need for you to be here any longer. Would you kindly head on down to the San Juan beach and take some more video footage. I will conclude my business here and meet you in about half an hour."

On this occasion, I could genuinely speak for Carlos and say that we both couldn't wait to get out of there. It was obvious that those two men were going to have an extremely painful death, and we both didn't want to see this. So together and without saying a word, we did a quick about-turn and went back to the Bond mobile. From the car-lot, it was only a short drive down to San Juan beach and for some unexplained reason, we all just chatted as if nothing had just happened.

The story at San Juan beach was the same as the two other places we had stopped at, an abandoned, burnt out coastal town. I got the Phantom up in the air and did some filming, but I realized that unfortunately every town and beach across Tenerife was going to look the same. After about five minutes of filming, I spotted Senor García heading toward us, so hit the Phantoms return to home button and the drone flew safely back to the Bond mobile.

Looking very serious, Senor García got into the car and informed us we had a new destination to head for, it was a small inland town called Barrio Taucho. I put the information into my satnav and within a few minutes, we were soon on the twisting TF583 highway. As we travelled along this winding road, Senor García told us that we were looking for a tall but oddly shaped metal tower that had recently been erected in a hilly area, just before Barrio Taucho town. Other than that, Senor García didn't offer any other information, so we just keep our eyes peeled and sure enough, we soon spotted the tower. We estimated the tower stood about one hundred feet tall (thirty, point four eight meters) with a large domed top.

To get a closer look, I pulled the Bond mobile off the main highway and drove along a bumpy dirt track. The track led to a large compound area that had been fenced off with six-foot-tall (one point eight nine meters) corrugated panels with three lines of barbed wire on top of it. On every panel was a large notice that read, Excluir, Propiedad Privada (keep out, private property). Senor García then told us that he had recently had reports from the locals about this place. He said, the townspeople were concerned about the strange coming and going, odd lights that illuminate the night's sky, and uniformed armed guards patrolling the outer parameter of the fence. After listening to this, we all agreed that it was time to get the drone out and do a bit of aerial reconnaissance. While I got the Phantom into the air, Carlos turned on our military-style laptop that locked into a secure military severer. He told us he would use google earth and look for any recent satellite imagery of Barrio Taucho town and surrounding area.

The images coming through on the Phantom control monitor showed the compound had six mobile outbuildings, two Toyota pickups, and bang in the centre was the strange tower. All of a sudden, six guards came rushing out of one of the buildings and two with machine guns began firing at the Phantom. Despite my best effort to manoeuvre the Phantom to safety, a hail of bullets hit the drone and it tumbled to the ground. Fearing for our lives, we all scrambled back into the Bond mobile. Then with the pedal to the metal and throwing up a trail of dust, the Bond mobile launched forward and I drove as quickly as I could away from the tower.

However, the tower's guards had jumped into the two Toyota pickups and were in hot pursuit. Both Carlos and Senor García had handguns, but without debate, we agreed that this was time to get the heavy artillery out. So, with some clever bodily manoeuvring, Carlos managed to climb over the back seats to where the gun box was and called to me for the code. Using the code, he then opened the gun box and handed the Minimi Light Machine Gun to Senor García. He then passed the Glock to me while he chambered a round into the Diemaco C7 Assault Rifle. He then threw the bulletproof vests over and told Senora Valentina to put one.

By now, we were speeding along the TF583 highway towards Barrio Taucho town and Senor García was talking calmly on his mobile. He hung up and said that I should take the next right on to Carr Taucho road and stop at the Club El Almacigo. I did exactly as I was told; within a few minutes, I skidded the Bond mobile to a halt on the Club El Almacigo car park. Senor García with the Minimi Light Machine Gun in hand jumped out of our vehicle and shouted;

"B.J take my sister inside and keep her safe. Carlos, take those stairs at the side of the building to the roof and use the Assault Rifle to take out the drivers or the front tires of the Toyotas."

At that, Senor García sprinted across the road and took cover behind some large rocks. He had barely got to cover when the two Toyotas came into sight. Within less than a heartbeat, several shots rang out and I could see that Carlos had peppered the leading Toyotas bonnet and front passenger tyre with bullets. Both Toyotas screeched to a halt and as their occupants rapidly left their vehicles, they fired a few rounds towards the roof of Club El Almacigo but hit nothing.

I and Senora Valentina ran inside the Club El Almacigo and as I glanced out of the reception window, I realized that the tower guards were possible mercenaries and no fools. Tactically to maximize cover, they had positioned their vehicles in such a way that the one good Toyota was alongside the disabled one. However, what they didn't take into account was the cunning and might of Senor García. His earlier phone call had been to call for assistance from some of his men who lived in and around the Barrio Taucho area. And Oh boy, did they come. Within minutes several old trucks, well jalopies packed full of men armed to the teeth began to descend from the hills and surround the Club El Almacigo.

To my mind, the tower guards were now outmanned and outgunned, but they dug in and began firing at the oncoming trucks. Senor García had crept up to the rear of the guards. He was the first to return gunfire. As he sent out a hail of bullets from the Minimi Light Machine Gun, he hit two of the guards and fell to the ground. The other guards realized they had been outflanked and concentrated all their firepower on Senor García's position.

Now, I have seen my fair share of Rambo movies. And in the movies, every man and his dog have a Russian rocket-propelled grenade (often abbreviated RPG_7). However, this was Tenerife, and seeing the men Barrio Taucho town having these shoulder-firing anti-tank weapon systems was a surprise. I hasten to add, it was even more of a surprise to the guards. In unison, four of Senor García's men fired their RPG's and that was the end of the guards, Toyotas, and a big part of the road.

From behind his rocky cover, Senor García stood up, and to indicate he was Ok, he waved his gun in the air. Seeing this, cheers went out from his men, but those cheers only lasted a few seconds. The ground under our feet began to shake and that was followed by an explosion that was brighter and louder than anything I had experienced before. Instantly, clouds of dust filled the air and even though I and Senora Valentina were inside, we were all temporally blinded and deafened.

It took a minute or two for my vision to stabilize, but the loud explosion had buggered up my hearing. I could see that Senora Valentina was sitting close by me on the floor. So, I reached down tapped her on the shoulder and gave her the thumbs up. She returned the gesture but indicated that she could not hear. In a bit of made-up sign language, I also showed that I also couldn't hear.

By now the dust had settled and we both ventured outside and were greeted by an equally deaf, but dust-covered Carlos. With mouth and hand gestures, I could make out that Carlos was saying something like "fucking hell, what's just happened?" All we could do to respond is look vague and shrug. At that, from his vantage point across the cratered road, Senor García popped his head up from behind some rocks, dusted himself down, and seeing us, he gave us a wave. As he walked over to us, he was joined by several of his men who were all indicating that they too could not hear.

After clearing the dust off the Bond mobiles windows, we and Senor García men drove to the site of the strange tower. However, as we approached the area, to our astonishment, we could see that the tower had disappeared. All that was left of was a smoldering, cavernous hole in the ground. We left our vehicles and with guns at the ready, our small band then cautiously approach the area where the fence had once stood. All that was left to see was a few fragments of twisted metal, everything, including the six mobile units, had been almost atomized.

While everyone continued to carefully inspect the demolished zone, I launched the second Phantom and took some aerial footage of the area where the tower once stood. While this footage was good for S.T.O.P, it was something that Ms. Tarragon-Jones would also need to see. We then had a bit of good luck, one of Senor García's men found the wreckage of the other Phantom. The drone had three bullet holes in it and two of its rotors were smashed from its fall from the sky. But the good news was, the memory card was still in tacked. So, now I had some good video footage of the tower and surrounding area before and after it had been blown to smithereens.

We were just about to pack up when the cavalry arrived. Three Boeing AH-64 Apache gunship helicopters descended on the area, followed by several U.N and Spanish military trucks, full of armed soldiers that all looked pissed off. We that's everyone, were then detained for questioning. I guess they thought that we were responsible for the massive explosion and it didn't help that we were all still deaf. So, even though I flashed my diplomatic pass and Senor García and tried to talk to them in Spanish, there was a total breakdown in communications and a lot of gun-waving.

After a phone call by a senior U.N officer to the British embassy, things calmed down. Taking pity on my deafness, the same U.N officers got a note pad out and wrote a question asking why we were in this area? I explained that I, Senor García, and some of the locals were visiting the area because we had a report of a large strange tower lighting up the sky at night. I then went on to say that we were taken by surprise when we found the tower was guarded by armed mercenaries. Adding that upon seeing us, the mercenaries gave pursuit, and then tried to kill us. I then speculated that it was the same mercenaries or their associates that blew the tower and its surrounding area to pieces. Other than that, I declined to say any more.

While I was being quizzed, the Commanding Officer of the Spanish soldiers had established who Senor García was. Thankfully, that added a lot of credibility to our presence in the area, and as we were all deaf and of no assistance, we were allowed to go on our way.

Our drive back to the marina was going to take about thirty minutes. At that time Carlos fired up the laptop and because we were all temporally deaf, he began to make a presentation on some thoughts he had had. His first thought was the tower looked like a modern version of one invented by Nikola Tesla. He began the presentation with;

Senora Valentina mentioned in her television interview that Tesla designed the alternating-current (AC) electrical system., However, he did lots more, for example, in eighteen ninety-three, Tesla made pronouncements on the possibility of wireless communications with his devices. Tesla tried to put these ideas to practical use in his unfinished Wardenclyffe Tower project, an intercontinental wireless communication and power transmitter, but as I remember, the funding ran out before he could complete it. Now, that's where I remember the tower from.

However, in the late nineteenth century, Tesla then went on to patent the "Tesla coil," This coil laid the foundation for wireless technologies and is still used in radio technology today. The coil is classed as the heart of an electrical circuit. It works with a capacitor to resonate current and voltage from a power source across the circuit. Interestingly, this may or may not be connected to all the strange things that have been recently happening in Tenerife. But, Tesla himself used his coil to study fluorescence, x-rays, radio, wireless power, and electromagnetism in the earth and in its atmosphere.

To follow up on this line of thought, Carlos continued to investigate Tesla's work and found another interesting connection. After quickly analysing what he had found, he then added the following to his presentation.

It seems Tesla was not the only one with brilliant ideas. A man called Jonathan Zenneck was one of the first known scientists to study electromagnetic wave propagation over the surface of the earth. With Zenneck surface waves, electrical power is directed along the earth's surface, in much the same way that electrical power is directed through conventional transmission lines using electromagnetic waves. According to what I have just read, in the early years of the twentieth century, two theories of electromagnetic wave theory co-existed. One was the classic Hertzian radiated waves (ground waves) which are transmitted via conventional antennae on a line of sight path and dissipate over a distance into space. And the other was the Zenneck Surface Waves which use the surface of the earth as a waveguide and travel at high levels of efficiency.

It is theorized that the surface wave is impervious to weather effects such as lightning geomagnetic disturbance or electromagnetic pulses (EMP), including those associated with a nuclear detonation. Unlike a wired grid, the Zenneck wave cannot be physically attacked or indeed cyber-attacked through any wired network., The wireless power system will employ a "transmitter probe," located near a power generation plant, to launch a Zenneck carrier wave. Now to make this system work globally, receiver antennae's will then be positioned appropriately around the world to receive the signal and download the power into a local microgrid or conventional grid architecture.

Carlos concluded his presentation with a summary that read;

OK people, just stop and think for a moment. When the major storms hit Tenerife, all the electrical power on the island went down. Mobile phone communications were disrupted and for quite a while we had no internet. If my theory is correct, the only ones who would still have power, internet, and Mobile phone communications would be the ones using Zenneck carrier wave technology. Therefore, whoever is behind this, has immense power and wealth, state of the art technology, and some catastrophic agenda that we don't know about yet."

As soon as we got back to the marina, we followed the very eager Carlos into S.T.O. P's computer room. There we were greeted by Juan José and our team who were confused as to why we were all deaf? However, after a short verbal and hand sign explanation, they understood. Then, without any further delays, Juan José helped Carlos cast his presentation onto one of the computer's large monitors. With a mixture of anticipation and dread, we all pulled up a chair, huddled around the screen, and read the presentation. It was certainly something of a revelation. We all gasped, wowed, and said a few swear words as we individually assessed Carlos's theories.

To follow the presentation, Carlos had previously removed the memory cards from both Phantom's and he popped them into the commuter's memory card reader. Within a minute we were all able to watch the video footage of the before and after of the tower. I have to say it was good to have some fresh eyes on this. Juan José instantly picked up on the deep cavern that was left after the tower had been destroyed. Using a keyboard and Microsoft word, so us deaf people could follow. Juan José then typed on the screen the following; The builders of the tower must have excavated this out first and put the power generation plant in before building the tower. He then entered; It was probable that the power generation plant was destroyed seconds before the tower. That theory certainly made sense as to why we felt the ground tremble before the bright flash of light, deafening sound, and debris cloud.

After seeing what Juan José had just typed, Senor García then took over the keyboard and inputted the following; My friends it looks like we have stumbled onto something of great significance. Let's first get the U.N, Spanish, and U.K governments involved with this and as soon as we can. We also need to upload all of this on our web and media sites as soon as we can. It's going to be interesting to see if any of our S.T.O.P members around the world have seen similar towers or indeed if they have any further information.

Chapter Fourteen, Towers

The following day my hearing had improved a bit, but now I could hear a constant, but faint ringing, that was driving me crazy. I also knew I was in trouble as I had missed a few calls from Ms. Tarragon-Jones. I'm sure she would think I was a total idiot if she found out that with all the excitement of yesterday, I forgot and had left my diplomatic phone in the Bond mobile overnight. Now to equal that, my mobile was dead and needed charging. So, with cap in hand, I gave her a call and to my surprise, she answered and said;

"Mr. Jameson I am so, so glad to hear your voice. I and all of the embassy staff have been really worried about you. May I also say, we are also very proud of you. What you and your team did yesterday goes well beyond the call of duty."

She then did something very old fashioned and very British, she and who was every in her office cheered and said;

"Hip, hip hooray, Hip, hip hooray, Hip, hip hooray.

Well bugger me, I was glad that we weren't using skype. I could feel my eyes welling up and I got all emotional. To cover up for this, I pretended that the phone signal had gone faint for a while, but I suspected the astute Ms. Tarragon-Jones had rumbled me. She graciously gave me a moment, and said;

"Now Mr. Jameson, let's get down to business. I have passed your video footage of the tower onto the relevant intelligence agencies for analysis. At this point, we cannot conclusively say that the tower is related to what happened in Tenerife but be assured, this will be investigated fully.

As for today, I do have some cheering news for you. With the help of the British Government, we have been able to get clearance for you with the Spanish and British aviation authorities to bring your wife's body back to the U.K. For that, you can utilize Senor García's private jet, or we can arrange to have her brought home in an RAF transporter. Additionally, you can bring your range rover and its contents with you. This, however, will have to be brought to the U.K in the RAF transporter. All of this can be arranged as early as tomorrow, please call me back with your wishes and I will make the necessary arrangements."

With that, Ms. Tarragon-Jones hung up.

OMG, I knew this was going to happen, but my heart and mind began racing. Taking a few deep breaths, I tried to calm myself down, but it didn't work, a zillion thoughts on funeral plans were going through my head. Carlos was on deck having a few moments in the sun, so I rushed up and told him the news. Immediately he could see I was in a bit of flap and said;

"B.J, it's great news. Now, I think it would be a good idea if we sat down and made a priority list of things that are needed to be done."

With my head still in turmoil, that sounded like a good idea. So, with the help of a laptop, for the next half hour, we made up a priority list. While I went over the list for the umpteenth time, Carlos telephoned the García's and brought them up to speed. Needless to say, they were one hundred percent behind me. The only objection the García's had was bringing Shelia's body to be brought back in an RAF transporter. They said, and I had to agree, that it would be more dignified to bring her back in García's private jet. I was also pleased to hear that they could arrange a nice coffin for her transport and all of this could do this as early as tomorrow afternoon.

The top of the list of priorities was face timing my daughters and letting them know the news. Within seconds of telling them, they both went into a mental panic. Well, being their parent, I didn't admit that's exactly what I did. So, in a stress-free voice, I told them to calm down and said I Carlos had composed a list of all the things that needed to be done and would I email them a copy. After that, I telephoned Ms. Tarragon-Jones and between us, we finalized that it would be tomorrow for the transportation of Shelia's body and we would fly out of Tenerife in the García's private jet at two in the afternoon.

Shortly after my telephone conversation with Ms. Tarragon-Jones, she sent me an email confirming the arrangements. She also said that when we arrived at the airport, we should ask for a U.N officer named, First Lieutenant Karl Barlow. It was Lieutenant Barlow who I spoke with when we were detained for questioning at the blown-up tower. Now this made me laugh out loud, I had to give Lieutenant Barlow a password which was; Happy holidaymaker. Well, I wasn't sure if this was a wind-up or not, but if the good Lieutenant Barlow asked for one then that's the answer I was to give.

Previously when we spoke, my two daughters had said they would handle Shelia's cremation. However, it was upsetting my youngest, so her big sister stepped up and took over the arrangements. To my surprise, she emailed me saying that although there was a long waiting list at the local crematorium, thanks to some intervention by Ms. Tarragon-Jones, we were been given special consideration and the service has been scheduled a ten-thirty am, in two days' time. Emma, my daughter also included in her email that Ms. Tarragon-Jones had booked the Birmingham North Moor Hall Hotel for the funeral reception with had reserved twenty rooms. With my martial arts and fitness clubs based around the Midlands, I have to say Moor Hall Hotel was perfect as it had easy access to Birmingham city centre and the motorways.

Although it was short notice, I then sent a standard email and text message to all my club Sensei's (teachers), family, friends, and students inviting them to Shelia's funeral. I also had to consider our vast association with the global martial arts community, over many years, we had made many internet friends. So, I posted an edited version of my email on Facebook. In it, I just let our martial friends know about Shelia's death and the funeral arrangement. This allowed our friends to post their thoughts and condolences online.

Through the power of the internet, the word soon got around that the S.T.O.P team was traveling to England. With that, poor Senora Valentina García was inundated with requests wanting her to do television, radio, blogs, and newspaper interviews. However, the icing on the cake for this was an actual half-hour T.V show on the BBC. Senora Valentina thought this was brilliant and was adamant that during our visit to the U.K she would try to fit in as many interviews as possible. To cope with this extra workload, Senora Valentina thought that although Juan José was still recovering from his leg injuries and in a wheelchair, it would be a good idea to ask him to come along as her assistant. Without hesitation, we all agreed that Juan José would be an asset and that being in a wheelchair wasn't a problem.

As if my head wasn't spinning enough, we then had another piece of information from our internet friend Anonymous, who gave us something really big to think about. The post read;

Hi all at S.T.O.P,

Having read what has happened to you with the tower in Tenerife, I began to investigate if other countries have similar Towers using Zenneck surface waves technology. To date, I have found that England, Ireland, Scotland, Wales, France, Germany, Spain, Greece, Russia, India, China, and the U.S.A all have towers that are already constructed or in the process of being constructed.

Strangely, each country has different construction companies, technology companies, and investors involved with them.

My searches to date have revealed that while on the surface big companies like Fran-power seemed to be legitimate concerns, others, however, are fronted by real people, but they have no past internet history. I have attached several links so S.T.O.P can do its own investigation into this.

Now, this might just be nothing, but with all the strange earthly things going on, it's worth mentioning and possibly investigating. A group of six towers three miles high have been discovered on the moon by conspiracy theorists who believe they could have been built by aliens. Footage taken from Google Moon, which is collected by Nasa satellites orbiting the moon and taking images of the lunar surface, appears to show several rocks standing high above ground level.

A Soviet Union space probe named Zond 3 made its way to the moon thirty-three hours after being launched on the eighteenth July nineteen sixty-five. In one of the images of the far side of the moon, a mysterious tower-shaped structure can be seen protruding from the lunar surface. In its vicinity, no other similar structures are seen, and Ufoligist's believe that the mysterious 'tower' seen in the Zond 3 image is a crucial piece of evidence supporting their theory that there are alien structures on the far side of Earth's moon.

More to come soon

Anonymous.

After a brief discussion with Carlos, we agreed that the first part of Anonymous's post needed further investigation, so we asked our S.T.O.P team to have a dig around the internet and see what else they could find. I also sent the list of countries with these strange towers to Ms. Tarragon-Jones and asked if she or the appropriate government agencies could look into this. As to the second part, as crazy as it sounded, it just could not be ruled out. So, Carlos agreed to do a discreet investigation and see if there were any merits to this.

It was mid-afternoon before the García's arrived at the marina, and as normal they brought their wonderful cook Paula with them. After our exploits yesterday and going to the U.K tomorrow, Senor García thought we needed feeding up. Somehow, he had acquired some fresh extra-large T-boned steaks with all the trimmings and we were going to have this treat with all the delicious accompaniments. While Paula busied herself in the galley, we sat and chatted.

I could see Senor García was relaxed asked for his thoughts on Anonymous's latest post and his response to the alien towers on the moon took me and the others by surprise. With a Spanish mafia bosses' composure, he said;

"Yes B.J, a copy of this post was sent to me. While I think some of the hypothetical conjecture about aliens is rubbish, we also have to have an open mind to certain possibilities. On December eleventh, nineteen seventy-two, Apollo seventeen touched down on the Moon. This was not only our final Moon landing but to my knowledge the last time we left low Earth orbit. One has to ask why did these missions stop? Many answers to this have been put forward, but one conspiracy is the moon and indeed other planets within our solar system have many aliens or alien artifacts on them.

Now let's just say these aliens or artifacts are real. We as humans on this planet would have to accept that at some stage our solar system, galaxy, and the universe has other intelligent life forms in it. That would then lead to further speculation about the origins of life on earth and indeed our beliefs in all past and present religions.

One of the big questions is, are we as species ready to accept all of this without any logical or spiritual answers? Well, the consensus is we are not ready. Disclosure of this nature would cause a global meltdown in the structure of our civilizations. What is reassuring is, an alliance of government and religions has been monitoring this and other off-world activities for many years and preparing to put forward some pre-emptive, re-assuring answers.

Now as to the alleged towers on the moon, we at S.T.O.P like the alliance of government's and religions have to prepare for all eventualities."

With one of his big toothy smiles, Carlos then spoke and said what Senor García said just said was brilliant. He then went on to say;

"If you don't mind me bringing this up, I have been doing a bit of investigation and I want to tell you about an odd place called Chaco Canyon.

By now we all knew that Carlos would throw something interesting into our nearly full zany pot, so we all nodded and taking on his college teacher look, he continued;

"Chaco Canyon is located in the Four Corners region of New Mexico; Chaco Canyon is a shallow canyon that was once home to ancient Native American peoples about a thousand years ago. What remains of the civilization indicates a highly sophisticated infrastructure that appears to have been constructed in alignment with various celestial bodies. Enormous, elaborate stone buildings housing roughly seven hundred rooms and numerous underground ceremonial halls known as "kivas are just some of the features that make Chaco Canyon such an extraordinary place.

NASA and other institutes began researching Pueblo Bonito, translated that's Spanish meaning beautiful town, and Chaco Canyon in the 1970s when they discovered some three hundred kilometres of sophisticated roadways and underground kivas through multispectral scanning technology. These elaborate roads and kivas aren't visible to the naked eye or even through aerial photography. What's curious about the Chaco Canyon roads which were overbuilt, underutilized, and constructed without reaching any sort of destination is until later, they appeared to have no functional purpose. Now speculation grows that they are indeed a type of conductor for Zenneck surface waves. Now that has to be of interest to us, but Nasa has other interests in Chaco Canyon.

They and other interested parties are doing extensive research on the canyon and Pueblo Bonito the celestial linearity of the ancient architecture that resides there. The Chaco Canyon inhabitants not only had high expertise in celestial studies. It is believed they could have also known about advanced space travel. I should add, although the canyon was inhabited for roughly four hundred years by these highly intelligent and sophisticated people, all of its residents vanished without a trace. Amazingly, except for one small room, no other burial grounds or graveyards have been discovered in this isolated canyon and researchers remain puzzled by the sudden disappearance of this ancient society.

Theories have been put forward that the Chacoan race used their intelligence and aptitude for astronomy to escape an upcoming cataclysm, or colossal catastrophe, of some sort. According to ancient Sanskrit texts, the earth cycles through four yugas, or epochs. The fourth and final age is known as "kali yuga," which translates to "age of the demon" and is the final era before some sort of cataclysm takes place to start the Earth's cycle anew.

It is believed that we are currently living in the kali yuga, which is characterized by a human preoccupation with the self, sin, greed, and materialism. Between drastic climate change, political upheaval, and ongoing violence across the globe, is it possible that we will soon be facing a modern-day cataclysm?"

Carlos then paused, looked at our faces that must have read astonishment on them. Then for some obscure reason, he began laughing loudly. With tears of laughter now rolling down his face he said;

"On top of everything else, a cataclysm is coming. So, unless we unravel the secrets of the Chacoan race, build a spacecraft and vacate this planet as soon as possible, it looks we're all going to die."

Well, that got us all going, I started with a chuckle and ended up rolling on the cabin floor. Senor García laughed so much he thought his sides were going to burst and poor Senora Valentina had to rush to the loo, as she thought she might pee herself.

Chapter Fifteen, Back to Blighty

Before I and Shelia travelled to Tenerife, I would have been classed as a very calm, cool, and collected kind of person. However, I knew later today I would have to collect my beautiful wife's body and take it back to England and it didn't just upset me, it terrified me. I don't know if it was the thought of seeing her body in a coffin or having to meet my girls in the UK with their dead mom. But this cool dudes' hands would not stop trembling and my stomach was making immensely loud groaning noises. Now when I say loud, it was so embarrassing as Carlos could hear them vibrate throughout his boat. Nevertheless, he did, however, show some sympathy to me and mixed me a concoction to drink of milk with peppermint in it to help calm down my turbulent tummy. I can't say the potion helped much, but it did make me belch a lot.

After failing to eat some breakfast, I packed mine and Carlos's luggage into the Bond mobile. We then headed over to S.T.O. P's offices to pick up Juan José. We also needed to take care of any last-minute business, and I gave our staff a quick pep talk. Well, it was more a stomach rumble, look after the shop, see you all in a few days kind of talk. Despite me not mentioning, well avoiding it, they all knew it was a difficult day for me, so before I left, they all gave me a group hug, and the cool, calm, collected guy left with tears in his eyes.

Within minutes of exiting S.T.O. P's offices the García's turned up and they climbed into the Bond mobile and we all headed over to Tenerife's south airport. Needless to say, on the journey over I didn't want to talk much, but embarrassingly, my stomach had plenty to say. In an attempt to save my embarrassment, Carlos jumped in and explained that it was pre-funeral nerves and he had given to a peppermint drink to help calm my stomach down.

In life one thing always leads to another, disconcertingly my stomach-churning turned to flatulence. The descriptive meaning of the word flatulence refers to the accumulation of gas in the alimentary canal. Well, I had enough gas in my alimentary canal to fill several hot air balloons and it needed to be released. To hide this, I had to suffer severe stomach pains for several bum clenching miles. However, as soon as we got to the airport's military checkpoint, I had to jump out of the Bond mobile and let out the loudest and longest fart in the history of all man and womankind. Fortunately for me, it was just wind and nothing else.

Luckily for me, the soldiers manning the checkpoint had a good sense of humour. After approaching me cautiously and asking me for some identification, laughing the soldier said,

"Sir, if you would have released that inside of the car, the car would have exploded and it would have instantly killed all the occupants."

His mate on the other side of the car called over and joked about now having to wear hazmat suits while on duty. Life didn't get any easier when I got back into the car, my "good friend" Carlos was having hysterical convulsions. Despite this, I apologized and graciously the García's and Juan José tried to hide their amusement, however, they too cracked up when Carlos asked if the outside air smelt of peppermint!

The soldiers at the checkpoint must have telephoned ahead because a military Landover came to greet us with First Lieutenant Karl Barlow in it. He then escorted us directly to the García's private jet. At the side of the jet was a Black Funeral Hurst carrying my wife's coffin in it. I couldn't help but gasp upon seeing this. Then I went to pieces, my whole body just went limp, I cried and I could not get out of the car. Carlos was the first to come to my rescue, however hot on his heel was Senor García. With my two friends supporting me, I managed to get out of the car, and then I had an emotional time. With First Lieutenant Karl Barlow leading them, six soldiers dressed in their regiments dress uniforms saluted me and, in a fashion, befitting a fallen soldier, they loaded Sheila's coffin loaded onto the aircraft.

With shaky legs, I stumbled up the aircraft's steps and was greeted by the Captain and Stewardess who both offered their condolences. The stewardess then directed me to my seat and gave me a well-needed glass of water. While I sat and looked out of the airplanes side window, I could see Carlos helping to get ours, Juan José, and the García's luggage on board. The García's had made their way onboard and so had First Lieutenant Karl Barlow. He came over to me and said;

"Mr. Jameson, please accept my commiserations on the passing of your wife. At Ms. Theresa Tarragon-Jone's request, I will be traveling with you to the U.K and I will be head of yours and your team's security detail for the next few days. She has also organized to have your vehicle put on an R.A.F transporter. It will be delivered to the Birmingham North Moor Hall Hotel."

I was, to say the least, a little puzzled, so looking at First Lieutenant Barlow, I asked;

"Why in god's name would we need a security detail? Were just going to my wife's funeral."

The First Lieutenant exhaled and replied;

"Mr. Jameson when we first meet, you and your team had just been in a firefight with a well-armed mercenary force. As a result of this, a rather expensive communication tower was destroyed. Luckily for you, you had support through Senor García's men. It would be fair to say that these mercenaries were on the pay role of some big global organization that has a network in the U.K. Now bearing this in mind, and the fact that you are a British Diplomat, I and my team will endeavour to keep you, your family, and friends safe while you are on British soil."

First Lieutenant Karl Barlow could see the look of dread in my eyes and in a softer tone continued to say;

"You never thought about this, did you?"

With some embarrassment, I just shook my head from side to side.

To reassure me, he placed his hand on my shoulder and added;

"Don't worry old boy, you will still have your own firepower in the boot of Range rover and I have a good team, who are extremely professional and will be very discrete."

My gaze went over to Senor García, who smiled and gave me one of those, mafia bosses, don't worry, I have it in hand looks. Despite this, it did worry me and I could not believe how naïve I had been. How could I have put my family and friends in such jeopardy?

Carlos then boarded the airplane and seeing that I was looking a tad distressed, came and over and inquired;

"B.J, how are you doing?

I just shook my head from side to side and replied;

"Not so good. On top of Shelia's funeral, I think I am bringing a lot of bad trouble to my family's doorstep."

Not saying anything, Carlos sat beside me and I told him about my conversation with First Lieutenant Barlow. After listening he just nodded and replied;

"Unfortunately, B.J, First Lieutenant Barlow is right. You, I the García's and all the other victims on Tenerife of this catastrophe, will have realized that life from now on will never be the same. And yes, until we stop these atmospheric lunatics, there is going to be a danger to you and everyone around you. However, despite what has happened to you and your wife. You, my kiss ass Karate friend have to count yourself one of the lucky ones. There are not many people who have the ability and resources to protect their loved ones. And while I think about this, you also have the capability of fighting back with your government's blessing."

Well that told me and I have to say, he was right. It was no use moping around feeling sorry for myself. I was indeed one of the lucky ones, and I intended to use that luck and the U.K government's resources to the full. I thanked Carlos for his wise words and as the plane took off, I settled into my luxury seat and fell into a deep, well-needed sleep.

Before I knew it, Carlos nudged me and said we would be landing in thirty minutes. I just had time to pop to the loo, wash my face, and have a drink of coffee before we touched down at Birmingham International airport.

As we taxied along the runway, I could see it was a gloomy, wet day in Birmingham and typically, although it was summer, it was only fourteen degrees outside. Our private jet headed towards the arrival terminal where a small area had been coordained off to allow Shelia's coffin could be loaded into the waiting Hurst. We all watch this and headed into the arrival's terminal building, where we passed quickly through passport control and into the arrivals area. There we were greeted by a hoard of T.V, media, and press reporters. In what seemed like an absolute frenzy, they all wanted to know how I felt about bringing my dead wife back home, my involvement with S.T.O.P, and my job as a British diplomat?

It was Juan José who rushed forward and took control of the situation. In a calm, but controlled voice, he told the frenzied T.V and press reporters;

"Ladies and Gentlemen, thank you for coming here today As I am sure you are aware, this is a distressing time for Senor Jameson and his family. However, he is extremely grateful to the British Government, his friends here and in Tenerife, for helping to arrange to bring his loving wife back to her home country. I am pleased to inform you that all the arrangements have now been made for Mrs. Jameson's funeral and it will be a private affair for family and friends, Members of the press and media, I would ask that you respect this.

Today is not the best time for Senor Jameson to give a full press report on his involvement with S.T.O.P or his position as a British Diplomat. However, as S.T.O. P's press secretary, I would be happy to set up a formal group interview with you all within the next day or so."

While Juan José then took out his iPad and began arranging dates for the press interviews, we slipped by and exited the arrivals. Once outside, we were greeted by my two daughters and my new family member, Ms. Theresa Tarragon-Jones. My daughters ran to me and for a few moments, we just hugged, cried and we all said how much we all missed their mom. Ms. Theresa Tarragon-Jones also decided to show affection by running up to Carlos and passionately kissing him on the lips. Needless to say, the hot-blooded Spaniard seemed to enjoy this and let his hand slip down to Ms. Theresa Tarragon-Jone's bottom. Reluctantly, breaking from her embrace, she then tapped me on the shoulder and said she had cars waiting to take us to the hotel.

Allowing for the evening traffic, I estimated that the journey to the hotel would take about fifty minutes or so. In that time, I decided to bring my daughters up to speed on all that had happened in Tenerife, how I got involved with the García's, S.T.O.P, my appointment to the diplomatic core, and why we would have security officers looking after us for the next few days. It was a tall order, but they both listened intently. Then after a brief discussion, they both agreed that whoever had carried out this act of barbarism, needed to be stopped or brought to justice.

When we arrived at the hotel, Ms. Tarragon-Jones busied herself directing us to our allocated rooms and making sure our luggage was quickly sent up to us. She also informed everyone that we had half an hour to freshen up as she had arranged for an evening meal for us all in the main restaurant. The meal was a carvery buffet and as I was ravenous, I had a selection of beef, pork, chicken piled up with roasted potatoes, parsnips, mashed potatoes, a heap of steaming hot vegetables, and what seemed like a gallon of onion gravy to help wash this down. However, I made sure there was space left for pudding and the apple crumble with custard and a scoop of ice cream filled that space nicely.

Once we were all watered and fed, we sat in the lounge area and discussed what we had scheduled for the next two days. Juan José told me he had set up a press conference tomorrow morning at nine o'clock. I asked if everyone thought it was a good idea to have this as a Jameson family interview and everybody agreed. With his iPad on his lap, Juan José then rattled off numerous interviews he had arranged for Senora Valentina and told her the BBC one would be live at the Birmingham studios tomorrow evening. She seemed very pleased with this and as a typical woman, said she would now take her to leave as she needed to prepare her wardrobe for tomorrow's events. Now that sparked off my two daughters, they went into a lady's panic about, hair, makeup, and what they would wear for tomorrow's interview. In the end, they too retreated, and that left the men and Ms. Tarragon-Jones who seemed as cool as a cucumber about everything.

First Lieutenant Barlow then came and joined us and I took the opportunity to run a few things by him. First, I told him that after tomorrow's press interview, I wanted to go and visit my main Martial arts and fitness centres and I would like Carlos to come as well. He said that was fine and he and one of his team would accompany us. Secondly, I wanted to know what security he had provided for my daughters and immediate family? With a confident look on his face he told me;

"Mr. Jameson, we have a team of twenty, ten males and females. There are on call twenty-four hours a day, Oh, and hasten to add, that most will be working incognito."

That sounded OK with me and partly answered my next inquiry, however, this was the big one for me and my family so I asked;

"Will the same work around my wife's funeral?

Nodding he replied;

"Yes Sir, it will. I have already been in touch with the Co-op funeral directors who have provided, times of pick up, routes, crematorium details, and drop-offs."

He then added;

"Mr. Jameson, we know you and your family have been through hell. However, I want to reassure you, Sir, that we and going to do everything we can to make sure that your wife's funeral goes without a hitch."

From his mannerisms and what he had said, I could see that the First Lieutenant was a professional at what he does and I respected him for that. However, I thought we needed to drop the formalities and told him to address me as B.J and I would address him as Karl. He then smiled, saluted, and replied;

"That's fine by me, Sir."

We all had laughed and for the next half an hour we just relaxed and enjoyed each other's company. It was Ms. Tarragon-Jones, who with a wry smile on her face broke up our gathering by declaring that it was time for her and Carlos to hit the sack. My horny friend raised no objections, he just raised his eyebrows, gave everyone one of his big toothy grins, stood up, put an arm around Ms. Tarragon-Jones waist, and after saying good night, they both left.

Senor García asked if we would like a brandy before retiring? I declined to say I too need my bed now. As I stood up, I jokingly asked Karl if he would like to escort me to my room for my safety. Laughing, he told me to piss off and with that, I left him and Senor García to have a one for the road glass of brandy.

After having a good night's sleep, I woke up just before six. I planned to go for a long run, but it was bucketing with rain outside. So, I turned to plan B and headed on down to the hotel gym and have a good workout. To my surprise, Carlos and Ms. Tarragon-Jones were already there. After saying good morning, I discreetly enquired if Carlos had slept well and with one of his super big toothy smiles, he said he had had a very energetic night. At that, we both laughed and then got stuck into our workouts. I have to say I felt so much better after my workout. I then headed back up to my room for a shower and a shave. Then at seven-thirty, we all meet up for a hearty, full English breakfast. When we were finished, Ms. Tarragon-Jones approached and in her very efficient way she informed me that my car had been delivered, members of the press and media were already arriving, and were being directed to the main conference room by Juan José. Then almost whispering in my ear, she also added that the reason Karl was not at breakfast was, he and some of his team handling the press conference security. That to my mind was all good positive news and I thanked her.

As I looked across at my two daughters, they looked a little edgy. Understandably, they were a little anxious over the family press interview. They both knew that they were not just representing our family, they were going to be the voices of all Tenerife victims' families. Although, as their dad, I tried my best to reassure them that no matter what they said it will be OK, it was Senora Valentina who came to my rescue and said;

"Emma, Oliva, your mother loves you both very much and she is so, so proud of what you are going to do today. She says she will be in your hearts as you speak to the world today."

Well, that brought a few tears of both sadness and joy. My girls then had to rush to the ladies to tidy up their eye makeup and once they were ready, we headed over to the hotel's main conference room. Juan José met us at the conference room entrance and then took us to a large desk with chairs behind it that faced the press. The desk had numerous microphones on it and before we could start, we had to run through the normal one, two, three sound checks. With that over, Juan José called to get everyone's attention, and one by one he introduced the Jameson family. He then invited questions to be asked and the first from a man from Sky news was a humdinger;

"Mr. Jameson, I have been a press officer for many years and yet, I am amazed at the level of security you and your family have. Can you explain why?

A silence fell in the room and all eyes and cameras were fixed on me. I slowly looked into the lens of each camera and replied;

"In the catastrophe that happened on Tenerife, my wife was the first to die. After that thousands were killed, but to date, no one has any explanations. The world now faces the same threat and as a British subject with involvement with S.T.O.P an organization that is investigating this calamity, I have been deemed worthy to be of some service to the British Government. That service has already put my mine and other members of S.T.O. P's lives at risk and that's why we have been given the level of security you see."

Sensitivity is something reporters seem to forsake when they are on the trail of a story. The next question was directed to my daughters from the sun newspaper, and it was lower than low. With no compassion in her voice, the lady reporter asked:

"I understand that this was the first time your mom and dad had gone on holiday without you. Was this because they were having trouble in their relationship and wanted a holiday to sort things out? Or was it because they needed a break because of inner family problems?"

Both my daughters looked at each other and began to laugh. They then had a brief chat about who was going to answer this question and decided it would be my eldest Emma. Composing herself, she answered;

"The only reason mom and dad went away was, it was their twenty-fifth wedding anniversary. Dad bought this holiday for mom as a surprise present Now for the record, we the Jameson's have had a fabulous, loving family life and a big part of that life has been taken away from us. Mom and thousands of other innocent people were needlessly killed. The families of all those people are grieving and want answers. What they and we do not want is the press asking silly questions that can only cause more heartache.

Dad loved my mom with all his heart and he is now demonstrating his eternal love for her by trying to track down hers and all the other victim's killers and then bring them to justice."

While Emma's words melted my heart, the hard-hearted press continued and any other reporter asked;

"You have all mentioned that Mrs. Jameson was the first to die in the Tenerife catastrophe. However, it looks to me as if Mrs. Jameson's death was no more than a tragic accident."

The Jameson family didn't need to discuss this, it was back to me to answer this one. Looking directly at the reporter, I replied;

"Initially I would have agreed with you, however, your assumption is wrong. As events unfolded and S.T.O.P did more investigations, it was more than evident that my wife's murder was done by manipulating a thunderstorm that created focused lightning bolts was the opening prelude to all the other Tenerife murders. I would like to stress that this evaluation has not been fully endorsed by the governments of the world, but at the same time it certainly has not been ruled out."

That was three tough questions answered, I wondered if the next one would be easier, but it wasn't. A man stood up and introduced himself as Timothy Ailing, a correspondent for religious affairs from the Times and Sunday Times. Mr. Ailing asked;

"We understand that S.T.O.P is also investigating some paranormal activity that involves the late Mrs. Jameson and others who recently died on Tenerife. Would you like to comment on this?"

Fortunately, Juan José was still in the conference room and he was quick to answer this with;

"Senor Ailing, as your newspaper is aware, S.T.O.P has a specialist on board who is heading this side of our investigations. Senora Valentina García is as we speak giving interviews with members of the press and media. She would be delighted to do one for your newspaper. If you see me at the end of the Jameson family interview, I will gladly set up an interview for you."

While I thought this was a reasonable answer, suddenly, Mr. Ailing became very agitated. Then, without warning, he ran from where he was standing, lunged across our press table, and attempted to attack me with his fists! Luckily for me, at almost sixty years of age and quite out of condition, Mr. Ailing was no fighter. So, I easily blocked his blows and soon had him in a simple arm restraint. However, within seconds, this seemed to insight all the other reporters and their teams at the press conference and in mass, they all charged towards our press desk!

This is where you have to put the skills of a trained martial artist in the right context. First, forget all the martial art movies. All fight scenes are staged, rehearsed, and shot with different camera angles and then edited in the cutting room. Next, the element of surprise is always on the side of the attacker, or in our case, a crazy mob intent on killing us. Finally, our martial arts fighting code of ethics teaches us to be calm and exercise control and restraint. Well bugger that, within seconds, we were fighting for our lives, it was a free for all.

I seemed to be the main target and despite landing one or two good blows, I was soon battered to the floor where kicks, punches, and someone biting me persisted. My only saving grace was, Carlos, Senor García, Karl, and his team were on hand and they all waded in. It took them what seemed like an eternity to restrained everyone, but finally, the last few were dragged off me. At first, everything was quite bleary and I had trouble standing, but all of that was quickly put aside when I saw my two daughters lying bloodied and groaning on the floor.

It was obvious that they had both taken quite a beating, but they managed to sit up. Wiping some of the blood away from her eyes, Emma half laughing, half crying said;

"Dad, that's the last press inter-view I'm ever giving."

Oliva wasn't feeling at all humorous, her finger was probing the gap where her front teeth had been kicked out. As she stood up, she booted a restrained male reported in his bollocks who was still shouting he wanted to kill us. He screamed in agony and one of Karl's lady security officers had to pull Oliva back before she repeated the process.

As I looked around the conference room. I was pleased to see that Carlos, Juan José, who was still in his wheelchair and Senor García were a little ruffled but unharmed from helping fight off our attackers. It also appeared that Ms. Tarragon-Jones had joined in and despite having someone else's blood on her rather expensive white shirt, she too was uninjured.

While the large portion of Karl's squad stayed to guard the S.T.O.P team against a still extremely hostile press. Karl escorted, no helped me because I was having difficulty standing in an unoccupied smaller conference room. Then, my daughters were brought in and we were given medical assistance from two of his squad who were field medics. Karl then insisted that we go to the Queen Elizabeth Hospital for a full check-up and he had an air ambulance on standby for that. I told him that that was a bit of an overkill, but he replied and said;

"B.J, it's not an overkill. You might all have concussions or internal damage. Oh, and if you don't believe me, go take a look in the mirror on the wall."

He then helped me to my feet and as I stood in front of the mirror, I couldn't believe what I was looking at. My face looked like I had gone fifty rounds with a bare-knuckle boxer and it was only then that my body began to feel that the bare-knuckle boxer might have been wielding a baseball bat!

My Amigo Carlos then came in and was holding something in his right hand. He went over to the one lady medic and gave whatever he was holding to her and then came over to me. He slumped into a chair and with a sombre face he said;

"The storm has passed, there is total confusion in the main conference room. All the reporters have no recollection of what they did to you and your family. This situation, it's just crazy!"

With all the blows I had received to my head, I was having trouble focusing, but did I just hear right? A storm, what storm? I too slumped into a chair and looking at Carlos, I told him I hadn't got a clue what he was talking about with a storm. To gather his thoughts, he inhaled and slowly replied;

"B.J, when I got up it was raining heavily, I just thought we Spanish always hear from our British tourists that it always rains in England and this was the norm. However, while you and the members of the press were in the press conference, the winds picked up and a powerful thunderstorm moved in. You and your girls were wrapped up with the press interviewing you and didn't hear it.

Now, my friend, this is scary, really scary. I think whoever attacked Tenerife with HAAPP weather mind manipulation techniques, has now pushed that technology forward. I am guessing from the press's amnesia, that the storm we just experienced was the same, but it was targeted directly at you and your family. B.J, this is not fiction! Whoever is doing this, now can target individuals.!"

In the old days when a boxer went back to his corner after taking some heavy blows, the old method of reviving him was giving him smelling salts, pouring ice-cold over his head and down the front of his shorts. Well with what Carlos had said, that just happened to me. My head was now clear and after attacking my family, I wanted to come out fighting, but my opponent was not yet visible to me. I first looked at my girls all bloodied and battered and my heart sank. Then I looked at Carlos and yes, I was angry, but making a scene now would only upset my girls more, so I shook my head and said nothing. Carlos gave me a nod back to indicate he understood my quandary. Then, he informed me that he had found Olivia's teeth and had given them medics.

As a martial artist we both know from experience that if a student's tooth or teeth are knocked out, the nerves and blood vessels can't be repaired. That is why all avulsed teeth will need a root canal. However, the bone can reattach to the root of the tooth once it's put back into place. The odds of saving a tooth are highest in young children, but adult teeth can be saved as well. So, with a bit of luck, Olivia's teeth might be saved. I thank Carlos for this and before we could discuss anything else, Karl said the air ambulance had just arrived and he and his team would escort us outside.

It was a bit embarrassing to be strapped into a wheeled stretcher, but apparently, that's the procedure for patients who travel in an air ambulance. So once all three of us were secured, the air ambulance took off and we headed for the Queen Elizabeth hospital. As I was lying down, I took the opportunity to close my eyes for a few minutes and have a think about what had happened. However, my thoughts were soon disrupted by my daughter Emma saying;

"Dad, we need to talk."

Opening my eyes, I looked at Emma who was lying next to me, and inquired;

"OK Emma, what's on your mind."

She began to cry and said;

"Dad we both know that that was a deliberate attack on our lives and without the help of the security provided, we would have been Killed!"

Emma was no fool, she would have quickly assessed the situation That assessment would have brought the realization that until the day we stop these terrorists, we as a family are always going to be directly in the firing line. I reached over and held her hand and said;

"Yes, you are right and I, S.T.O.P, and the governments of the world are not going to rest until these lunatics are brought to justice."

She squeezed my hand tightly and replied;

"If you want two new members for the U.K branch of S.T.O.P sign me and Oliva up."

Under the circumstances, it was a courageous thing to say, but our tête-à-tête had sparked off another concern. It would not be just us three who would be targeted, we would have to look at the security of the whole family, that's my daughters' partners, my brothers and sisters, aunts, uncles, close friends, and so on. I decided as soon we landed and got seen too, I would have to contact Karl and Senor García and see what could be done.

On arrival, I have to say the Queen Elizabeth Hospital is remarkable. No sooner than we touched down on the helipad, a full medical team was already waiting and we were whisked inside and given a thorough once over. Apparently, for any injured British troops, this is one of the major U.K treatment hospitals. Although we had plenty of cuts, swellings, mega bruises, and Olivia had lost a few teeth, we all seemed medically intact. The only bad news was, we all had suspected concussions and would have to stay overnight for observations. After a short delay, we were taken to ward in the hospital's new wing and that's where Karl, with a very glum face, was waiting for me.

He asked the ward manager if we could have some privacy and she obliged by giving us her office. Once inside Karl asked me to sit down as he had some bad news for me. Instantly my heart sank and as I perched with trepidation on the edge of a seat, he placed his hand on my shoulder and said;

"B.J, I am sorry to have to inform you that your house and all your businesses have been attacked by arsonists. As yet, I do not have a full report on the extent of the fires, but from what I have been told from the senior fire officers and police on each scene that the fires are extensive and they are not hopeful of saving much. The only good news I can offer you is, as far as we know, no one has been injured"

In all my life, I had never felt low and vulnerable. I and my family were only just coming to terms with the terrible death of my wife. Then, a few hours ago in what should have been a genial press conference, it turned out into the press conference from hell where we were all nearly killed by crazed media and press reporters. Now we just hit an all-time low, and somehow. with my heart racing and head pounding, I had to drag myself out of this seat and go tell my daughters that our family home and business were all gone. However, even that went amiss. As I tried to stand up, my legs gave way from underneath me and I collapsed to the floor. After that, things became very confusing, all I could hear was muffled voices, then everything went dark.

When I came around, the day had become night and I had an Intravenous drip attached to my left arm. Apparently, after chatting to the hospital doctor, I had had a bit of a seizure due to stress and becoming dehydrated. However, the saline running through my system did not alleviate my anxiety. I explained to the doctor that it was my wife's funeral tomorrow and I and my daughters needed to be discharged as soon as possible. Professionally, he told me to calm down and if all is well, we will all be discharged first thing in the morning.

No sooner than the doctor left the room my daughter came in to see me and needless to say, we had an emotional time. This was the first time they had ever seen me laid up in a hospital bed and all things considered, they put on a brave face, told me they loved me and gave me lots of tearful hugs. They also told me not to worry about the house and businesses, saying all of these things could in time be replaced, but their dad couldn't. With that, Carlos and my new family member, Ms. Theresa Tarragon-Jones burst into the room. Almost jumping onto the bed, they both rushed overthrew their arms around me and showered me with words of kindness and kisses.

Now a few kisses on the cheek from Ms. Theresa Tarragon-Jones is acceptable, but when you have a mad Spanish male friend who continually kisses you, it's time to put the breaks on. Laughing, I pushed him away and said;

"Carlos my good friend, save some of your kisses for the lovely Ms. Theresa Tarragon-Jones."

He stood up, looked at me, and then tears filled his eyes and with a very sad face he said;

"B.J, when you collapsed, I thought you had had a heart attack and was going to die."

Well, those words set a spark off and in no time we all were crying. I tried to say it was just a bit of a seizure, but I was inundated with lots more hugs and kisses. After a few minutes we all settled down and my girls began to talk about their moms' funeral arrangements. It then hit me that other than my holiday clothes, all my other clothes were at my home and now destroyed in the fire. So, other than some slacks, shorts and a few t-shirts and casual shirts, I hadn't even got a jack, trousers or suit to wear to my wife's funeral.

Before I got too melancholy on this, Senor and Senora García came in to visit me. With their normal thoughtfulness, they brought flowers, an array of different fruits, and some rather expensive chocolates. While Carlos shared out these yummy delights, Senor García said he had some important news for us. He began;

"Today has been a terrible day for B.J and his family and sadly, these events cannot be undone. However, we must not waiver in our quest to stop these people. To this end, I have discussed with First Lieutenant Karl Barlow increasing security and he said that under the circumstances he has been allocated an additional ten officers. We have also agreed that I provide personal security contractors who will support First Lieutenant Karl Barlow's team.

Now B.J, today you lost your home and business and I understand that you English have insurance to help cover your losses. However, with my understanding of the insurance industry, this will drag on for months if not years. Now to help with this, I have the resources and finances and will put them at your immediate disposal.

Now tomorrow is a very important day and B.J my sister suspects that all of your formal clothing has been destroyed in your house fire. So, we have taken the liberty of doing some shopping for you and have a selection of off-the-peg suits, jackets, trousers, shirts, ties, shoes, and socks for you to try on. The ones you don't want or do not fit will be returned.

Now, as to future press conferences and interviews for S.T.O.P., We cannot back down, therefore I would like to propose that we continue these. However, for our security, we will only do these by Webcam, Podcast, Skype, FaceTime, Zoom, Web X, or other media communications methods. If this is agreed, then Juan José can reschedule the ones my sister will be doing and also arrange any future ones for S.T.O.P and the Jameson family "

Once again, I was indebted to Senor García and Senora García's generosity, thoughtfulness, and kindness and thanked them for this. Collectively, we then discussed Senor Garcia's proposal at press conferences and despite today's setback, we all agreed we should continue. The only proviso was, we would all do them under the conditions laid out by Senor García, but we would not disclose our locations.

With all the well wishes and business for the day sorted out, slowly after a few more hugs and kisses everyone left and I tried to settle down in my hospital bed. This proved ludicrously difficult due to the sheets being tucked in so tight, I could not move. Then there were comings and goings of a busy hospital followed by being monitored every few hours by the very diligent nursing staff. So, by five-thirty in the morning, I only had managed a few cat naps. Although I was feeling tired, I knew had a long, busy day ahead. I got one of the nurses to disconnect the Intravenous drip, got myself up, struggled into the shower cubical, showered, and shaved my swollen, battered face as best as I could.

Soon after that, the doctor came in and said he was happy to discharge me, however, he insisted on prescribing some pills to help relax me. That made me smile inwardly as I have had hardly ever taken any medication and had no intention of changing this now. However, to get a quick discharge, I thanked the doctor and before he left, I asked if my daughter was also being discharged. To my delight, he said they were and that was his next port of call. Once the doc had left, I asked one of my security guards to contact First Lieutenant Karl Barlow and let him know we would all be ready to leave in about an hour. Then, it was time for a much-needed coffee and I began to sort out my clothes for Shelia's funeral.

Senor García and Senora García had chosen some very expensive off the peg clothes and after a quick rummage, I put on a Gucci white shirt and black tie, Armani black suit, black silk socks, and a beautiful pair of Berluti black soft leather shoes. I have to say they all fitted well and I felt like a million dollars. The only let down was my swollen face and two black eyes. However, the Garcia's had thought of everything, they had gotten me a pair of Cartier Panthere sunglasses.

When my girls arrived, they gave me the once over and in unison, gave me a wolf whistle. That made us laugh. To carry on the much-needed pre-funeral jollities, Emma had gotten hold of three large medical paper bags. Using a nurse's scissors, she had cut eyes holes, and mouths in each one, and laughing she said that we should all wear these at mom's funeral as with our battered faces we all looked like zombies out of the tv serious, the walking dead. For a bit more fun, we all put them on, I added my sunglasses and then we took a family selfie. While we were still wearing our paper masks, Karl walked in, took one look at us, and burst out laughing. Joking, he then said that when we leave the hospital, we should wear them and tell the hospital staff that these are now being prescribed by the NHS to help victims get over facial traumas.

Putting the laughter to one side, he then went on to tell us about our security for the day. The first bit was our transit from the hospital to our hotel. He said traveling through Birmingham's early morning traffic by car was a security nightmare, so he had arranged a helicopter to transport us. Next on the agenda was our journey to and from the crematorium, for this Karl had arranged an armed police escort and his team would-be drivers in all of the funeral cars. To top this, a helicopter and four unmarked cars would be constantly monitoring our route. Karl then half frowned, half smiled, and said;

"I have to say, I have never worked with outside security firms before, but Senor García has been in contact with me and throughout the day, he will also be providing some additional security. To make this work, I have provided him with a plan of what security will be going on today.

I had some concerns about the legality of this and civilians carrying firearms. However, just before I arrived, Senor García confirmed that his men and women will be working within the guiding principles of British law, in support of the with the West Midlands police and my security team."

That sounded like a reasonable plan to me, but I had one major concern. I knew lots of family, friends, and club members would want to attend Shelia's funeral service and the reception afterward. I wanted to know how Karl or Senor García was going to monitor all those wanting to be at both functions?

Karl nodded and told me that a medium-sized visitor's marquee had been set up out the front of the crematorium and Hotel reception. All those who wish to attend either function will enter through the marquee, be photographed with facial recognition software, and be issued with a badge of approval subject to me or my daughters' consent. He then produced a laptop and explained that consent or rejection would be just a matter of clicking on the faces as they appear in the face recognition software.

I couldn't help but smile, the security software he spoke about has been used widely for passengers on cruise liners for years, but this must have been the first at a funeral. Although we needed it, even Shelia would have seen the funny side of this.

Karl's radio then burst into life and a female voice said;

"This is mother bird; we have just touched down on the helipad nest. Are my hatchlings ready to fly?

With a big grin on his face, Karl replied;

"Hatchlings feed, watered, chirping, and ready to fly mother bird."

Well, how could you not laugh at that? We all had a good chuckle and on Karl's OK, we followed him and with our security team surrounding us out to mother birds' helicopter. Mother birds take off was extremely smooth and within about ten minutes of flight over Birmingham City and out towards Sutton Coalfield, we touched down on the hotel's grounds. There we were greeted by Carlos and Ms. Theresa Tarragon-Jones who gave us all a hug and then ushered us inside to the main reception area. Once inside they had arranged for teas and coffees and said we had about half an hour before the funeral cars would arrive.

While my girls went into a lady's panic and rushed off with Ms. Theresa Tarragon-Jones to put on some additional makeup to help conceal their facial injuries, I took a moment just to sit, sip a coffee gather my thoughts, and get my emotions into tow, before having to face my wife final journey. After about ten minutes, Juan José and Senor Garcia came into the reception area and both came over to me, nodded, and sat with me. It was one of those occasions where nobody knew what to say, so until the funeral cars arrived, we all just sat in silence.

It was Senora Valentina who broke the silence by announcing to us that the funeral cars had just arrived. That sent a chill down my spine. However, just before we were about to leave, Senora Valentina said she wanted to speak with me and my two daughters. She escorted us into a quiet corner of the reception area and asked us to hold hands. Before all this happened, I would have thought this to be a bit stupid, but now I knew differently and immediately took my daughter's hands. Looking calmly at us all, Senora Valentina then said;

"Earlier this morning I spoke with Shelia, she sends her love and says she misses you all. However, she has also told me that you should not be sad today, today you are just having a funeral for her physical body. She says, she wants you all to be strong and wanted to remind you, that she like all the other victims are still trapped in an unknown void and is relying on you to rescue them."

I felt my girls tighten their grip on my hands and without speaking, we knew at that moment that despite our latest setback, we had to battle on.

We thanked Senora Valentina for speaking with Shelia and under armed guard, we headed out to the funeral cars. The first car we could see was Shelia's black funeral car. In the back was Shelia's funeral casket and appropriately, it had been draped with a white cloth that displayed our martial arts centres Logo. On top of the casket was a large round wreath of red and white flowers that were shaped into a yin and yang. Seeing all this upset me, I tried to fight it by repeating in my head Shelia's words about not being sad today and being strong, but my eyes let me down, and soon tears rolled down my face.

Now as you can imagine, my tears had a snowball effect and within seconds, my daughters began to cry. That spurred Carlos to start and I could even see Ms. Theresa Tarragon-Jones Juan José and the Garcia's passing around tissues to wipe their eyes. The only one who was calm was Karl. He gave us a few moments and then tactfully he directed us to the appropriate cars. Once onboard, we buckled up, and, in a convoy, we head toward Sutton Coalfields' crematorium. The police cars to our front and rear of the convoy had their blue lights flashing and that deterred any of the busy traffic from cutting in.

The convoy took over twenty minutes to get to the crematorium, in that time, I and my daughters had a chance to look at Karl's laptop and approve of those who had come to pay their respects today. When we arrived, I was pleased to see that all of my students had turned up in their Gi's. (martial arts suits). The senior black belts were wearing black Kimono Jackets, Hakamas, (baggy black trousers) and each had a Katana, (Japanese sword) strung through their obi, (belt). With Karl's approval after being vetted, the seniors then lined up, drew their swords, and formed an arched guard of honour so that the pallbearers of Shelia's coffin and close family and friends could pass through. I knew that Shelia would love this, this was the highest respect any deceased martial artist could ever get.

Shelia's coffin was then wheeled to the front of the crematorium and once everyone was in the chapel of rest, I walked to the front to say a few words. As I looked around the chapel of rest, I was overwhelmed to see so many attending. It took me a few moments and a few deep breaths to compose myself, then I began;

> "First, on behalf of Shelia and the Jameson family, please accept our sincere thanks for coming here today. We were all shocked and saddened by the sudden death of my wife's death, but I want you to join in with me in a moment of silence to remember all the others who died in Tenerife just after Shelia's passing."

At that, I lowered my head and stood still for about a minute. Then raising my head, I continued to say;

"Thank you for that, I am sure the families who also lost a loved one will appreciate that our thoughts are with them.

It's hard, to sum up, someone you love and has loved you back, given you many, many years of happiness, two beautiful children, been your best friend, training, and business partner. Well, Shelia was all of this and more. She wasn't just a mother to my two girls. she was the mother to everyone who studied martial arts with us, her heart was big and she could always see good in everyone. One of her great passions was fitness and martial arts. As I look around here today, I see many faces of those who attended her classes, I think you will all agree that Shelia that she radiated enthusiasm and threw her heart and soul into them.

I have always been a down-to-earth kind of man, but Shelia had a unique way of making everything look sophisticated, and even a workingman's budget, she made our home look classy. To say she was a great cook would be an understatement. She took pride in the presentation of every dish. Even a plate of egg, sausage, and chips looked as though it had been made by a five-star Michelin chef.

Everyone laughed at this. I suppose by now I was just prattling on, but it helped to talk about her and I needed to say much more;

"Shelia's love of animals extended to us doing lots of fund-raising events in our clubs for many animal sanctuaries and trusts. As a couple, we both loved the outdoors, wildlife, and spent many happy hours just walking through woodlands. One of our joys was tending to our garden. We must have twenty bird feeders in it and each day Shelia would diligently fill each one. Sadly, that, our beautiful home, our martial arts, and fitness clubs were destroyed by arsonists yesterday."

At this stage I didn't want to say too much about Shelia essence, soul, or whatever it's called being trapped in a strange unknown void, so until I knew more, I had to camouflage the beginning of the next sentence by saying;

> "I know it my heart and mind that Shelia would not want us the Jameson's to give in. So, to all my Senior martial arts and fitness instructors, I want you to go out and hire local facilities and use these until we can find new premises. Further, I would ask that every club member support their local instructors in this. For that support, I promise you that I will open new, superbly equipped dojos and fitness centres as soon as humanly possible.
>
> Finally, to honour the memory of my wife, mother to my children, and friend to so many, I would like to name the first Centre we open, the Shelia Jameson Martial Arts and Fitness Centre."

Now, I am not sure what etiquette is used in a Chapel of Rest, but this was met with rapturous cheers and applause. Although it was a very sad day, the rest of the day went without a clinch, well except for one that popped up later in the day.

As funeral receptions go, Shelia's reception went well and it gave me a chance to catch up with members of mine and Shelia's family, and all of our friends. Each offered their condolences and support in helping rebuild our lives. I did, however, notice Ms. Theresa Tarragon-Jones was missing for some considerable time and when she returned, she asked if she could have a few words with the members of S.T.O.P.

While my daughters held the fort, I and the S.T.O.P team managed to slip away and meet up in the hotel's small conference rooms. There, Ms. Theresa Tarragon-Jones had set up a T.V and it was on the B.B.C new channel. She looked at me and said;

> "B.J, you are your family are headline news."

As we watched the B.B.C news presenter verbally related the story of our attack followed by some gruesome video footage.

As this was yesterday's news, the relevance of this story did not hit home until he followed up with;

> "Given the seriousness of what happened yesterday and until this incident can be investigated fully, the British Prime Minister has announced in Parliament today that all live press conferences for government officials will be suspended. The Prime Minister then went on to say that the British Government is at this stage also advising any groups or individuals to only take part in press interviews by Webcam, Podcast, Skype, FaceTime, or other media communications methods."

The screen then went a video of the British Prime Minister addressing Parliament and stating the same. After this, the B.B.C reporter stated that reports were coming in of other countries voicing their concerns about this attack and also looking at banning live press conferences. Some even spoke about the possibility of suspending large public gatherings and sporting events. It was covid 19 all over again.

Chapter Sixteen, The other side

From the dawning of mankind, wealth and power are the two main features that dominated those who classed themselves as the elite of the human race. As a child, Francisco Martìnez had observed this, but as he lived in a small cabin on the outskirts of Alto village, New Mexico, he knew that he would never achieve that status unless he chose both of the following routes. The first was a serious crime and the second was arduous studies.

Although Francisco was extremely intelligent, profitable work was short in a village that had a population of just over two thousand. Therefore, his papa and mama were dirt poor and did not have the means to send him to a good school, college, and on to the likes of Yale University. So, Francisco financed this himself through his criminal and business exploits.

At the age of ten Francisco had already killed, no in his words, assassinated his first man. The man was a local small-time drug dealer and he had Francisco doing some minor drug dealing with the local adults and school children for him. Francisco could see this man for what he was, a pervert, and even as a child, it sickened him. So, one night Francisco sneaked into the man's house, waited for the man to have his way with one of the local boys. While Senor pervert was having a cigarette on the first-floor balcony, Francisco rushed up behind him and with a mighty push, launch the man over the balcony rail. The man fell to his death and his demise was recorded by the local police as an unfortunate accident. However, they and the local community were glad to see the back of him. Francisco never admitted or had any remorse in this evil man's death. However, Francisco always carefully analysed his actions and knew from this that if planned things out carefully he could get away with murder. And he did, time, and time again.

As a teenager' Francisco had become quite the criminal academic. By most criminals' standards, Francisco's crimes were, ingenious, extremely well-executed, and through his studies of forensic science, almost impossible to solve. One of Francisco's many passions was physics and chemistry, when he was not planning a robbery or assignation, he relaxed by reviewing the chemistry of Louis Pasteur, Alfred Noble, and Michael Faraday and the theorizing of Isaac Newton, Tesla Einstein, Planck, Hawking and many more.

From an early age, Francisco could see that the supply and demand for illegal drugs brought in vast profits and that's what he needed. However, he could also see that in most cases the suppliers were total idiots and were only one step ahead of the law, a bullet or a lifetime behind bars. Therefore, after leaving Yale University he decided to do things differently. Through his criminal exploits, he had already accumulated a reasonable amount of money and with it, he opened a pharmacy that dealt under counter drugs to those who wanted them. This was so successful that within a few years he owned a chain of pharmacies. Finally, he sold his pharmaceutical chain for several million and opened Franco a multinational pharmaceutical company with a research facility. This company legitimately supplied drugs and medications to governments, hospitals, and trusts globally and behind the scenes, manufactured all types of non-regulated and illegal drugs.

Over the years Francisco's desire for wealth and power expanded into all types of legal and illegal enterprises. Another company he set up was Franarms Inc. This company dealt with the global sale of all types of armaments and land, sea, and air militarised equipment. As you can guess, Francisco over the counter sales did very well and his under-the-counter sales did even better.

The sales of armaments did so well that Francisco saw a fantastic opportunity to capitalize on this and he opened Fran-freight. This company specialized in the secure road delivery of armaments and militarised equipment across the U.S.A.

Fran-freight soon expanded into Fran-air and with its fleet of heavy lifting helicopters and small and large cargo planes, it opened up a global armament delivery market. For the extra-large militarised equipment Francisco needed ships and Fran-shipping was created. Each of Fran-shipping container ships cost a whooping seventy-five million dollars and Francisco had six of them. Needless to say, as a side-line, Fran-freight, Fran-air, and Fran-shipping also delivered from Franco legal and illegal drugs and weapons.

Francisco could also see that the stock market could bring in some healthy profits. On the downside, he could also see that if you played it wrongly, you stood to lose a fortune. So, he decided he would not gamble his hard-earned cash, what he would do is let others play the market and he would reap from their profits. To do this, Francisco created an algorithm computer program that helped predict stock market trends and sold it under contract for several million. Part of the contract agreement was Francisco would maintain and update the algorithm program for a fee of three percent of the gross profit of each punter. Now, some did make small to large losses. But on the whole, the majority of punters made some reasonable gains, and a few hit the million-dollar jackpot. This fact was widely advertised and Francisco's program was a big hit globally. Before long, the fee of three percent of the gross profit of each punter earned Francisco several more millions of dollars.,

As his wealth grew, his status also grew and those with profitable investments came knocking at his door. We all know that money makes money and before Francisco was thirty-five, he was already a multi-billionaire. However, life had become too easy, he missed his early days of danger and assassinating his opposition. It was at that time that he cast his mind back to his home in Alto, New Mexico. He recalled one of the assets of New Mexico was the Pueblo Bonito cultural site in Chaco Canyon. Francisco had fond memories of the place and how during his late teens he would explore this ancient site. Francisco smiled to himself as he remembered spending hours walking around the site, taking photos, and making notes.

Out of curiosity Francisco did a google search on Pueblo Bonito the major cultural site in Chaco Canyon. What he found surprised him. He already knew that the area was a national monument and a world heritage cultural centre. But what he didn't know was several years ago, NASA and other agencies had taken an interest in this ancient site and were still carrying out investigations. Over the years Francisco had had some dealing with NASA and he knew that if a space agency was investigating things on the planet earth, there was a good reason for it. It was then that Francisco decided Pueblo Bonito and Chaco Canyon had many mysteries that had not yet been solved and he was going to be the one to unlock them.

Chapter Seventeen, Power opens doors

Before Francisco set off for Alto, New Mexico, he contacted the directors of United Nations Educational, Scientific and Cultural Organization or UNESCO for short. He told them as a child he lived in Alto and wanted to visit the area and was particularly interested in the Pueblo Bonito cultural site and the Chaco Canyon. Shrewdly, he also dropped out that if he was pleased with the work UNESCO was doing on the site, he would consider making a substantial donation to UNESCO. Next, he contacted the administrative director of NASA who he knew personally, and repeated what he had said to UNESCO. Both organizations welcomed this entrepreneur's interest in Pueblo Bonito and the Chaco Canyon and with the thought of extra funding, they readily agreed to give him the grand tour.

To carry out his investigations, Francisco needed a place to stay and his family home was perfect for that. Some years ago, he had the family's home cabin completely gutted and modernized. Then until the deaths of his papa and mama, both his parents lived in what you would call an extremely luxurious lodge. Alto and its surrounding areas is a place of extreme beauty and from time to time, the lodge was let out to wealthy tourists. Therefore, the lodge and grounds were in pristine condition and it had every modern convenience known to man, that suited Francisco.

On arrival at the Chaco Canyon tourist centre, both organizations had representatives on hand to welcome Francisco and although they did not have a red carpet, they made the boy from Alto feel like a Hollywood star. The tour staff along with NASA representative gave Francisco a detailed tour of the Pueblo Bonito and the Chaco Canyon by driving him around in an almost brand-new Grand Jeep Cherokee. To accommodate him, they stopped at every point of interest, so that Francisco could snap a few photos and take notes. Then halfway through the day, they gave him an executive lunch. On the final leg of the tour, Francisco met with some of the local press and lots of pictures were taken. Then, to conclude Francisco's visit, Francisco was presented with a VIP pass that allowed him access to all of Pueblo Bonito, and the Chaco Canyons wonders, and his pass even allowed him into the restricted areas.

Francisco did not want to waste time or re-invent the wheel. So, once he was back at his family's home, he used his computer skills to hack into NASA's data files on Pueblo Bonito and the Chaco Canyon. All the files were heavily encrypted, but some were quite old and those proved easy to hack. That's when he came across a section of files from nineteen eight two under the heading of Energy and marked, top-secret.

Each file had a subfile name and that name indicated the content of the file. The first was Anasazi Surface Waves, that file had a series of sub-files attached and showed data collected from numerous tests carried out. Just glancing through this, Francisco could feel his heart rate quicken, to him, this was exciting stuff. However, he soon learned that these files were just the tip of a massive iceberg. Pueblo Bonito and the Chaco Canyon were not the only ancient sites under investigation by NASA and each ancient site had its special connection to some form of unexplained technology? Francisco wondered about this 'unexplained technology' and wanted to know more.

However, despite his best efforts, Francisco found the newer files difficult to hack using his Desktop computer that has six NVIDIA GTX295 dual-GPU cards and one GTX275 single-GPU card that adds up to a respectable12TFLOPS of computing power. What he needed to crunch through these firewalls of NASA's highly encrypted codes was access to his super commuter appropriately named Fran-com.

This computer with its unique AI came in at a staggering two hundred million dollars to build and has a LINPAC benchmark score of one hundred and forty-three point five PFLOPS. Francisco used the supercomputer for his for research at Franco pharmaceutical company, to maintain his stock market algorithm program and do logistics on his armament's transportation business.

For some serious extra income, Francisco also hired out Fran-com computing abilities to various government agencies including the U.S air force, U.S army, U.S navy, NASA, Space X, and several major research companies. At a premium fee, Francisco also provided a computing service for those who would be classed as international criminals or radicals. Although all the data collated was supposed to be highly confidential, the multiwall firewall protected and when finished, completely erased from Fran-com data files. Fran-com however had a secret duplication program that worked deep in the background. So if and when he wanted to, Francisco could have a peak and sometimes illegally utilize the hirer's data and computer research information.

For now, he just laughed to himself as the Fran-com computer was housed in the highly secure basement at his at Fran-tower Offices, New York. Despite Francisco's initial enthusiasm to find out more, he knew he needed to stay in Alto and finish his exploration of Pueblo Bonito and the Chaco Canyon for a few more days. He was a man of strong intuition and with other snippets of information he had gathered from Fran-com computing, his guts told him he was onto something really big. So big that with patience, careful preparation, and long-term strategy, he could turn his meagre billions turned into several trillion.

With the sun just rising the next day, Francisco packed the equipment needed into his rented jeep and headed back out to Chaco Canyon. His first task was to explore the Anasazi ley line, which precisely connects the Aztec Ruins and Casas Grandes along with Longitude 107° 57'. He was intrigued as the engineering of the site is still unexplained and large amounts of stone were moved miraculously. The first question he wanted answers to was, did Chacoans learn how to harness the energy of ley lines, vortices, and magnetic fields? To do this, he paused at regular intervals along the ley line and took numerous, very deep soil and rock samples. Once he was back in New York, he would have these analysed at his Fran-com headquarters.

The cunning criminal already knew that Nasa and other agencies would have done the same and even more exploration. But, to utilize all their years of research, he had to pretend to do some realistic field and chemical analyses of his own. So, after eating his packed lunch, his next point to visit was the visitor's restricted site, Fajada Butte (Banded Butte).

As a boy he had visited this rock that rises one hundred and thirty-five meters above the canyon floor. He also knew all about its spiritual and astrological significance and had read the published data of an investigation by Anna Sofaer in nineteen seventy-seven. It showed with some accuracy that the spirals also track the eighteen-point six-year lunar cycle He fondly remembered the boy with his notebook in hand walking through the ruins of small cliff dwellings in the higher regions of the butte. But now, years later, the erosion of this wonder was evident. With sweat pouring from his brow, he clambered up what remains of a ninety-five-meter-high, two hundred and thirty-meter-long ramp. As he approached the top, he could see the set of spiral petroglyphs pecked into a cliff face behind three giant slabs of rock had shifted and their astrological alignment had been spoiled.

However, Francisco was already aware of this. What he needed now, was some high-quality digital video footage of the spiral petroglyphs pecked into a cliff face behind three giant slabs of rock. So, he set up his HD digital camcorder and carefully took video footage from several angles. The video footage would be uploaded to Fran-com and the computer would re-create the three giant slabs of rock into their correct alignment and then analyse the data of the eighteen-point six-year lunar cycle.

Once Francisco had finished filming the three giant slabs of rock, he pointed his video camera onto the canyon and took quite a lot of video footage of it all he could see. He took out his notebook and a digital voice recorder and made a verbal record of his finding so far. Speaking into the recorder, he said;

"I am at the top of Fajada Butte, looking out across Chaco Canyon. The former Anasazi empire now lies across portions of the four modern states of New Mexico, Arizona, Utah, and Colorado. Chaco Canyon contains more than twenty-four thousand archaeological sites within thirty-two square miles.

Being the central hub of Puebloan society, Chaco Canyon possessed twelve multi-story great houses made of stone and wood, a dozen great kivas, and hundreds of smaller housing sites. Great houses were constructed of sandstone and timber with veneer masonry and ranged from eighty to five hundred and eighty rooms. Small houses were of simpler stonework and averaged about 20 rooms each. Both types were domestic structures, but also contained round rooms used for religious ceremonies, known as kivas. "Great kivas," up to eighteen meters in diameter, were the largest buildings in the Americas until the nineteenth century.

The Chacoan's architecture, as well as their arts, was among their greatest achievements. They painted and carved on the canyon's walls and decorated the walls of rooms and kivas with paintings as well. They left behind pieces of painted wood, stone and clay, and ornaments of shell, turquoise, and other rare materials. Many consider their occupational items such as the basketry, textiles, and painted pottery to be art too".

Over the years Francisco had acquired legally and illegally many rare, expensive works of art and precious artifacts. In his collection, he had a few pieces of Chacoan art, but for his grand plan to work, he decided he would need more. However, these and other artifacts from around the world would be for display purposes. Putting that thought aside, for the time being, he cleared his throat and continued his dictation;

"However, it is Chaco Canyon's petroglyphs or rock art, that has caused the most controversy in the pseudo archaeological community.

For my verbal records, Pseudoarchaeology is alternative archaeology, where people make interpretations of the past from outside of the archaeological science community. People who believe in the Ancient Alien Astronauts theory believe that all advanced civilizations were created with the help of a superior race, in this case, aliens. It is speculated that they gave humans instructions on how to become a more advanced society.

Ancient Astronaut theorists believe the proof is simply the grand scale of an ancient society's architecture, as well as in their art, weapons, pottery, agriculture, etc. Their belief stems from the assumption that ancient man is too primitive and not intelligent enough to have an advanced culture similar in ways to our own.

A famous petroglyph named the Sun Dagger, that I have just filmed has caused the most scepticism amongst pseudo archaeologists. However, a popular Alien Astronaut theory is that the spirals petroglyphs represent galaxies which would mean that the Puebloans are capable of self-awareness. Astronaut theorists then assume that there is no way the Pueblo peoples could have figured it out on their own, therefore they had help from "the teacher in the sky" who passed on the knowledge to them. And while the spiral petroglyphs are proof that Chacoans have met aliens from other galaxies, the image next to it is said to be an alien astronaut with antennas sticking out from its head.

Another point of view is, the figure with antennas is a shaman holding a solstice while being surrounded by animals common in the Pueblo region. Paintings of animals, religious ceremonies, and figures–like shamans, are incredibly common in Pueblo art.

Ancient Astronaut theorists also find it hard to believe how a prehistoric community like the Chacoans could have survived in its barren, dry landscape. Despite the region's arid land and harsh temperatures, Puebloans have routinely produced agriculture surpluses large enough to develop and sustain an incredibly rich social and ceremonial life. Chacoan people, like all other Pueblo peoples of the Southwest, depended on corn, beans, and squash for sustenance. The "advanced" farming technique of Pueblo peoples was no coincidence, it was mastered by their ancestors over thousands of years and entirely feasible. The myth of the disappearing "Anasazi" or early Pueblo people, induced by the many spectacular, abandoned sites (like Chaco Canyon) is very persistent and hard to dispel.

There is however another possibility. The sites were abandoned at several different periods in time and the central Puebloan region was depopulated permanently around thirteen hundred C.E. But these people did not disappear, instead they migrated to new homes to the east, south, and west joining their Pueblo brethren's communities Also, the number of residential rooms in Chaco Canyon suggests a population far larger than that which could have been supported by the land available. Meaning it is possible that most people did not live there year-round and there were possibly large commutes to Chaco for religious ceremonies once Chaco dispersed, they returned home.

The construction of these cultured, brick structures did not begin immediately, the inhabitants first lived in very basic dwellings but by about eleven fifty AD, twelve magnificence structure's like Pueblo Bonito was built. And yet in other parts of the world at the same period, they were living in wooden hovels. That is indeed odd?

A major question needs to be answered; Anasazi culture spread almost forty thousand square miles. However, no obvious indications that the depopulation of the canyon in the 13th century was caused by any specific cultural practices or natural events".

Francisco paused for a moment, flicked through his notes, and found an item he had downloaded. Reading this out loud he then added;

"Pseudoarchaeology believe it is possible that the Chacoan race used their intelligence and aptitude for astronomy to escape an upcoming cataclysm, or colossal catastrophe, of some sort. According to ancient Sanskrit texts, the earth cycles through 4 yugas, or epochs. The fourth and final age is known as "kali yuga," which translates to "age of the demon" and is the final era before some sort of cataclysm takes place to start the Earth's cycle anew.

It is believed that we are currently living in the kali yuga, which is characterized by a human preoccupation with the self, sin, greed, and materialism. Between drastic climate change, political upheaval, and ongoing violence across the globe, is it possible that we will soon be facing a modern-day cataclysm?

If the Chacoan peoples knew a cataclysm was coming, did they use their astronomical knowledge to depart the planet beforehand? More importantly, does NASA have a similar motive for investigating Chaco Canyon?"

From a flask, Francisco quenched his thirst with a drink of water and hit the playback button on the voice recorder. Attentively, he listened to what he had just said recorded and thought his assessment of Chaco Canyon was reasonably comprehensive. Once back, he would upload this onto Fran-com later for some final editing and then use it as an introduction into his research into the mysteries that surround Chaco Canyon.

However, Francisco knew that his quest was only just starting. He now had a wide-ranging plan and part of it was to visit and explore other ancient sites around the world that had anonymities and possible alien interventions locked into their distant passage of time. So, after another day of exploration of his doorstep mysterious site, enthusiastically he headed back to Fran-com headquarter and with ease, hacked through the firewalls of NASA's highly encrypted codes.

Each file revealed insights into NASA's discoveries and although some files were somewhat speculative in their findings. Others indicated a definite hot trail to extra-terrestrials having visited the planet earth, many times, over thousands of years. Furthermore, alien diagrams and artifacts had been found by NASA and other agencies. Although it had taken several years, the diagrams had been successfully deciphered by professional linguists, and now scientists and engineers trying to replicate them. As to the artifacts, these were still being studied in various Labourites. But, to Francisco's delight, the files contained detailed photos and exact blueprints of each artifact. That meant Fran-com could replicate them using the latest laser 3D print technology. The only downside to this was, while it was easy to replicate the alien artifacts, determining their actual usage and power source was something that at this point Fran-com did not have the data to do. That being said, that did not mean they were discarded. To the contra, each replicated artifact was placed in a secured chamber and Fran-com constantly tried to study the purpose of the alien object.

For Francisco to legitimately and illegally move forward, he decided to create three new companies. The first was Fran-power. This company would research all kinds of alternative energy sources. However, to begin, its prime objective would be to investigate Zenneck surface waves technology and if viable, build or sub-contract to build surface wave power stations.

The next company would be named Fran-global and would largely cover conventional communications methods, Fran-global would also have a facility for research and implementation of alternative earth and space communications systems.

Finally, the most ambitious, extravagant, and expensive was Fran-Expansum, (Expansum is modern Latin for expanse). Although this company would initially be an absolute money pit, with Francisco's business and influential connections, many, many doors would open. He was more than confident that he would not have to put up much money himself. Once he put out his structured business proposal on controlling global warming, countless extremely rich individual investors, corporations and governments would throw tons of money into this.

Over the years Francisco had supplied and distributed various chemicals and components for numerous clouds seeding and HAAPP projects, so he already had his foot in this lucrative door. What he was now offering was to have to launch a series of satellites set up in a grid around the globe. Each satellite would be powered by the sun's solar energy and then, in turn, utilize the latest onboard advanced HAAPP technology. The main goal would be to control global warming, but the same technology could also control localized weather conditions.

However, being a visionary and criminal, Francisco had two more plans that were the icing on Fran-Expansum's cake. The first was even with the current technology available, his satellites could be used as electromagnetic weapons and mass or individual mind control weapons. Now if you add in a bit of NASA's 'secret off-world technology', the market for this alone would be huge. Better still, for his wealth, the financial benefits would be of any wall street scale.

And finally, for Francisco, this was the big one. Once he proved that the global warming and weather control system was successful, he wanted to expand the program to terraform the earth's moon and then the planet mars. After that, with the technology he could now get his hands on, Fran-Expansum would set its sights on planets way beyond our solar system.

As Francisco laid out his plans, he could not help but laugh. He had just remembered a James Bond movie, Dr. No. In the film, James Bond is sent to Jamaica to investigate the disappearance of a fellow British agent. The trail leads him to the underground base of Dr. No, who is plotting to disrupt an early American space launch with a radio beam weapon. Francisco mused that perhaps if he was ever caught for his criminal activities a bond movie might be made about him. Putting this rather amusing thought aside, Francisco knew he was far too clever and continued to finalize his supreme master plans.

Chapter Eighteen, It all takes time

Over the next few years, Francisco worked diligently at setting up his three new companies. Each had its obstacles, but through good business practice, extortion, and "a bit of luck" certain people inexplicably died or just went missing. Francisco could see the financial light at the end of the tunnel.

These new business ventures took him to many countries around the world. Although this sounds great, he had to attend endless business meetings that ran to long evenings sitting inexpensive restaurants pandering to his potential business investors and government bureaucrats' whims and fancies. To offset these tedious formalities, whenever he could, Francisco went off to explore ancient geological sites of interest to his projects. Whilst on a visit to some European countries, Francisco took the time to explore the Bosnian pyramid complex. The hills are located near the town of Visoko, northwest of Sarajevo. The town was Bosnia's capital during the Middle Ages, and the ruins of a medieval fortress are located on top of Visočica hill.

Many scholarly people have tried to discredit this site; however, Francisco's interest was not in a claim that these are the largest human-made ancient pyramids on Earth. He was interested in the claim that unexplained waves had been detected at the top of the largest of the hills and could be reached out into deep space. If true, these waves can travel faster than light and possibly prove the existence of a cosmic internet that allows for intergalactic communication. While Francisco was a little sceptical, he knew NASA had two operatives secretly investigating these claims, so he thought that doing some investigative research was worth doing.

The Bosnian pyramid complex had now become quite a tourist attraction and the tourist route was not what Francisco wanted.

So, Francisco contacted a well-known Bosnian businessman now based in Houston, Texas. Over many years this man had done lots of research and initiated excavations of the site and with his help, Francisco engaged some local experts. With his small ground team and with some rather expensive equipment that linked into Fran-com AI and one of his Fran-Expansum satellites, he carried out some extensive tests of his own. However, even using this amount of Hi-Tec hard and software, detecting these waves proved extremely difficult.

Fran-coms hardware and software were continuously being updated. The computer's AI was now constantly re-writing its algorithms, automatically linking in with similar computers for data and coming up with suggestions for hardware upgrades. After reviewing several negative results, the AI computer suggested a test for waves at an extremely low frequency or ELF for short. To carry out the detection of ELF waves is pretty straightforward. A basic circuit consists of an antenna to pick up the initial emissions, a 'choke' usually made of ferrite to remove the higher frequency signals. An amplifier is used to amplify and filter signals in the band you are looking for, and a second amplifier to output a signal that can be displayed on an oscilloscope or interpreted by a computer using the relevant software.

It only took a short time for Fran-coms AI to design advanced schematics for the manufacture of a small field machine that could detect ELF, incorporate an oscilloscope and link up directly with Fran-com and Fran-Expansum satellites After that, it just took a few more hours for the solid parts to be made using a 3D printer and at the same time, the circuitry was produced by Fran-power electronic division. With Fran-freight acting as a currier, the ELF detector was delivered to Francisco and his Bosnian ground team the following day. They, in turn, unpacked the machine and without any delay set off up the largest hills to begin testing for any ELF waves.

As soon as the new ELF detector was turned on, readings showed that ELF waves were present, but they were extremely weak. This puzzled Francisco as he knew any system that ran ELF required a powerful power supply. Putting that aside, for the time being, Francisco wanted to find the source of the ELF waves. Understanding that due to their extremely long wavelength, ELF waves can diffract around large obstacles, and are not blocked by mountain ranges. Therefore, Francisco had a hunch that the source could be hidden in an unexplored underground cavern off one of the tunnels around the hill complex. These tunnels have been named Ravne tunnels and are an ancient man-made underground network. So, after some financial enticements, he was issued with a special permit to enter and explore the network of tunnels that spread for over two point four miles.

Those local officials issuing the permit knew that for decades numerous archaeologists had trawled over every inch of the Ravne tunnels. So, in their minds, the chances of finding anything of archaeological or monetary value were extremely low. However, fortunately for Francisco, NASA had quite recently used one of the USA air force satellites to do a deep earth scan of the Bosnian pyramid complex and through a little indiscrete computer hacking, he had been able to obtain an up to date map of the network of tunnels. More interestingly, the satellites scan revealed several unexplored caverns that run off some of the tunnels.

To gain access to the caverns Francisco knew he would need some heavy-duty mining equipment and a small team of miners who could operate them. He, therefore, hired the team and all the equipment needed from a Polish mining company who were happy to work for cash and would ask no questions. Within a few hours of the equipment arriving, the mining team began the long hard haul of heavy equipment down the sometimes very narrow and low passages. Meanwhile, Francisco set off ahead of them. Using his NASA map, he soon found a solid rock face that had a cavern behind it. He then turned on the ELF detector, but no ELF waves were detectable. Francisco wanted the mining team to come back later and create an opening into the cavern as there could be undiscovered artifacts in the cavern. So, he marked the co-ordinance onto his map and headed off to the point of interest on the NASA map.

For the next few hours Francisco explored the tunnels, searching for the source of the ELF waves. Then finally at one of the rock faces of a hidden cavern, the ELF detector blinked into life. Again, the single was relatively weak, but with excitement, Francisco let out a loud cheer. He then radioed the mining team leader that he wanted them here as soon as possible and within just over an hour and thirty minutes they arrived with their mining equipment. Initial examinations of the rock face were carried out and it was determined that to get to the cavern, they would possibly have to blast or cut through over three meters of solid rock.

Normally, rock samples would be taken, analysed and a plan laid out setting out the most cost-effective and safest way forward before such an operation took place. But, for this excavation, Francisco had to rely on the impromptu expertise of his mining crew. After a brief discussion, they agreed that blasting through the rock face was too dangerous as the tunnels could easily collapse. So, they chose to employ a slower, safer method. A small, one-meter diameter tunnel boring machine would be used as it works in most kinds of mining, from consolidated sands to very hard rock. The team leader estimated that to bore through the three meters of thick rock with the machine they were using would take about fifteen to twenty hours. So, knowing he could do no more, for now, Francisco left them to it and went back to his hotel to relax and use the hotel's rather good spa, heated swimming pool, and a little later, the hotel's outstanding restaurant.

Just after sunrise the following morning, Francisco had a telephone call from Aleksander the mining team leader informing him that the rock was not as hard as they thought. They had worked through the night and were close to breaking through the rock face. He then informed Francisco that they would hold back until he arrived. Francisco quickly got dressed and headed back to the tunnels around the Bosnian pyramid complex. Once there, the boring machine was turned back on and after about twenty minutes the circular cutters broke through the last bit of rock.

After the boring machine was withdrawn, a large airline was inserted and it began to pump fresh air into the darkness of the cavern. The mining team leader, Aleksander estimated that to have good breathable air would take well over an hour. However, he had a few self-contained breathing apparatus (SCBA), and knowing that Francisco was keen to get into the cavern, he gave him some basic instructions on the SCBA usage and then put it on him. For safety, he also insisted that he be connected to their mobile field communications system that uses wireless radios, wear, overalls, safety boots, heavy-duty gloves, and a miner's hard hat that had a rather useful LED head torch attached to it. With his safety kit on, Francisco then climbed into the round one and a half meter-wide hole and on his hands and knees, made his way towards the dark cavern.

Aleksander followed Francisco and using his radio he told him to pause before exiting the drilled hole, saying;

"Boss, shine your head torch downward and make sure there is some ground to step on and not a deep chasm".

Francisco did as he was told and sure enough, the torch-lit up a nice solid rocky floor. Before exiting Francisco slowly moved his head around and began to examine the cavern. It was vast, beautiful, and had numerous large stalagmites and stalactites. As he focused the light on the walls, he could see the distinctive ancient painting on the walls around the cavern. Straight away he knew this was a major archaeological find. Carefully, he then eased himself out and onto the floor, and for a few moments, he sat motionlessly and tried to take in all he could see. Aleksander joined him and both men smiled, shook hands, and together they just gazed at the beauty they had uncovered.

It was Aleksander who broke the silence by talking through his radio and saying;

"Boss, I have been a miner for over thirty years. I started as a boy as a pits miner and then moved to open face mining. I have blown and cut through this earth, but truly, to open up this cavern and see all that we are looking at is just amazing."

Aleksander then got up and said he would start to bring through the equipment Francisco needed. He also recommended that as this was a major archaeological find, only he and Francisco should be allowed into the cavern. That way everything would be left untouched until Francisco decided what he wanted to do with this major discovery. That sounded sensible to Francisco and while Aleksander brought through some large portable lights, the ELF detector, and various cameras, Francisco set about exploring the cavern.

While many of the ancient wall paintings and hieroglyphic texts were fascinating, one painting caught Francisco's eye. It was of a large black pyramid that had several wavy lines coming out of it. The lines sprayed outward from the top of the pyramid and linked to several different coloured spheres. Each sphere was distributed at various distances. Francisco guessed that a large black triangle could be the ELF wave transmitter and the wavy lines the ELF wave sent to our moon or planets in or out of our solar system. The only problem Francisco could see with this ancient painting was, the Earth is surrounded by a layer of charged particles (ions) in the atmosphere at an altitude of about sixty km at the bottom of the ionosphere, called the D layer.

The Earth's surface and the conductive D layer acts as a parallel-plate waveguide that confines ELF waves, allowing them to propagate long distances, but without escaping into space. So, the question Francisco needed answers for was, what advanced technology was used to thrust the ELF waves through the earth's ionosphere, into space, and possibly way beyond our solar system? While he was pondering this, Aleksander called to him on his radio and said he was just about to turn on two of the big LED floodlights. Aleksander then did a countdown befitting a miner about to blow something very big up. He called at the top of his voice, "three, two, one," and for the first time for possibly hundreds, if not thousands of years, light-filled the front part of the cavern.

He and Francisco cheered as this happened. Once again, the two men stopped and gazed around the cavern. From where they were standing, they could see that the ceiling reached up at least twenty meters and where the rock ceiling was so what lower, the stalagmites and stalactites almost touching the roof or floor. Aleksander then informed his boss that all the equipment had now been brought through. Excitedly, Francisco came over picked up the ELF detector and turned it on. Instantly the detector picked up a low reading of ELF waves. Francisco nodded at Aleksander and he then began slowly pointing it around the cavern. The ELF waves seemed stronger deeper into the cavern, so holding the detector in front of him Francisco leads the way followed by Aleksander, who knows had a very powerful handheld torch.

Both men slowly made their way around some of the large stalagmites and stalactites and realized that the cavern narrowed into a small passage. Cautiously they passed through this passageway and entered a much larger chamber. Aleksander gradually shone his torch around the chamber and stopped when he came to a narrow-based, one-meter wide, two-meter-tall, glass-like surface, black pyramid object resting on the rocky floor in the middle of the chamber. With smiles on their faces, the two men gave a cheer and stopped for a moment to absorb their latest find. Then Aleksander handed the torch to Francisco and using his radio he said he would go and fetch two more of the big LED floodlights.

Now alone, Francisco walked over to where the pyramid object was. He then placed the large LED torch on the floor and angled it so it shone on the mysterious black artifact. Then using the ELF detector, Francisco slowly walked around the object and took more reading. To his surprise the signals were still quite low, however, this was the source of the ELF waves. While it was still scanning, Francisco then placed the ELF detector on the ground and took out his mobile phone, and placed it near the mysterious black artifact. Then using the voice command, he made a call to his office in New York. It was a remote chance but, he wanted to see if the radio waves from the mobile phone interacted with it, but the readings on the detector remained the same.

Next, on his agenda was taking videos and still pictures of the black artifact but, before he did this, he wanted to touch its smooth surface. First, he did this with his heavy-duty gloves on but as he could feel nothing, he then removed them and gently placed one of his hands on the glass-like surface. The surface was extremely cold to the touch but, at the same time, Francisco thought he could feel a slight tingling through his fingers. He removed his hand and inspected it. Seeing nothing unusual, he put the tingling sensation down to static electricity. He placed his hand back on the artifact and began running his hand slowly back and forth. Once again, he could feel the slight tingling. So, his curiosity rose and he then placed both hands on the black artifact. Instantly, a surge of energy shot through his hands and strange images flashed through his mind.

This shocked Francisco and he could hear himself yell;

"Fucking hell"

At the same time, his natural survival instincts set in and he pulled his hand away from the black artifact. Repeating his words several times, he took a few rapid steps backward and inspected his hands. Francisco was pleased to see except them trembling, everything was intact. He wanted to tear his mask off and take a few deep breaths but, he knew this was not possible. So, breathing slowly through his nose and then out through his mouth, Francisco began to re-compose himself.

At that, Aleksander came back into the chamber with two more Large LED floodlights. Oblivious as to what had just happened, he just gave Francisco the thumbs up, positioned the lights, and turned them on. Although this chamber was vast, compared with what they first encountered, it was just a big rocky, pretty dull cave with a high vaulted but curved roof. From an archaeological point of view, its only saving grace was the mysterious black artifact. However, there was something about the vaulted curved roof that puzzled Francisco? It looked like it had been deliberately manufactured. He then pondered if this curved roof helped with the transmission of ELF waves? This was something he would look into later.

Although Francisco was still a little stunned from his "hands-on" experience with the black artifact. He told Aleksander that he wanted it taken immediately to the surface and that before anyone tried to move or touched the artifact, he wanted it covered in with a thick tarpaulin. Francisco also added that he wanted the whole removal videoed and Aleksander would have to set up remote cameras for this. Without question, Aleksander cheerfully went off to make the necessary arrangements. Francisco now had what he wanted and he wanted it kept as quiet as possible.

First, he began making arrangements with Fran-Freight to have the artifact transported to Fran-Com HQ for analysis. Next, he decided that the ancient wall paintings and hieroglyphics texts in the first cavern would only raise archaeological suspicions. Therefore, he would have Aleksander make it look as if the cavern collapsed as they were trying to bore their way through. This rock formation instability would also give him a good reason to abandon any further archaeological investigations into the Bosnian pyramid complex.

Finally, there was Aleksander and his mining team. He liked Aleksander but, he and his team were a liability to his plans and they had to go. He knew that when they had finished, they were going to fly back to Poland on an airplane chartered by Fran-Freight. It was conceivable that some chartered airplanes were not always serviced to the highest standards. Consequently, a serious fault could develop that would lead to an absolute tragedy, where all lives are lost. This sounded like a plan that would work and Francisco decided that as he liked Aleksander; he would look after his family after his sad demise.

Chapter Nineteen, It's all in a day's work

One of the first things Aleksander had to do in removing and shipping the strange artifact was to calculate its total weight. As the two-meter-tall object looked completely solid and made of an unknown material, Aleksander decided to carefully use a hydraulic jack, jack up each corner of its pyramid base, and then once raised, slide an industrial weighing scale under it and then lower it back down on to the scales. After setting up the remote video cameras and carefully covering the artifact with a heavy-duty tarpaulin, Aleksander started at one corner and began to ease the first hydraulic jack in place. It was then that he realized that the artifact was indeed quite light. After a little more investigation and a bit of manhandling, when he got it on the scales, the whole thing only weighted sixty kilos or a tad over one hundred and thirty-two pounds.

Bearing in mind his bosses' instructions that he wanted the ceiling to collapse in and the cavern sealed off, Aleksander didn't have to worry about getting the artifact around some of the large stalagmites and stalactites, he just smashed them apart. After that, it was easy to transport the artifact to the surface. He then packed the strange relic in a large wooden crate that Francisco had lined with layers of lead and thick aluminium foil. Then with some haste, he headed back down to the cavern with some good old-fashioned sticks of dynamite.

Once Aleksander was back inside the first cavern, he set about drilling several holes in strategic places and placed a stick of dynamite in each of them. Next, he rigged up long lengths of fuse wire and attached it to each stick of dynamite. Each length of fuse wire was wired up to the detonator that was at a safe distance, well outside the cavern.

One of the considerations Aleksander had to take on board was that the bedrock and earth above the caverns would subside once he detonated the dynamite. This in itself wasn't a major problem, the problem was sightseers, walking parties and, cyclists. So, before he could carry out the detonation, he had his team discreetly scoured the land above for any persons wandering or cycling around and when he got the all-clear, he hit the detonation button. As soon as he deemed it was safe, and the dust had settled, Aleksander went back down the passages to where the cavern was. He was pleased to see the pyramid passage walls close to the cavern had not collapsed and still looked sturdy.

What delighted Aleksander, even more, was, the explosion had done exactly what he had planned. Even if there was a formal investigation, it just looked like the cavern rocky ceiling had structural weaknesses and had collapsed as they drilled into the cavern. Aleksander walked away from there feeling rather pleased with himself. He knew he was good at his job and this just proved it. Better still, he and his team could now pack up their mining equipment and head back to Poland with some good wages and for the personal "explosive" work he had just done he would get a super big bonus.

To make it look like a total surprise, Francisco had gathered up his original team of guides and were exploring some of the Ravne tunnels when they all heard the thunder of bedrock and earth collapsing into the cavern. As his team of guides had no idea what had just happened, they thought it might be an earthquake! With Francisco in tow, they quickly exited the Ravne tunnels.

As they left the tunnels, the main guide used his radio to contact the tourist information centre to try to find out what had happened? After chatting with someone on the other end for about a minute, he announced that one of the mining team had just reported that the ceiling of the cavern that they were trying to gain access to had collapsed. Looking and sounding very concerned, Francisco asked if anyone had been hurt? His guide assured him everyone was safe. At that, Francisco did an Oscar performance and acted relieved. His guide then announced, for safety, the whole area needed to be evacuated. The Ravne tunnels and surrounding areas were being closed to everyone and would only be re-opened once it is deemed safe.

Still looking very concerned, Francisco thanked his guides and said he would go head off back to his hotel. On the way back, he telephoned Aleksander, and still keeping up the act in case the telephone call was monitored, he asked the miner what had happened? Aleksander was in on this and over the telephone he too gave a command performance and related that in his opinion there must have been quite a structural weakness in the rock above the cavern. He then went on to surmise that the vibration from the machine they were using to bore through the rock must have triggered the collapse of the roof of the cavern.

Keeping up the pretence, Francisco said he was just glad to hear that Aleksander and his team were all safe. He then added, in light of what had just happened, they would have to abandon any further mining work at the Bosnian pyramid complex but, everyone would get paid in full. At that, Francisco ended his call and without a mental pause, he began to mull over the plan with a few thought-provoking modifications in it for the demise of the Polish mining team. To set the plan in motion would take a few days, but Francisco's knew time was on his side. It had worked in his favour that the mining project finished earlier than expected. Now, it would take about a week for the miners to pack up all their equipment for transportation back to Poland and at that time, Francisco would weave his terminal plot.

Without delay, Francisco headed back to Fran-Com headquarters. His priority was to have his new Bosnian artifact analysed by the Fran-Com. To do this, he had a special doomed room constructed that would allow ELF waves to flow through it easily. For this, the doom was made of dense metal sheeting and as air slows down ELF waves, the air was extracted out of it. One thing Francisco couldn't do was replicate the vast size of the cavern. So, after some careful calculations, he settled for the doom that was substantially smaller than the cavern he found it in. Then to maximize any flow of ELF waves, the metal doom was situated on the tower block roof that housed Fran-Com HQ. As the construction was prefabricated, it was erected within a day and as soon as it was ready, the pyramid artifact was placed dead centre and Fran-Com began to carry out various tests.

The first one was to investigate what this strange object was made of? Normally, this would be done by taking a sample of the object and then determining from that sample its molecular mass. However, this was not possible as the pyramid object surface could not be penetrated by any means known to man, and that included an incredibly powerful laser. Fran-com speculated that the exterior was possibly made of unknown monatomic elements that have unique physical and energetic characteristics.

Fran-Com then tested if the artifact would react to sound waves at different frequencies? Now considering that it was giving off a constant flow of ELF waves, the artifact did not respond to any sound waves, at every known frequency. However, Fran-Com did deduce from using ultra-high intensity sound waves that the artifact had several chambers inside. Fran-Com then mapped out its internal construction showing one chamber at the top which was a pyramid, another at the bottom was flat and all the one in between was of a honeycombed construction. As to what this signified, Fran-Com and Francisco had no idea?

One thing that did come to Francisco's mind was when he touched the artifact, some images flashed through his mind. Could those images be related to what Fran-Com has seen in the high-intensity sound waves scan? He then pondered on Fran-com's conjecture about the exterior being made of unknown monatomic elements that have unique physical and energetic characteristics. He decided that there was only one way to find out and that was to touch the surface of the artifact again. Now one thing Francisco wasn't and that was reckless. He knew he could get one of his staff to be a Guinea pig, but that had risks. Would the experience kill them? That in itself wasn't a problem, however, trying to explain the death of an employee would attract unwanted attention. Another possibility of using a human Guinea pig was, if and this was a big if, what if the alien artifact locked on to that person's DNA. Would they be the only person who could communicate or operate its unknown power? Now that in Francisco's mind was not acceptable.

After giving the matter some thought, Francisco decided it would have to be him who re-touched the alien artifact. But, before he would do this, he wanted as many safety nets in place as possible. First, he needed an oxygen mask and in case of unforeseen electrical or other abnormal activity, he wanted an instant oxygen backup supply coming from an external source. Then, he had himself attached to an ECG (electrocardiogram) that was monitored by Fran-Com. To back this up, outside the dome he had a paramedic team on standby along with a helicopter. The helicopter was needed if he had to be transported to the hospital. Finally, at the hospital, he had a team of doctors on high alert that specialized in various traumas.

All that was left for Francisco was to enter the metal dome and touch the artifact. To calm himself down he took a few deep breaths through his oxygen mask. Then, still feeling a little anxious he opened the airlock door, entered, and closed the airlock behind him. Once inside, he looked at one of the CCTV's and promptly Fran-Com voice control confirmed that all monitoring systems were active and when Francisco was ready, he should proceed.

Like a brave man walking to his execution, Francisco took the last few paces, and with an air of bravado, he placed both his hands on the black smooth surface. Instantly he felt a surge of energy through his hands and his mind filled with shapes and images. He had a strong desire to pull his hands away but, he knew he had to carry on. As he held on, the flow of energy began to creep up his arms and steadily fill his body. He just had time to take a deep breath when he heard Fran-Com offering reassurance by stating that everything was well within acceptable parameters.

After that, the weirdest thing happened, Francisco felt a mental detachment and to his surprise, his mind was on another plain and he was having an out-of-body experience. Now from his mind's eye, he could see himself standing in front of the artifact. What was even stranger was, the artifact was no longer black, it was transparent and he could see all the chambers inside. He then realized that the pyramids, box-like honeycombed sections were the ones that had flashed through his mind. However, at this stage, their significance was still puzzling?

For Francisco, this out-of-body experience wasn't unpleasant and after a while, he enjoyed being able to mentally wander around the inside of the domed room. Then he had a strange compulsion to explore the interior of the now transparent pyramid. The area he was first drawn to was the transparent base of the pyramid. Having no physical boundaries, his mind easily entered the space at the bottom of the pyramid.

However, upon entering, he was amazed by how immense the space was. The first thought that popped into his head was this is just like a Tardis from the science fiction series, Dr. Who. "It's bigger on the inside". That being thought, the Tardis always had a centre console and interior walls. The space he was in had nothing but what could only be described as lots of something that resembled plasma light that kept changing colour?

A scary thought then came into Francisco's mind and that was, without any visual references, how would he find his way back out? For a split second, Francisco began to panic and then he realized that all the tiny beams of light were focussed on his mental being. Within a millisecond each of the three chambers' purposes became clear to him and he also understood how this piece of alien technology could enhance his plans. Without any further mental investigations or fear of escaping the base of the pyramid. Francisco mentally concentrated his mind on re-joining his body and once that was done, he left the dome, and enthusiastically began to amend his numerous financial and murderous campaigns.

Chapter Twenty, Homeward bound

It only took four days for the Polish mining team to pack up all their equipment. Now, as they still had a few days to spare before flying back to Poland they took the opportunity to view some of Bosnia's cultural sites. Well, that's what they would tell their loved ones back home. Bosnia's cultural sites to them were to visit as many of Bosnia's bars as they could find and there were plenty.

Still feeling the effects of their alcoholic binge, they all boarded the executive jet chartered by Fran-Freight. However, before the airplane had left the runway, the crew opened a bottle of Belvedere one of Poland's finest Vodka. The stewardess told Aleksander and his team that this was a gift from Francisco for all the hard work they had done. Well, being polite, the Polish miners soon drained the bottle and settled down in their comfy chairs for the flight back home.

The late nights, excessive alcohol, and a good slug of fine Vodka had taken its toll on Aleksander and while his younger team members played cards, he decided to have a bit of shut-eye. Despite the bravado, manly laughter, and cussing going on in the background, it didn't take long for Aleksander to fall into a deep sleep. However, his sleep was a troubled sleep and one of extreme anger. The rage got so bad that he forced himself awake only to find that his team had begun to brawl. Without thinking he immediately shot up out of his seat, grabbed the empty Vodka bottle, and smashed it across the skull of one of his men. Instantly the man fell to the aisle's way of the aircraft with blood gushing out of his head but, the rage drove Aleksander on. He then used the now broken bottle to repeatedly stab the man in his back.

Despite the luxurious tables top being well secured, one of the miners had been able to tear one from its fixings and he used this as a shield against an onslaught of attacks from another two miners. Sadly, he was so engaged in defending himself from his workmates he did not see Aleksander from the rear. Without any hesitation, Aleksander lunged the sharply pointed broken bottle into the base of the man's spine. As the man screams in pain, Aleksander grabbed the man's hair, pulled his head backward, and cuts his throat from ear to ear.

While this bloodshed was going on, the pilot and co-pilot were able to secure their door to the pilot's cabin. However, the two- cabin crew members were women. were not so lucky. In desperation, they tried to hide behind a small curtain in their galley but, Aleksander and the two miners surviving soon turned their crazed attention to them. It's very difficult to know what goes through a person's mind when they know they are in imminent danger but, for the two women their first thoughts were this was going initially be sexual. However, they were completely wrong. The only thought in all three men's minds was to kill them with extreme pain.

The attacks began with some pretty heavy punching and kicking, but despite the screams of their helpless victims, instantly all three men knew that this did not satisfy their murderous lust. So, Aleksander opened a litre bottle of Brandy from the drinks bar, had a good swig of it, and then poured the rest over the now hysterical air hostesses. He then produced a cigarette lighter from his pocket and to the delight of his companions, he set the two ladies alight. As the flames engulfed their prey, without consideration for the consequences, eagerly the other two miners followed Aleksander's lead and callously dowsed the burning women in more alcohol.

Before long the whole galley was ablaze, but all Aleksander wanted to do now killed his two workmates. That same thought was on each of the miner's minds. As the flames spread into the main cabin all three men ignored this and entered a final bloody clash that soon ended as the smoke, heat, and flames overwhelmed them. Despite the pilot's efforts to plan an immediate landing, the internal temperature sored so high that within seconds, the fuel tanks ruptured atomizing the aviation fuel. Consequently, the jet aircraft exploded in a fireball, sending flaming debris over several miles.

In modern times with high-tech forensics, what Francisco had just committed was several brutal but completely untraceable assignations. That thought alone should have pleased Francisco. Nevertheless, it didn't. With his newfound technology and knowledge, he knew that there had been several others of alien and human origin that had done executions, assignation, and mass killings many, many times before.

On one of his mind links with the alien artifact, he had discovered that there were indeed several of these artifacts dotted around the surface of the planet earth. They had been installed on the planet several thousand years ago and were used originally by their alien designers as a way of controlling and enslaving the then un-civilized humans. The devices were also powerful communication devices that could send and receive data and messages from well beyond our galaxy.

As the alien artifact revealed its macabre earthly history, Francisco was somewhat surprised to find that all the artifacts on earth are powered by pure energy, and on earth, this was in abundance in the life force of human beings. One of the easiest ways was to collect this pure energy was through human sacrifices. Consequently, with some mind control, the Aliens convinced the heads of states and spiritual leaders of ancient nations that they were indeed gods. One of the major things they instilled was to spare their nations from unimaginable suffering was to appease these gods from the heavens with regular human sacrifices.

Whilst there were no actual sacrificial numbers, images revealed human sacrifices going back to the Iron Age and were most prolific across the whole of Europe. Then Francisco had images of sacrifices in the Aztec period from about the year fourteen forty where the aliens seemed to have escalated the ritual of human sacrifice. After that, Francisco's mind was bombarded with images of mass human sacrifices that were a particular feature of the Egyptian pharaohs. Suddenly all the ancient images stopped? Before he had time to contemplate the significance of this, time jumped forward several hundreds of years and the imagery that came into his mind next were completely unexpected.

Vivid pictures of Adolf Hitler's Third Reich flooded Francisco's mind. In an instant, Francisco understood that the Third Reich had been using one of the alien artifacts left on the planet earth to control the minds of the German populace. However, morbidly to do this, the artifacts needed a vast amount of human life forces, and the easiest way to supply this was through the usage of gas death chambers!

Whilst this revelation would have sickened the average person, Francisco was far from being a normal person. He felt euphoric and could not wait to test this technology out. That's how he executed the demise of Aleksander, his mining team, and all of the crew on the commercial aircraft tragedy. However, that was successfully done and now it was time to arrange a new experiment, something he believed had never been done before. He wanted to see if the alien artifact would work in conjunction with some advanced technologies created on the planet earth.

With Fran-com monitoring everything, Francisco used his hands to link himself to the black artifact. Within a moment he began to have an out-of-body experience and through thought alone, he directed ELF waves given off by the alien artifact to one of the high satellites that were in low earth orbit that had the latest HAARP technology onboard. Fran-com then activated HAARP's high-power, high-frequency transmitter and began to manipulate the ionosphere just above the mountain Teide in the Canary Island of Tenerife, Spain. Though Francisco's mind's eye he could not only see the build-up of density in the cloud formation, he could also feel its electrical power.

As the clouds formed into a thunderous rage, the HAARP equipment onboard the Fran-Expansum satellite manipulated the storm to head for Tenerife's island coastline. Francisco's mind's eye moved with the storm and to his excitement, a lone figure rose from the blue seas below. Instantly, Francisco knew this was his test victim. He focused on the target and as the storm discharged a bolt of lightning, he directed it to his prey. The bolt of lightning hit the person parascending squarely in the chest and within seconds, the parachute deflated sending the person tumbling towards the now turbulent seas. With a high degree of contentment, Francisco re-joined his body and knew with this small success he could now attempt to execute the next more exciting and ambitious part of his plan.

Looking externally at the pyramid-shaped artifact, you would never have known that in one of its honeycombed chambers was all of the life forces of the Polish mining team and the crew of the commercial aircraft. Now, however, one of the other chambers had a new single occupant. He and Fran-com had tried in vain to understand the technology behind this alien artifact, but to date, it baffled them.

After a lightning bolt shot down the lone parascender, Francisco had gotten Fran-com the scan the European news channels for information about the tragic lightning incident. He soon found his victim was a mother of two, named Shelia Jameson. Francisco knew that she and the other life forces trapped in the honeycombed chambers could not hear him, but he did a courteous bow and with a smile on his face he said;

"Welcome dear lady to your new home. Please don't be concerned, although to you the void you are in seems infinite, in my reality, it's quite small. You might also like to know that you do indeed have neighbours. But I guess from where you are that's another universe's distance away.

Now, Mrs. Jameson, I do have some good news for you, very soon, other kindred souls are going to join you."

With a smile on his face, Francisco walked away from his wonderous alien artifact and immediately began to activate what he would describe as his most ambitious mass assassination operation to date.

Chapter Twenty-one,
Operation Tenerife

Based on the last two test operations, statistically, Fran-com predicted a ninety-five percent chance of success with operation Tenerife. With this in mind and what the artifact had revealed throughout its time on earth, Francisco connected himself to the artifact and ordered Fran-com to begin the program that was about to change the world.

Stage one was to create a massive electrical storm across the island that would disrupt the island's power stations and temporally immobilize all forms of communications. That stage was easily achieved with the use of the HAARP equipment onboard the Fran-Expansum satellites.

Stage two was a little complicated as the plan was to target the minds of all multi-nation tourists that were holidaying on the island of Tenerife. However, to get over this, Fran-com had some advanced software for multi-lingual translations. So, while Francisco controlled ELF waves that carried the first subliminal message that all holidaymakers should attack, maim and kill all Spanish hotel staff, Fran-com provided the all-important translations. To make sure the subliminal message was received by as many of the holidaymakers as possible, Francisco then kept bombarding the Canary island with ELF waves that carried the subliminal message for several hours.

While the electrical storm and subliminal bombardment were going on, Fran-com monitored and analysed all global news channels for the worldwide reaction to the Tenerife disaster. Then after Francisco had finished his mind manipulations, he got Fran-com to playback all that he classed as the relevant data back to him. The initial reports on the death rates were very encouraging and what was even better was, the deaths list was growing steadily by the minute. Francisco was also pleased with how creative some of the killings had been. That in itself would insight public outrage, but on the brighter side, the press loved gruesome deaths. However, one thing that did disturb him was the amount of female and male rapes that had been reported. To Francisco's mind, this was not acceptable. He, therefore, made a mental note that when he sent out future subliminal messages, he would eliminate such deplorable behaviour.

One thing that puzzled Francisco was, how much pure energy does the alien artifact use for missions like operation Tenerife? Well, after mentally linking with the artifact, he was pleased to see that the total energy expended was less than the deaths of life forces captured from the demised miners and aircrew. That bit of news excited Francisco, it now meant that the pure energy now being collected into Mrs. Jameson's chamber would power a full global mission.

Putting that aside until a later date, while murders, mayhem, and communicational chaos continued on Tenerife island, Francisco wanted to test out his newly installed Zenneck Surface Wave communications unit at the small town of Barrio Taucho. So that nothing could be traced back to him or Fran-power, he had set up a bogus company with bogus directors and employees.

As an extra precaution, he only ran tests for an hour and then shut down the installation. However, to his delight, all the tests were one hundred percent successful. In fact, despite the storm's atmospheric disruption, torrential rain, and high winds, all television, telephone, internet, broadband, radio, and other multi-media communications running through the Zenneck Surface Wave unit worked perfectly.

With the tests completed, Francisco knew that it would only be a matter of time before the local authorities became suspicious of this odd-looking installation. Therefore, to him, this installation was now disposable. He had a team of mercenaries on site and had them wire the whole place with some untraceable, rather old, large sticks of dynamite. Being professionals, for a more explosive effect, the mercenaries then attached the sticks of dynamite to several large propane gas cylinders and placed them strategically around the installation. Their orders were to stay put, wait, ward off any intruders and as a last resort, destroy the installation if it looked the installation parameter walls were going to be breached.

That night, Francisco retired to bed and as normal, he expected a sound night's sleep. However, something strange happened, just as he closed his eyes his mind travelled to Tenerife Island. As his mind wandered through a resort named Los Cristianos, he could see hotels on fire, shops being looted and on entering a hotel, he could see dead bodies strewn around the reception area. This strange experience did not faze Francisco, he enjoyed it.

After a while, he opened his eyes and found that he had never left the comfort of his bed. Francisco had heard of certain gifted people who could remote viewing (RV). RV is the practice of seeking impressions about distant or unseen targets, purportedly using extrasensory perception (ESP) or "sensing" with the mind. Now it seemed that the alien artifact had opened his mind to this ability. With that thought in his head, he closed his eyes and let his mind take him back to the Los Cristianos resort. Once again and in all its glory, he witnessed the destruction of a resort that only an hour ago was a thriving tourist destination.

It was obvious to Francisco that what was witnessing was in real-time and the aftermath of his operation. Oh, how he would have loved to have had this gift a few hours ago when all the killings were taking place. He then had a nice thought that when he ran his next operation, he might just be able to witness all the killings at first hand. Keeping this thought in his head, he drifted out of remote viewing state and off into a peaceful night's sleep.

While Francisco slept, the chaos continued on the island of Tenerife and Fran-com program, operation Tenerife was monitoring everything. It had now built up some comprehensive individual statistics on the initial Spanish governments and global government's responses and reactions, financial disruptions to the Islands tourist industry, rebuilding and repairing hotels and shops, and updating the death tolls along with those who had sustained serious, life-threatening injuries. Fran-com programming knew that when Francisco woke up, he would want an immediate update and therefore the supercomputer was constantly revaluating these statistics. Fran-com had calculated that in less than twenty-four hours the chaos in monetary terms had already exceeded over one trillion dollars. However, that figure was growing by the second.

The penthouse suite Francisco had at Fran-com headquarters occupied one whole floor and although it was extremely luxurious, it was also a wonderment of modern technology. Now we are not just talking about sensor lights and an Alexa unit. We are talking about a state-of-the-art bed that senses when you wake up and slowly raises you up to view your wall to ceiling multimedia monitors that are built into every wall and window around the penthouse.

First on Francisco's agenda was to get a comprehensive update from Fran-com. Fran-com presented the update in actual video footage, news, and multimedia reports from around the world and statistical graphs. After hearing all the positive news on operation Tenerife, he used the voice command to order a hearty breakfast from his in-house chef and he asked that the multi-headed rain shower be turned on in thirty minutes after he used the state-of-the-art gym next to his bedroom.

Good quality clothes and shoes were something Francisco had an abundance of. To house his expensive clothing and shoe collection, he has a one hundred square meter walk-in wardrobe with a computerized delivery system. The system was linked to every touch screen monitor in the penthouse. So, all Francisco had to do was scroll through his itemized wardrobe, click on what he wanted and the items of clothing or shoes were delivered to him.

As he dressed, he spoke with Fran-com and asked if any items in operation Tenerife had been red-flagged? Fran-com reported that only one item had been reg flagged and asked if Francisco would like a report of this? Francisco wanted to keep on top of everything that was happening and asked Fran-com to proceed. Fran-com instantly reported the following;

"As law and order has broken down, a man named Alejandro García who is known as the head of criminal organization on the island of Tenerife is trying to restore some order in the Los Cristianos area. He and a large team of men who work for him, seem to have been successful in ejecting hostile tourists from several hotels and shops and other establishments."

Fran-com then added;

"I have already made up a comprehensive file on this man and the García family. How would you like to proceed?

It made Francisco laugh to think that a fellow criminal was the one to help return law and order to the island. No, he thought, this man García is only looking after his own illegal enterprises. Then another thought popped into his head;

"It's only what I would do and I Francisco can live with that".

So, he told Fran-com for the time being;

"For the time being, let's just keep monitoring him and his family and let us see what develops".

After eating a nutritious breakfast, Francisco wanted to conduct a small experiment, he headed to the roof where the artifact was and linked into it in the normal way. Within a few moments he was outside his body and then using the power of the artifact, he focused his mind on his new remote viewing ability, his target area was Los Cristianos. Amazingly his experience was the same as he had the night before in bed.

For a while, he let his mind remote view around the devastated area. However, it soon became boring as he was only seeing what he had seen before. Then a thought came to him and he focused on the man Alejandro García. In an instant, he was in the reception area of a hotel and he could see a tall slim man with a machine gun, he guessed this must be García. To Francisco's delight, García and his men opened fire and shot dead three-armed men who were just about to attack two other men. After that, Francisco watched as Alejandro García walked over and chatted with two men and that's when he heard the name, Jameson!

From what Francisco quickly gathered, this was the husband of Shelia Jameson, the woman whose life force was now in one of the alien artifacts chambers. Normally, this would not have been of any interest to Francisco, but this was too much of a coincidence and he did not like coincidences. So, without seeing any more, he then ended his remote viewing experiment and immediately got Fran-com to do a background check on Mr. Brian Jameson and Senor Carlos López.

Simple everyday background checks can be done using search engines like Google, but Fran-com went way, way deeper. First, it hacked into both men's and their family's medical records. Then it accessed everyone's school, college, and university results. Tracking careers and work records was easy by first getting hold of national insurance and personal tax information. From their Fran-com found out where each individual worked and their annual incomes.

Once you can hack into the world of governmental, banking, commerce's and multimedia's computerized systems, a supercomputer like Fran-com can easily gain full access to everything. So, banking, credit or debit card, loans, and any household bills information are a doddle. Oh, and don't think for a minute that bank account numbers and passwords are safe, Fran-com accessed these in a nano-second. The same applied to government tax, national insurance, house and business rates, police records, marriages, and family death records, Fran-com accessed them all with ease. Finally, Fran-com carried out a worldwide web search on all multimedia sites and copied every photo, video, and posting that had ever been done on B Jameson, C López, and their respected family's. All of this was done in under thirty seconds and ready for Francisco to view at his leisure.

Rather than read through file after laborious file, Francisco asked Fran-com to do synopsizes of Brian Jameson, Carlos López, Alejandro García, and his psychic sister. He then reviewed these summaries and decided that all four would become extremely useful in unwittingly implementing his plans.

For the next few days, Francisco relaxed and let the aftermath of his Tenerife experiment unfold. As far as all the analyses went, this had been a massive success and the icing on the cake was, his "team of four" had now banded together and set up an internet organization called S.T.O.P. Instantly he knew that this would gain massive momentum and with a little manipulation, S.T.O.P was a perfect world wide platform for spreading propaganda.

Chapter Twenty-two, The team

With all the funeral guests gone, I and my two daughters, Carlos and Theresa Tarragon-Jones, and Garcia's sat in the lounge and took a few minutes just to relax. In general chit-chat, we all agreed that Shelia's service went well. On top of that, despite the complexities of the funeral arrangement, we also agreed that our security team had done a fabulous job.

I was just generally talking when suddenly a haze hit my mind. My first thoughts were, I was going into a relapse from what had happened yesterday. Although I tried to fight it and tell the others what was happening, my vision was blurred and my speech sounded slurred. Then within a second, my whole body went limp; all the mental lights went out and I went unconscious.

Now I'm not sure how long I was unconscious, but as the haze lifted from my mind, I realized I was still in the hotel lounge. However, as I tried to stand up from the armchair I was sitting in, I found that my arms and legs had been bound with plastic restraints! Although my vision was still somewhat blurry, I could see Carlos and Senor Garcia were also now semi-conscious and they too were bound the same as I was.

Struggling to try to free himself, Carlos called to me and asked;

"B.J, what the fuck has happened. How have we been knocked out and restrained and more importantly, where are the ladies?"

Through the fogginess of my brain, I hadn't thought about my daughters or the other two women, so the last part of Carlos's question shook me rigid. I had no answers and I hate to admit it but, panic set in. Desperately I tried to break my restraints, however, I of all people should have known better. Throughout my martial arts career, I had taught numerous police forces and private agencies about restraint methods. Additionally, I taught the correct procedures in the technique of applying plastic restraints to immobilize threatening or violent people. It was with this in mind that I knew that without a sharp implement or some snips, my struggling was in vain.

Suddenly, the young man who had been serving drinks to us popped his head up from behind the bar, rubbed his eyes a few times, and asked what had happened? Then without any further questions, he could see that we had been tied up and after a moment he called;

"Hang on their gentlemen, I have something behind here that will cut through those restraints."

Within a few seconds and with a half-smile on his face he rushed from the back of the bar and began cutting us free with the bar knife used to cut the fresh lemon and oranges. As he cut through my bonds, I questioned him about what had happened, but as it turned out he was clueless as we were. Without taking, the three of us rushed out of the hotel's lounge area and into the reception. There we were dumbfounded to find First Lieutenant Karl Barlow and four of his security team restrained, weapons removed, and still unconscious! Earlier, without thinking my survival instincts had set in and I had taken the bar knife from the barman. I flashed it to Carlos and while I cut Karl's and his team restraints off, Carlos followed up by checking their pulses to see if they were still alive. After a few moments, I got the thumbs up from Carlos indicating that all five were still in this mortal world.

Slowly Karl and the security team began to gain consciousness, but it was immediately obvious from their faces and initial talk that they were as confused as we were as to what had happened? However, as a true professional Karl shrugged off his drowsiness and began to evaluate the situation. First, he asked if we had also been knocked out and he also inquired as to where the ladies were? It was Senor García who answered him;

> "To answer you, all three of us were all rendered unconscious and then restrained. The lounge barman was also rendered unconscious, but he was not restrained. As to the four ladies that were with us, they are no longer in the lounge Therefore I strongly suggest that you and your security teams do an extensive search for them. I too will contact my men and assist in the search."

Karl nodded and while Senor García got out his mobile phone to contact his men, Karl turned on his walkie-talkie to contact the security teams inside and outside the hotel. Both men then froze in the realization that their devices were dead. Seeing what was happening, Carlos and I rummaged through our pockets and pulled out our mobile phones, however, they too were just showing blank screens. Thinking on his feet, Karl then rushed behind the reception desk and tried the hotel's landline, he then scrunched his face, looked over at us, put his both hands in the air to indicated that the line was dead. Calmly, he then said;

> "We have two unconscious receptionists behind here, Carlos can you come and give them some assistance."

He then paused, looked attentively around the reception, tried a few switches, and added;

> "It looks like all the electricity in the hotel in the Hotel is out, I'm guessing that with all our communication devices down and no power, the building has been hit with an electromagnetic bomb. Now let's not waste any more time, we need to split up and look for the ladies."

However, before any of us could move, to our surprise a mobile phone began to ring? Without looking our ears simultaneously located the phone on a table at the far side of the reception. I walked over to pick it up and put it into answer call mode. A robotic voice informed me that I had one new message and by pressing the number three I could retrieve the message. So that everyone could hear, I put the phone on speaker and hit the number three button. A machinelike man's voice then said;

"It can be presumed by now the incapacitating agent has worn off and you are all gathered in the hotel's reception area. So, let's begin. Four hostages have been taken, they are; Theresa Tarragon-Jones, Valentina García, and Emma and Oliva Jameson. At this stage all four are unharmed, but to show that we are indeed very serious. You will find a fifth woman whose body parts are in the mini-fridges in rooms from one to twenty. She was one of First Lieutenant Karl Barlow's team. Fortunately, these rooms have the old-fashioned key entry and are not dependent on a key card that requires electricity. You will find a master key on the first shelf behind the reception desk. Go check on this and await further instructional messages."

At that, the message ended and the phone went dead. For once Karl looked quite pale and I could see he was upset at the thought of what he was about to witness. So, I offered to go, but he was her Senior Officer and the soldier down was one of his close colleagues. I'm sure I could see tears forming in his eyes as he graciously declined my offer. With his head lowered, he picked up the passkey and left the reception area.

As he walked away, all I could focus on was Emma and Oliva, however, the realization that Theresa and Valentina were also in serious peril terrified me. I looked over at Carlos and Senor García and instantly knew they were thinking the same. It was Senor García who spoke first;

"Senor's, it is obvious that all of this has been carefully thought out. Sadly, the instigators at this point in time have the upper hand. I, therefore, recommend that it is best to try to remain calm and do our utmost to get our loved ones back safely. B.J, I am so sorry to hear that you two daughters have also been taken."

He then walked over to me and to my surprise, he gave me a big hug. As he did this, he whispered in my ear;

"I think the hotel has been bugged, they might have hidden surveillance cameras and microphones."

He then broke his embrace and turned to Carlos saying;

My friend, my beautiful sister has been taken and I am heartbroken. I am sure you feel the same about the lovely Theresa Tarragon-Jones. We must do everything we can to get our loved ones back safely."

Carlos had already twigged that the Spanish mafia boss was up to something, so he came forward and hugged Senor García. The two men then realized that First Lieutenant Karl Barlow had just re-entered the reception area and they ended their manly embrace to listen to what Karl had got to say.

As good a soldier as First Lieutenant Karl Barlow was, we could all see he was struggling to control his emotions. Putting his hand on the reception counter to steady himself, he announced;

"Corporal Victoria Penton died in the line of duty last night. I can confirm that her body parts are indeed where the message said they were. Further, through a video recording left on this iPad, I can confirm that despite being dismembered whilst still being alive, Corporal Victoria Penton's bravery was outstanding."

He then stood to attention, saluted, and said;

"Corporal Victoria Penton it has been an honour to serve with you."

At that, he just broke down. The four-man security team that had been left in the reception rushed to his side to offer their own tearful support. Then one of the corporals broke away, walked over to us, and through his tears, emotionally in quite a tone he informed us;

"Gentlemen, I don't know if you are aware, but Victoria was the First Lieutenant's girlfriend; they were due to be married at the end of this year."

Well, we were already just mortified at the horrific death of this poor woman, then with that shocking news on top, it brought a flood of tears to mine and Carlos's eyes. Even the ice-cool Senor García's lips trembled and he too had tears in his eyes. However, even though his sadness, I could see that if he could have gotten hold of the person or persons who killed Corporal Victoria Penton, their deaths would be far, far worse than hers! Then to our surprise, we were abruptly interrupted by the mobile phone on the table bursting back into life. Everyone froze for a split second, then in unity, they looked to me to answer it.

Wiping the tears from my eyes, I walked over and answered it. Just like the last time, I was informed that I had one new message and I had to press three to retrieve it. As I hit the number three, I once again switched on the speaker so everyone could hear the latest message. The machinelike man's voice began;

"Now that we have established that the hostages taken will be un-mercifully executed if you do not do follow our instructions. We shall begin.

Senor García, until this is over, the hotel will become ours and S.T.O. P's base of operations. Your first job is to move every guest and member of staff out of the hotel. Before they are allowed to leave, they must be informed that if they speak to the police, security services press, or comment on any social media, they, their families, and friends will be killed.

To set up the base of operations, you will need to source the necessary office equipment. All desktop computers, laptops, tablets, and mobile phones within a two-mile area drives and data storage have been destroyed, therefore you will need new ones. Do not skimp on the specifications on any of these. The operations centre will be set up in the main conference area.

We also want you and your men to handle all of the hotel's internal security. No one will be allowed in or out of the hotel without our authorization. If for any reason an attempt is made to breach through your security zone, they must be shot dead on sight.

First Lieutenant Karl Barlow, will be in charge of the hotel's external security. We know in this field that you are highly proficient. However, to ensure your complete co-operation, we have taken four of your soldiers who were guarding the parameter as hostages.

Your orders are to set up an armed control point at the front of the hotel. From there, you will monitor the air space around the hotel and patrol the grounds twenty-four seven. Without authorization, no one will be allowed to pass your control point. Anyone or any group attempting to violate the air space or trespass on the hotel's grounds will be dispatched with fatal force.

Carlos López you along with Juan José, who is restrained with the others in the conference room will continue to run S.T.O.P. Your first assignment will be to publish on S.T.O. P's website and all social media sites an exact account of what has transpired so far. You will be sent videos, photographs, and statements of our intentions. They will be published across all social media without question.

Mr. Jameson, as you are a British Government envoy, you will immediately contact the British Government and inform them that they have exactly six hours to transfer Ten billion pounds sterling into a swiss bank account. The account number will be sent to the laptop that was issued to you by the British government. The email has been sent to your consular email address.

If this money is not transferred exactly six hours from now, four of the major cities in the UK with suffering a complete unrepairable power outage. This will include power supplies from nuclear and conventional power plants. All communications across each city will stop. This will include Telephone, Mobile, Television, Radio, multimedia, short wave radio, and so on. Every computer's hard drive will be destroyed and data files irreversibly corrupted. Cars and any other road vehicle electronics will fail. In short, it will be chaotic.

We understand that there will be some scientism of our ability to do this. So, to show that this can be done easily, the Royal Town of Sutton Coldfield one-minute ago has been targeted. In addition to the town-wide chaos, Good Hope Hospital is now without power, its backup systems are not working. All hospital Computer' hard drives have been fried and all communications are down. Oh, and we believe three commercial aircraft heading for Birmingham airport are due to fly over the Sutton Coldfield area about now. If this is the case, their onboard computers and electronic systems will be destroyed."

As we gasped at this final disclosure, the mobile phone message ended and a thunderous noise filled everyone's ears. After that, there were several other loud explosions. At this point, we had no way of finding out what just happened. However, after listening to the last part of that message, we all guessed that one of the aircraft had just crashed fairly close to the hotel! Without saying anything you could read what everyone was thinking; "Fucking hell". Then that thought must have changed, a silence fell over the reception as we all expected to hear further explosions from the other two aircraft. However, thankfully the only noises we then heard were the distant sounds of police cars, ambulances, and fire engines.

It was Senor García who broke the silence by saying;

"We have all been given tasks to do, for the safety of our loved ones, let's just get on with them."

He then headed for the conference room. I, Carlos, and Karl lingered for a few moments longer and to our surprise, the hotel's power was restored. It was me who then said;

"Well, I guess that's our cue to start work. I know we have many questions that need to be answered. However, Senor García is right, for the safety of our loved ones, or in your case, Karl, your colleagues, the clock is ticking, so let's get on with our given tasks."

Without any discussion, both men nodded in agreement and we all set off to begin our tasks. Theresa Tarragon-Jones had been my sole contact with Her Majesty's Government. So, I was clueless as to who I should contact in the British Government. In times like this, you sometimes have to try anything. So, I headed up to my room and tried to turn on my government-supplied laptop. To my surprise, it hadn't been zapped and within moments I was notified that I had mail. The one nice thing about an official British Government email address is, you do not get junk mail. On opening the first email from an "unknown sender" it itemized all the demands laid out for the Ten Billion Pounds Stirling and at the bottom of the page, it gave the details of the swiss bank account.

I guess the second email I opened was sent because the "unknown senders" knew I was a Governmental moron. The email contained several Government Department telephone contact numbers and their relevant email addresses. The first telephone number that caught my attention was for the Ministry of Defence. However, to phone them, I needed a working phone. My robust-looking mobile phone provided for me was on the bed, so I switched it on, and to my surprise that too hadn't been cooked by the E.M.B. A thought then shot into my head. somehow this and my laptop had been shielded while everything else in the hotel had been zapped. I knew then that all of this had been planned well in advance.

While those thoughts were upsetting, I put them aside for the time being. I then range the Ministry of Defence number and quoted my Diplomatic Number. Instantly, I was put through to The Rt Hon Prudence Marlow MP, Secretary of State. She then told me;

Mr. Jameson, thank god one of ours in the field, it's a shit storm where you are right now. You need to be debriefed right away. If you have power to your laptop, turn it on now and hit the video conference icon."

I did as I was told and the Secretary of State popped up on my screen. She nodded to me and informed me;

"Mr. Jameson before we begin, I need to bring a few more people into this conversation."

My screen then added three more people, the British Prime Minister, the head of MI5, and MI6. With all four acknowledging a secure connection. The Secretary of State then told me that as of one day ago, she was up to date with reports from Ms. Theresa Tarragon-Jones. So now what she needed from me was a comprehensive report on all that had transpired since Ms. Theresa Tarragon-Jones's last report. I took a deep breath and began. While I spoke, all four kept silent and had the best poker faces I have ever seen. However, as soon as I stopped taking The Rt Hon Prudence Marlow MP erupted with some explosive and surprising language; "Fuck, fuck, fuck she yelled and then she in our video conference she added;

"Mr. Prime Minister, this is a total fuck up. Whoever is responsible for this has our Country by the bollocks. These cock suckers have killed one of our soldiers, kidnapped our envoy plus three other women and four other soldiers, brought the town of Sutton Coldfield to its knees, and killed hundreds in a deliberate air crash. On top of that, these bastards want Ten Billion Pounds Stirling or they will do what they have done to Sutton Coldfield but to four of our Cities."

The P.M didn't seem bothered at Secretary of State profound language, he just agreed with her summary of what had so far happened and asked me;

"Mr. Jameson have you or any members of S.T.O.P have any idea what kind of technology is being used to cause these events?

That question should have been directed to our science professional, Carlos But I threw my two pennies worth in and answered;

"Mr. Prime Minister, I am not a scientist, but I believe that each attack that has happened has been using several different types of advanced technology. In Tenerife, my wife was killed with a technology that can harness lightning. I then witnessed a tremendous storm and mind control technology; the latter set tourists against the island's hotel staff. Here in the UK, I have seen and was injured when the storm, followed by mind control was used at a press conference.

Now, Mr. Prime Minister, that brings us to the latest attacks. First, whoever is responsible has been able to overcome the British force's highly trained security detail and a private security team by using some sort of advanced incapacitating agent. Secondly, they were able to easily take several hostages including my two daughters. Thirdly, they were able to isolate this hotel's power and the surrounding area's power, then destroy that power and all local communications. Fourthly, they easily scaled the technology up and targeted Sutton Coldfield Town.

I would speculate that the only technology close to one that affects electrical currents is one called Zenneck surface waves in which electrical power is directed along the earth's surface. Once again, I can only speculate Mr. Prime Minister that this technology has somehow been reversed and draws electrical power away from its source. As to how it then destroys the actual source is beyond my technical comprehension."

There were a few moments of silence as I guess the P.M took in what I had said. He then replied;

"Thank you for that Mr. Jameson. You certainly have given He Majesties Government something to think about."

Before the P.M could say any more, The Rt Hon Prudence Marlow MP had been stewing for a while and burst in with;

"Prime Minister, tell the bastards to go fuck themselves. The British Government doesn't bow down to low-life criminals or terrorists. Also, what's to stop these fuck heads from reneging if we did pay up?"

I could see the P. M's poker face and a small smile crept in. he then responded by saying;

"Prue darling, we will certainly discuss all possibilities of this. However, before any decisions are made, we need to gather as much intelligence as possible."

At that, the gentleman whose name I didn't catch from MI5 spoke.

"Mr. Jameson, do you think your hotel and indeed your laptop and phone are secure?

My answer was simple;

"No Sir, I believe everywhere has been cleverly bugged. I do however have some thoughts for you all to consider on paying the ten billion. I assure you; these thoughts will not compromise any security protocols."

It was the P.M that jumped in this time;

"I for one would love to hear your thoughts on this, please continue."

This for me was a big moment, I was fighting for my girls' lives. To cap that, I, B.J a nobody was about to give some advice to the P.M, Secretary of State, and heads of MI5 and MI6. With heart rate elevated, I took one big gulp of air in and began;

"The concerns voiced by the Secretary of State are indeed valid. If the British Government agreed to their demands, what is there to stop these racketeers trying to exploit further monies from the British Government? Well, I think I might have an answer. It seems to me that their motivation is for financial gain and nothing else.

Now I conclude because, whoever is instigating these gross acts of violence are is using S.T.O.P to publish videos, photos of all their acts of violence, and destruction across all forms of media. They also want their written demands to the British Government published.

All that has transpired in the U.K so far has been seen by the rest of the world and by each nation's government. The whole world is now waiting to see how the British Government reacts to these demands. Further, if the British Government submitted to these demands and hostilities continue after the deadline, it would tell other Governments that if they too have a deal with this group, they cannot be trusted. And that would be the end of a potential global money tree."

Before the P.M could catch his breath, the Secretary of State dived in with;

"Fucking hell, you know Prime Minister, I think this fellow Jameson might just have something. They could be using the United Kingdom as a stepping stone to Europe and beyond. If this is right, holy shit, these manipulating mother fuckers could be earning the biggest criminal jackpot in the history of the world."

With some humorous candor, the P.M interjected;

"Madam Secretary of State, I could not have summed Mr. Jameson's thoughts more eloquently myself. We have a few hours before our deadline, let's meet at number ten Downing Street and with our chiefs of staff and armed forces we can discuss this further.

In the meantime, Mr. Jameson, please be assured that the British Government will do its utmost to secure the safety of your daughters and the other hostages. Would you kindly keep this line open; we will need as much local intel as possible and I am sure we have lots more to discuss."

Well, I guess I had almost completed my task, so while I had time, I went to see how the others were doing. Senor García is quite a remarkable individual, he had managed to free and evacuate all the guests and staff out of the hotel. At the same time, he had been able to source from big businesses like PC World some top-of-the-range desktop computers, tablets, printers, mobile phones, and a box full of walkie-talkies that were being delivered by one of his men.

As soon as the office equipment arrived, we all helped unpack them. With a big push, we had our S.T.O.P and what I can only describe as our captured office up and running in about thirty minutes. Juan José was more than upset at the sight of the gruesome videos and photos that needed to be uploaded on to the S.T.O.P website, so Carlos handled it.

Although local news was sketchy, Juan José picked up some internet chatter about two passenger aircraft successfully doing an emergency landing at Birmingham International Airport. However, the internet chatter went on to speculate that the aircraft that had crashed, should have also been able to do an emergency landing at Birmingham International Airport. But, some of those who were posting online were actual eyewitnesses. Several of these claimed that they have seen an explosion from one of the aircraft's wings, thirty miles away from Sutton Coldfield Town Centre!

First reports in on the death toll stunned us all. It was estimated that the TIU flight had one hundred and eighty-nine passengers on board and they and all the crew had died. To make things worse, the aircraft had crashed into a large housing development and part of a primary school had been destroyed. We also had reports that a petrol station had caught fire and some of its tanks had exploded. The death toll on this was now several hundred and rising. I immediately emailed The Rt Hon Prudence Marlow MP, Secretary of State with this information and hoped it would have some bearing on the decisions she and the Prime Minister were having to make.

While we were setting up the S.T.O.P office, I noticed that Karl and his security team had remained outside the building, so I popped out to see how he and they were doing. Now I'm not sure exactly where that old British saying comes from, "keep a stiff upper lip, but Karl was remaining resolute and unemotional under extreme adversity. Seeing this, I decided that it would be best just to talk about business. So, I told him about my conversations with the Prime Minister and Secretary of State and then inquired about what orders he had received from his command? With a soldier's courteous tone, he replied;

"At this point, we have been ordered to follow the directive given and only guard the perimeter of the Hotel."

It was obvious that he knew more, but I suspected he did not want to divulge anything in case our conversations were being listened to, so I left it at that. Before I left, I told him one of Senor García's men was making teas and coffees and he would bring some fresh pots out to him and his team. Karl smiled and said;

"Ask him if he could rustle up a few biscuits, none of us have eaten for hours."

Now it's funny before food was mentioned, it had never entered my head. But, all of a sudden, my stomach screamed at me that it needed feeding. I headed back to the hotel, rounded up a few of Senor García's men and we went to the hotel's kitchen to see what we could find. Well, it was pleasing to find a very well-stocked kitchen. As it was still morning, we decided to cook and eat while you work breakfast, or in laymen's terms, egg, bacon, and sausage sandwiches.

When it comes to barbecues and breakfasts, every man is a five-star Michelin Chef. So, it didn't take us long to prepare some hearty "breakfast" sandwiches and we began to distribute them around the hotel. To keep them warm, I wrapped two large trays of them in tin foil and took them to Karl and the security team outside. As I was handed one of the trays over to Karl, he took the sandwiches off the tray and discreetly handed me a piece of paper. Knowing that we were being watched, I kept the paper under the tray. Jokingly, I then passed a few comments about how good the service had got in the hotel since the staff had left and headed back to the hotel's kitchen.

The kitchen had a large walk-in cold room and I guessed that was as secure as it gets. On the pretence that I was looking for items that would be suitable for lunch, I went in and read Karl's note, it read;

B.J, we believe the hotel and surrounding area are under some kind of advanced surveillance. It seems way beyond our technology. Therefore, be careful of what you and everyone else say or communicate through computers and the internet.

Satellite surveillance shows the attack on the hotel. First, extremely high-tech drones were used to gas everyone with an incapacitating agent that's chemical composition is similar to substance seventy-eight. This is an odourless military-grade incapacitating agent. Secondly, a team of forty moved in and spilt- up. Our satellite thermal imaging cameras show, one team removing the hostages from the hotel, while two other teams restrained all the security. The final team restrained all of us and then moved the hotel guests to the conference room.

Thirdly and lastly, the hostages were transported by a white transit van to a field close by where they were loaded onto a Chinook helicopter. After that, our satellite suffered a malfunction.

All of this information has been passed on by the M.O.D to the Secretary of State and Prime Minister.

Take care, Karl.

The thought of my two poor daughters, unconscious and bungled into a helicopter heading god only knows where got my heart pounding. However, I thought of Karl with his stiff upper lip and knew I had to battle on. Using my walkie-talkie, I called Carlos and Senor Garcia and asked them to meet me in the kitchen. Within minutes they arrived and I told them we needed to plan food for the rest of the day. I think they thought I had flipped my lid, but they graciously indulged me. We had a quick look around the kitchen and then I accompanied them into the walk-in cold room. There, I put my finger in front of my lips to indicate silence and showed them the note Karl had passed to me. Both men read it, nodded, and we began to discuss what was suitable for our next meal.

In the cold room, the hotel chef had left some big pieces of beef hanging for over twenty plus days, so we took these and put them in the oven along with some potatoes that we cut in quarters. Stacked in the corner were several trays of vegetables, so Senor García's men got to work cutting and dicing them up. While they busied themselves getting our next meal ready, I and Carlos went to the operations room to see what was happening. At the same time, Senor García then headed back to check on the hotel's security.

As soon as I walked into the conference room I could see Juan José pacing up and down and looking very concerned. I immediately inquired what was wrong and his answer was something we did not want to hear;

"B.J, Carlos this is not good. The United Kingdom Met Office has just issued an Orange alert storm warning for the U.K. Apparently, there has been a shift in the Jet Stream. They predict the main part of the storm will hit the central U.K around two o'clock this afternoon. That's when our deadline runs out!"

Instantly, with all that we had seen before, we knew this was no co-insistence. I looked at Carlos and all he could do was throw his hands in the air, shake his head from side to side and say;

"Imagine this, four major cities devoid of all power and communications, then you throw in a mega-storm and maybe some crowd mind control, the chaos will be just inconceivable. However, here's another unhappy thought, even if the British Government pays up, a big storm like this is going to reap havoc on all the local rescue efforts."

My head just nodded up and down in the agreement and then we all went silent. At that moment we knew S.T.O.P had for the time being been stopped. It might sound selfish given what had previously happened and what could soon happen. But all that was on my mind was the safe return of my daughters and I just felt helpless. I needed time to think and left the conference room and headed back to the room.

Chapter Twenty-three, S.T.O.P isn't going away, although the big boys have come out to play

Normally with my martial arts training, I can use some deep breathing exercises to help me relax. However, this time it just wasn't working, my mind was on high alert waiting for a decision from Her Majesties Government. For some reason, I just kept staring at my home office phone and laptop, hoping that one or the other would burst into life. But we all know times seemed to slow down when you are anxiously waiting for a call, message, or someone delivering a parcel to you at home. Also, we all know that staring at the device does not make the calls and messages come through any quicker. With all of this in mind, I went to have a shave and a shower but took my phone and laptop with me just in case.

After our beef lunch, which I could not eat and with only one hour left on the deadline, I finally got a call from the Secretary of State. With her normal expressiveness, she told me;

"Mr. Jameson, we have decided that we're fucked. Despite employing all of our Governmental resources and assistance from other countries, we cannot see a way out of this shit storm. The Prime Minister is as I speak addressing the nation and informing the country that Her Majesties Government has just paid ten billion pounds of ransom money to those cock sucking wankers. The P.M is also asking that all hostages will be freed, unharmed immediately, as Her Majesties Government has complied with all of their demands. Further, the proposed attacks on four of our major cities are cancelled.

We are hoping that you and the S.T.O.P team will get a message soon informing you as to the location of the hostages. If needed, we have a first-class medical team on standby. Let me know as soon as you hear anything, I will then pass it on to the P.M and our other intelligence agencies.

Now, as to this fucking storm that is heading our way, we have been approached by an American company, Fran-Expansum. They specialize in trying to control global warming using advanced satellite technology. Anyhow, these clever fuckers feel that the same technology could be used to deflect some storm away from the United Kingdom and are deploying these systems now."

At that, she ended her call. Without hesitation, I picked up my mobile phone and laptop and ran down to the conference room. There I was greeted with sounds of cheering followed by some hugs from Carlos, Karl, Juan José, and Senor García. Before the cheers and hugs ended, the terrorist mobile phone burst into life. Answering it, I was again informed that there was one new message. While an eerie silence fell over the conference room, I played the message on the phone's speaker so everyone could hear. It began;

"Our transaction with the British Government has been completed. To honour this, no more hostilities are forthcoming. As agreed, the hostages will be released unharmed.

The hostages can be found at a modern climate-controlled warehouse, just on the outskirts of East Midlands Airport. Location, Pegasus Business Park, Herald Way, Castle Donnington, Derby. Post Code, DE74 2TQ."

With that, the message ended and the mobile screen went blank again. Although I wanted to immediately jump into the Bond mobile, I had to restrain myself and let the Secretary of State know about the message. In her normal colourful way, she responded;

"Mr. Jameson, that's fucking good news. I will let the Prime Minister know immediately. Now, fuck off of this phone and get your arse over to that warehouse and give your girls a big hug from Aunty Prue.

Oh fuck, I nearly forgot. Teams from MI5, MI6, S.A.S bomb disposal, chemical warfare, and some medics will be dispatched. Don't enter the building or touch anything until they arrive and give you the all-clear. Mr. Jameson, this is just in case those fucking terrorist shit holes might have booby-trapped the building or surrounding area."

Well, I have to admit, in all my euphoria at seeing my daughters alive, I hadn't given a thought about this being a diabolical trap. Aunty Prue was quite right, I then had to go back and break the booby-trapped news to the team. Although they were as eager me to see our loved ones again, the thought of it being a deadly trap dampened everyone's spirits. However, putting the danger aside, nothing was going to stop us from going to the warehouse.

As we all headed on over to the Bond mobile it began to rain. Looking up, the skies above us didn't look extremely threatening, but I knew from experience that that could change in a heartbeat. However, before we drove off, Karl stopped us and informed us that we going to have police and military escorts. Forty-five minutes later, with sirens wailing and blue lights flashing we reached our destination. It looked like the cavalry had arrived minutes earlier and my god, they turned out in force. They were just setting up their mountains of equipment and above us in the rainy skies, every single move was being monitored by four A330 Puma air force helicopters.

Within minutes, one team had set up a hazardous chemical tent and had a dozen men and women standing by wearing hazmat suits. The team for bomb disposal was also suited and booted and was liaising with a special forces unit who were initially assessing the area. After using sniffer robots, they all agreed that the outer parameter was safe. And the SAS team began to assess the inside of the warehouse using some very high-tech drone scanners. Immediately, the scanner picked up the heat signatures of eight people in a room at the rear of the warehouse.

By now my heart was in my mouth and from the safety of being behind a large transportable bomb blast barrier, I watched a team of four SAS soldiers dressed in hazmat suits, move forward, and very slowly begin to examine a side door entrance for any hidden explosive devises. After a few minutes, an all-clear signal was given and cautiously they opened the door and placed the sniffer robot and small drone inside the warehouse to do an internal scan. As soon as the sniffer robots and drone operators said it was safe to enter, the four soldiers carefully entered the warehouse.

Ten minutes of absolute silence then passed before the big roller shutter door on the front of the warehouse began to open. Then, over a loud hailer, Karl gave the order, "Go, go, go" a wave of people rushed into the warehouse. Needless to say, I, Carlos, and Senor García were at the crest of that wave.

To mine and everyone else's surprise, except an office and toilet block at the rear, the warehouse was empty. We ran to the office block and were greeted by the team of SAS soldiers who informed us that all the hostage was alive, but had been heavily sedated. As I entered the small office, I could see all eight were unconscious and had been put on camp beds. Unconscious or not, I rushed over, kissed my girls, and held both their hands. In less than a minute an army of medics arrived and I stepped aside while my girls and the others were given a thorough checked over.

It wasn't long before the medics agreed that everyone's life signs were normal. However, as a precaution they wanted them airlifted to Birmingham's Queen Elizabeth's hospital until they became conscious. They also wanted tests carried out to see what drugs had been used to sedate the hostages and as an extra precaution, they wanted the hostages monitored for any nasty side effects. That all sounded good to me, Carlos and Senor García.

While a forensic team got to work inside the warehouse, the medic team put all the hostages on wheeled stretchers and took them out to two of the A330 Puma air force helicopters. We were then told that one of the other helicopters would transport us and the hostages to Queen Elizabeth's hospital. As we clambered in our pilot informed us that although it was still raining, the fierce weather storm had subsided, so we should be in for a smooth ride. That news made me think that the American satellite company mentioned by Aunty Prue had done its job, so well done to them. On top of that, the pilot was true to his word, we had a smooth ride and within twenty-five minutes, we were back in the Q.E hospital.

Now, a lot of people complain about the British National Health Service and maybe they are justified. But the service I and my daughter had had over the past few days was first class and that care of excellence continued. As soon as the helicopter's wheels touched down, teams rushed forward and whisked all the unconscious hostages to a hospital ward that had been specially prepared for them in the old part of the hospital.

It was quickly established that all the hostages had been rendered unconscious by a similar incapacitating agent that had been used on everyone in the hotel. They, however, had been given the incapacitating agent in a modified liquid form and injected into them at regular intervals. From that, we could only guess that all eight had been unconscious since the onset of this latest ordeal.

While we waited for our loved ones to regain consciousness, we decided we needed a coffee and headed down to the hospital's Costa Coffee. As this was a public area, we felt it was reasonably secure and safe to talk to. I kicked things off by saying;

"Is it me or do you also think we have all been played?"

Everyone nodded and with a very serious face, Senor García said;

"We have indeed lost a battle. Some of us have lost more than others. But I can only speak for myself, the war is not over yet."

A silence fell over us and for a moment as we all individually contemplated what those words meant to us. Then, I, Carlos, and Karl agreed that yes, our noses had been bloodied and eyes blackened. But we too were ready to fight until the end of the war.

Chapter Twenty-four, Fight, not quite what you thought

While a massive emergency operation to restore normality took place in and around the Town of Sutton Coldfield, we sat for several hours waiting for our loved one to regain consciousness. Then slowly one by one the incapacitating agent wore off and after a few more tests, we were finally able to see them. Well-being a dad I could not stop myself, I rushed over to them and gave them some big hugs and kisses.

However, not surprisingly, they were totally confused as to how they got to be in the hospital? When I told the girls what had happened, both Emma and Oliva were stunned. The same reaction also applied to the other hostages. Now, my girls have a great sense of humour, and shrugging off the last bits of drossiness, they both proclaimed it was the best sleep they had ever had and wanted the formula for the incapacitating agent.

While Carlos was still showering Theresa Tarragon-Jones with hugs and kisses, I noticed Valentina García had just given her brother a quick hug and was looking very stern and sitting bolt upright? I walked over to her and asked if she was OK? As she looked around the hospital ward, she beckoned me to come closer and whispered;

"B.J, I'm not sure if it's safe to talk. We have an "invisible espia" around us."

She could see from my facial reaction that I did not comprehend "invisible espia" so whispering, she translated;

"Invisible spy."

Trying to be polite, I nodded, but other than thinking that perhaps the hospital ward had been bugged, I hadn't got a clue what she was on about.

Pulling me even closer, her lips touched my ears and she whispered;

"B.J, it's an entity that can travel on the energy of a storm or electrical waves, but cannot be seen."

I stepped back a little, nodded, and knowing Valentina Garcia's background, I believed her. To everyone's surprise, I then took Valentina in my arms, told her I was pleased to see she was safe. Then with a big gasp from my daughters and a serious frown from Senor Garcia, I kissed her on the lips. Encouraging this, Valentina wrapped her arms around me and held the kiss for a few moment's and with a small smile on her face, she put her head on my shoulder and whispered;

"The things we have to do for the team."

She then added;

"I am not sure how to do this, but we need to let others know."

It was then my turn to smile and whispered back;

"I'm not kissing everyone, team, or not."

Well with the other looking on, we both had to laugh at that. We then broke our embrace and I said to Carlos that we all needed a cup of tea or coffee. To get him away from the group, I requested that he come with me to the hospital's Costa and we could bring some refreshments back for everyone. Carlos just nodded and after getting everyone's order, we then set off to the coffee shop. On the way I secretly told to Carlos what Valentina Garcia had told me While this sank in, he stayed silent, and then in very a hushed voice, he said;

"Wow B.J, no wonder we have always been three steps behind in everything we do. It's going to be difficult, but we must make a plan to get everyone up to speed. However, a group is easily targeted. We need to tell each member of the team individually."

He thought about this and as we entered Costa in a low tone, he added;

"How does this sound, you, I, and Valentina García need to make an excuse to get the others away from the group. Then when we are in a reasonably safe place, we tell them what is going on?"

That to me sounded like a reasonable plan and with a smile on my face I answered;

"Looks like we might be drinking lots of coffee or I can just passionately kiss everyone."

The latter made Carlos laugh and jokingly he responded;

"Keep those British lips away from Theresa Tarragon-Jones, she's all mine. However, mi amigo, you might have to do a bit of kissy, kissy to inform the Secretary of State and your Prime Minister."

Although this was said jokingly, in an instance we both realized that the Secretary of State and your Prime Minister were also going to be informed us of our suspicions, but that raised another problem. How were we going to do this?

After we all finished our refreshments, I asked Senor García and Karl if he would escort me to the hospital's chemists. They both looked a little strange at me. However, I explained to them that I needed to pick some medication the doctor had prescribed for me the other day and I wanted some security with me. Carlos's was less discreet; he just raised his eyebrows a few times, then looked at the vacant bathroom and he and Theresa Tarragon-Jones with a smile their faces disappeared. That left Valentina García with my daughters and we all know ladies never got to the loo alone. So, Valentina García and the girls headed to a loo, but as a precaution, they went to a loo in another part of the hospital.

After we had all been or done our bits of business, we all converged back in the hospital ward. There, we engaged in lots of small talk until a team of doctors came in and gave everyone the all-clear. Within minutes Karl had arranged two helicopters, one for us and one to transport those on his team who had been kidnapped back to their barracks. Within ninety minutes we were back at our hotel but as we left the helicopter Theresa Tarragon-Jones stayed onboard. In her best British accent, she stated;

"My government needs me, T.T.F.N."

She then gave us a wave befitting a queen and before we got inside the hotel, the helicopter took off. I and the others looked at Carlos and he gave us the two raised eyebrows single. Now, this didn't mean the same as when he did it with Theresa Tarragon-Jones, it meant, she was going to see Auntie Prue and the P.M.

While we had been away from the hotel, a team from MI5 had been doing a sweep to see if they could find any hidden bugs or spyware on any of the computers and other communication devices. Now to support this operation, they brought in the latest hi-Tec scanners and computer experts and after doing a deep scan they came up with nothing. This, however, supported what Valentina Garcia had said about it being an entity of unknown origin. So, with this in mind, we all had to be on our guard.

We all needed to know more about what Valentina García had said. So, the only way I could get her on her own and away from our "invisible spy" was to invite her to an impromptu meal in Birmingham City Centre. Knowing what I was up to she agreed to this and after a quick wash and change of clothes, we headed out to the car park. Fortunately, Karl had arranged to have the Bond mobile brought back for me and Karl's team had done a thorough search in case any bubs had been planted.

So, next, we needed a security detail. Senior Garcia's provided one of his men for Valentina García and Karl assigned one giant of a man as personal protection officer, who also insisted on driving. Therefore, I and Valentina sat in the back and we headed for the big city.

Now normally trying to park in Birmingham City Centre is a nightmare, but as a British diplomate, I had an ace up my sleeve, a diplomatic pass. Therefore, my vehicle was allowed to park anywhere without any time restrictions. Oh, and still, it must have frustrated the parking wardens, as they could not issue any parking tickets. The restaurant I chose was La Galleria restaurant, I had eaten there before, the food was excellent and I knew we could park quite close.

Although we hadn't pre-booked a table, we were fairly quickly seated in a quiet corner. However, the restaurant was quite full and as we walked to our table, we certainly got some curious glances from many of the dinners. But I suppose in all fairness, I would have done the same. First, our security detail checked out of the restaurant and its exits. Next, we are escorted to our table by the staff and our two burly security guards. But, the icing on the curiosity cake must have been my battered and bruised face and the gorgeous women I had with me. Valentina García looked stunning dressed in a black Carolina Herrera floral-print dress, black Saint Laurent shoes. And to compliment this, the accessories she wore were spectacular. Around her neck were a simple but stunning Bvlgari gold and black necklace. Now, my bank balance would have been screaming by now, but there were two more items. Her handbag was an elegant black Lady Dior lambskin and on her wrist was a gorgeous and quite expensive Gucci black and gold timeless watch.

Our lady waitress pulled our chairs out for us and once we sat down, we both had to laugh at the gazes we were getting. We then ordered some light refreshments and got down to the serious business of trying to decide what delights we would order off the menu. After looking at the menu for a few minutes, Valentina decided to have the same as me. Now I'm not a fancy eater and like big plated meals. So, the poor lady got the soup of the day to start, followed by the restaurant's rather delicious, large portioned Spaghetti Bolognese.

Once we finished our main meal, we were too full to order the dessert immediately and decided to let our stomachs rest for a while. It was then that Valentina García said she would like to tell me about how she knew about what happened to her after she was rendered unconscious by the incapacitating agent. She then took my hand, held it tightly, and began;

"As you are aware, the gift I have has been with me all my life. Others would be terrified of what I see every day. Saying that what happened when I went unconscious it was one of the scariest things I have ever seen in my life. The drugs must have affected my consciousness because my mind was on an energy plan, I had never experienced before. This is where I witnessed the entity and it had no physical form. I can only describe it as a blur of energy, but it was not of the spirit world. B.J, I am only guessing, but strangely I felt it had it also had a human form. Now this evil thing witnessed all of us being rendered unconscious and then eavesdropped in on conversations once you became conscious.

Now, this is when things got even stranger. As soon as the aircraft crashed locally killing all on board, I felt their energy leave their bodies, but instead of them going to the spirit world, something directed them to another void of non-reality? Now when I say non-reality, to me the spirit world is real, but this void is artificial. It is almost like an energy-holding cell that the recently passed energies are being held in. B.J, these voids can hold thousands of captured spirits."

Valentina then let go of my hand and for a few moments, she fidgeted with her necklace. I did not want to pressure her, but I was curious as to what she meant by "these voids". I could see she was distressed, so in a soft voice, I offered her a drink of water. Putting on a brave face, she took a sip of the water, took hold of my hand again, and continued;

"I know you would like an explanation to "these voids" and how many there are, but I have no answer. What I think is happening is; the energy of each soul captured is somehow used to power a device that can alter weather patterns and carry mind-altering wavelengths along with it.

Now before you ask any questions, I have some very important information for you. While I was unconscious, I found that Shelia is still trapped in one of these voids. It looks like it's first in, last out. Oddly, I was able to communicate with Shelia for some considerable time. She sends her eternal love to you and your two girls.

B.J, more importantly, we have sketched out a theory on how to release the trapped souls for these voids and if we are lucky, de-energize this soul-capturing device. To begin with, we will need to get unilateral co-operation from the governments of this world and their military forces. Then, we will need the brainpower of their top scientists. After that, I and Shelia will have to do our thing. And finally, B.J, for all of this to work, secrecy at every level will be of paramount importance."

It pleased me to know that Shelia was still able to pass on her eternal love message. But, OMG, wow, to come up with a plan from an unknown void to help save the world from a mysterious force. I had to laugh inwardly, only my Shelia and this elegant lady physic could do that. To cap this, if you are going to put a plan together, you might as well go for a big one, and this was the daddy of them all.

Seeing that the implications of what she had said were beginning to sink in, Valentina moved closer to me, kissed me on the cheek, and quietly said;

"To put this plan into action will take a lot of careful thought, that will involve everyone. B.J, I think you know that to avert any other catastrophes, this needs to be done as soon as possible. So, let's not discuss this right now and order some of those wonderful desserts, followed by a coffee. Then as soon as we get back to the hotel, we can activate our new S.T.O.P plan."

This sounded like good, positive thinking and I'm always up for that. So, as soon as I settled the bill with my government-issued gold debit card, we headed back to the hotel and began to secretively inform the S.T.O.P team and Karl of our suggestions.

Our main difficulty was finding secure places to talk. Nevertheless, our resident genius, Carlos came up with a solution. I left a note for Emma, Oliva, and Juan José to let them know we had popped out, then the rest of the team piled into the Bond mobile and we just drove around. Carlos's theory behind this was; if this entity was using some sort of energy wavelength to travel on, it would be difficult to direct the energy wave to a mobile object that is constantly changing direction. And as a few extra precautions, we all left our mobile phones at the hotel, and Karl had the vehicle's GPS and security tracker turned off.

Once we were on the road, Carlos said he already had some ideas on what kind of energy waves the entity was possibly using. With our ears pricked back, he explained;

"Mis amigos, extremely low-frequency waves, or ELF for short would be the easiest to use. This is due to their extremely long wavelengths. They can travel vast distances and can bend around extremely large obstacles. Tests need to be carried out to prove my theory, but I also believe that time is against us and we need to act now. All we need to stop the ELF waves are jamming devices and perhaps Karl can confirm this, but I think many naval ships and submarines already have them."

For security, Karl had insisted on being our driver. Keeping his eyes on the road ahead, he answered;

"As you are aware, I am not a Navy man. But I do have a little insight into ELF waves. During the Cold War, nuclear-powered submarines were developed that could stay submerged for months. Even today, transmitting messages to these submarines is an active area of research. Normally, they use very low frequency (VLF) radio waves that can penetrate seawater a few hundred feet to transmit communications. However, a few nations have built transmitters that use extremely low frequency (ELF) radio waves. These can easily penetrate seawater to reach submarines at operating depths, but they require huge antennas. These transmitters, receivers, and antennas would be installed on submarines, support vessels, and naval land bases. Now knowing our concerns for national security, I dare say they also have highly sophisticated ELF jamming devices."

Well, that was our first bit of good news. All we had to do now is find out what nations had these and get their cooperation to set up a way for a worldwide ELF jamming signal. Now, that was way above our pay grade, we would have to get the Prime Minister and Auntie Prue involved with this.

With all of our communication devices compromised and Theresa Tarragon-Jones already in London, we decided that we needed to drive straight to London. So, while we all got some shut-eye, our driver changed direction, and over the next three hours, he weaved his way through back roads until we arrived in the capital city. Our first stop was the Foreign and Commonwealth Office. There, Karl used a secure line to contact Theresa Tarragon-Jones. He then briefed her on our plan, and within twenty minutes, she had booked us an immediate appointment with the Prime Minister and Auntie Prue at number ten downing street.

We all hot-footed back out to the Bond mobile, and with our blue lights flashing and siren wailing, Karl put his foot to the metal and whisked us to downing street. There we were met by a security officer who directed us to the study room. Auntie Prue was the first to greet us by saying;

"Fucking hell, it's still the middle of the night. You know, I haven't had time to put my makeup on. I hope what you have got to say is good or I am going to be very fucking cross."

The Prime Minister was sitting in a chair, sipping a cup of earl grey tea. He then calmly stated;

"Prue my darling, calm down. These wonderful people have rushed here from Birmingham to help us in a time of extreme peril. Let's give them some tea, coffee, and biscuit's and we can then all sit, listen, and evaluate what they have to say."

We all knew Auntie Prue was just venting a little hot air. She nodded at the P.M and then mellowed. Smiling at us all, she came around gave each of us a hug and in true aunty style, she took orders for tea or coffee and dished out the biscuits. With the niceties over, we were joined by the heads of MI5 and MI6 and then got down to business. I did most of the talking, however, Carlos jumped in to explain the science technical side.

After our presentation, there was a brief silence while what we had said was being gauged. Then the head of M15 spoke first;

"Despite the U.K leaving the European Union, our relations with all of Europe are good. Therefore, I see no problem with them co-operating. I would also say the U.S.A, New Zealand, Australia, and India would be prepared to support our endeavours. As to China and its allies, we still have sanctions against them over Covid 19. On top of that, we have recently we have had some further political upsets with them. Needless to say, wounds are still sore, so now, they may or may not back us"

The last part of that statement riled The Rt Hon Prudence Marlow MP, Secretary of State, and in a fiery response, she replied;

"Well if they won't support us, Fuck them, what arseholes! Let them see what it's like to watch their towns and being destroyed by this group of crazy terrorists."

Once again, the P.M smiled at his Secretary of States passion and interjected;

"Ladies and Gentlemen, let's assume for the time being that globally we are all in the same sinking ship. Now with that in mind, let's see if we can rally all hands-on deck."

With that, the P.M and his entourage left the study and a few minutes later, to our surprise, M. S Theresa Tarragon-Jones popped her head in and said;

"Hi everyone, the Prime Minister wants you to stay for a while. Now, I guess by now you're all hungry, so I have arranged some breakfast for you. Please come with me to the kitchen."

We had hardly got our bums off the chairs when the Secretary of State burst in and proclaimed;

"Southern Ireland is under attack! Those fucking terrorists have just struck the coastal town Donegal with a complete power outage. The P.M is on the phone right now to the Southern Irelands Taoiseach and he wants all of you on a flight to Dublin. Theresa that also includes you. You will be transported to Heathrow airport by helicopter where an R.A.F transporter is ready to fly you over to Dublin Airport International. On arrival, we will have government officials and members of the Irish intelligent agencies waiting for you. They will brief you on the latest developments. Now get your arses in gear and hit the road. Oh, B.J, don't worry, I will get a message to your daughters and Juan José as to where you have gone"

As we rushed out of number ten and piled into the Bond mobile, Carlos looked at me and with a puzzled look asked;

"B.J, the García's and my English are quite good but, could you please translate what Irelands Taoiseach is?"

Even though we had just been thrown into a new unfolding dilemma, I liked that Carlos still had some clarity of mind, and replied so that the García's could hear as well;

"Irelands Taoiseach is the southern Irish name given to the person who heads the Irish cabinet of ministers, in other words, their Prime Minister.

Everyone nodded at that little gem of information and after a brief pause Carlos asked another question;

"I know this new attack has just been thrust at us, but does anyone have any thoughts on what we are going to do when we arrive in Southern Ireland?"

It was Theresa Tarragon-Jones who answered this;

"For now, we need to keep calm and just relax. When we arrive, we will have more intel and then we will be able to make a plan of action."

She then looked at Carlos and in a dusky voice said;

"Darling, don't you think it just great that we have been thrust together again."

Carlos looked at her smiled, then took her in his arms and gave her a big long, tongue-in-the-mouth kiss. To which we all reacted by pretending to vomit.

Chapter Twenty-five,
Eire's battleground

It only took two hours to transfer the S.T.O.P team from downing street to Dublin's International Airport. Upon arrival, we were greeted by a Senior Irish Diplomat, Connor O'Sullivan, and the Directorate of Military Intelligence, Dermot Byrne who told us that we were been taken directly to Donegal by helicopter and would be briefed as soon as we arrived. We then rushed across the tarmac and boarded a waiting Boeing CH-7 Chinook transport helicopter that took us to Aerfort Dhun na nGall, (Donegal airport).

As we approached the airport, Dermot Byrne told us that normally we would be looking at an airstrip that was voted the second most scenic in the world. However, on this morning, it looked like a battleground! An Aer Lingus aircraft had crashed into the main terminal building, and we could see numerous fire trucks trying to put out an enormous raging fire. At the same time, dozens of ambulances were tending those who have been pulled out of the terminal building and had miraculously survived.

As we touched down and viewed the devastation, Dermot Byrne said that there was a change in his plan. He had hoped to use one of the airport's outbuildings as a command centre, but with all this destruction, we were now going by minibus to the Central Hotel Donegal.

To take my mind off what we had just witnessed, I just looked out of the mini-bus's windows. I have to say, although we arrived in a storm, and the rain was lashing off the roads, the scenery along the way was stunning. From leaving the airport, it took us just over an hour to arrive at the hotel, however, despite the atrocious weather, my first impression of Donegal was, it's is a beautiful coastal town. The sad part was, with no power, no communications, and appalling weather conditions, the town was in utter chaos.

While we stayed in the mini-bus, Dermot Byrne and Connor O'Sullivan went to the reception to check us in and make sure that the hotel's ancillary power was functioning. It must have been all OK as Dermot Byrne stood at the hotel's front door and gestured us to come in. He then led us into the restaurant area and informed us we were about to have a fabulous Irish breakfast, and while we eating, he would brief us on what happening. So, as we tucked into our enormous meal, he began;

"First ladies and Gentlemen, you have the full backing of the Irish Government. Therefore, Connor and I will be on hand to assist you with anything you need. For security purposes, and your safety, until this is over, you will not use any computers, mobile phones, or any other communication device. Now, let me explain to you what has happened so far.

Like the attack on the English town, Sutton Coldfield, we had no warning. It's not unusual for Southern Ireland to have rain, but this storm whipped up in minutes and then we lost all electrical power, not just here in the town, but right up to the airport. At the same time, all communication went down.

Just before you touched down, our Taoiseach had an untraceable communication, this person or persons claimed responsibility for this and the attacks on English soil. The claimant then issued a demand that if we do not pay twenty billion euros within ten hours of receiving this communication, they will attack all major cities in Southern Ireland."

Connor O'Sullivan then added;

"Because of what has happened in the U.K, the Irish Government will in eight hours concede to the terrorist demands. However, we are leaving an open window of seven hours for you to try your plan. Now I know it's not long, but my office has had reassures that the British army, royal navy, air force, and some other European forces will help implement jamming the ELF waves. I can also confirm that secrecy is of paramount importance. Therefore, while you're in Ireland, you have been registered as international reporters and are here to report on the attack on Donegal."

Conner then handed each of us a folder, that to our surprise contained new identities for all of us. For a few minutes, we all browsed through the contents, then Conner asked;

"Now does anyone have any questions?"

I spoke up first and asked;

"With the members of the press attacking me, my family, and other members of S.T.O.P. Plus the fact that England's parliament has put a curtail on how many press officers you can have in one area; do you think this is a good idea?"

For a moment the air went cold, and the S.T.O.P team all looked at Conner for an explanation. Not looking at all worried he replied;

"It's a very valid question, and I should have explained why you are posing as reporters earlier, so, please accept my apologies."

He then continued;

"The whole world's focus is now off the U.K, the new terror hotspot is Southern Ireland. Therefore, the world press will want to report on how Southern Ireland's government is handling this attack. So, under the circumstances, having international reporters here in Donegal is quite reasonable.

Our Government is also aware that S.T.O.P members are of high interest to this individual or group of terrorists and what happened when members of the press attacked you. Consequently, to keep the terrorists off your trail, we looked at the one area that they would not think to try to trace you. Now that's why for the time being you are all International reporters."

Now that it was explained to us, we could all see the logic in what Conner had just said, and we all nodded in agreement. Conner then followed up by again asking;

"Now, does anyone have any further questions?"

Now, as if he were back in junior school, Carlos shot his hand into the air and asked;

"What is this bread? It's delicious."

Both Dermot and Connor laughed out loud at this, and through his laughter, Conner replied;

"That Francisco Ruiz, my Spanish reporter friend is Irish soda bread. We have a unique cooking method that results in the signature dense texture, hard crust, and slight sourness that soda bread is known for. You can also add other ingredients, such as butter, eggs, raisins, or nuts.

Now just for the technical-minded, the unique texture of this bread is the result of a reaction between the acid and baking soda that results in the formation of small bubbles of carbon dioxide within the dough."

Carlos gave Conner one of his big toothy grins and replied;

"Well Senor Conner, Francisco Ruiz would like to say, it's worth just coming to Ireland to taste this superb bread.

Oh, and the thought of having some raisins added is indeed a culinary delight. I must write about an article on this."

Well, we all had to laugh at that. Then, after this bit of light heartiness, it was back to business. Valentina, or under her new identity, the Italian reporter Angelica Romano got the ball rolling by saying;

"Dermot and Connor, jamming the ELF waves is indeed a priority, but with the power outage, have you investigated any sources of Zenneck surface waves across Southern Ireland?"

It was Dermot who replied saying;

"Irish Military Intelligence has been closely monitoring all of S.T.O. P's online activities and thanks to your endeavours, we have indeed located three new power plants that are testing this technology. Two are owned by Fran-power and seem legitimate. According to sources, both of these plants are not operational yet. However, just in case, we have teams on standby with Supreme court orders that state we are on the threshold of a national emergency, and until further notice, all work is to cease immediately, and all power sources must be closed down.

The other one is, however, a little more devious. The whole plant has been crowd-funded, and there have been some very substantial anonymous donations. We have a large strike force on standby, and when we know we can jam the ELF, the strike force will move in, and if necessary, forcibly close the power station down."

Valentina nodded, indicating she was more than satisfied with Dermot's answer but Alejandro García, who was now Angelica Romano's Italian photographer, Roberto Colombo, had something else on his mind and asked;

"Gentlemen, I am sincerely impressed at what you have said so far, but if I am to be a photographer, I need some photographic equipment, and we as a group need guns and a protection detail."

At that, Dermot asked to be excused for a few minutes. At the same time, Connor began to rummage through his ministry briefcase. He then produced a folder that as he explained had Irish firearms certificates for everyone. While he proceeded to hand these out, Dermot returned with two large metal cases and asked us to gather around him. He then opened one case and gave each of us a SIG Sauer M17 handgun and two boxes of ammunition. The other case he handed to Alejandro García and said;

"I think you will find the photographic equipment inside and a few extra weapons more than adequate. Now as to a security detail, for the time being, Military Intelligence has taken over this hotel. Therefore, all of the staff are the Army Ranger Wing. Now First Lieutenant Karl Barlow, or should I say, Nigel Hickman reporter for the Daily Mirror, I understand you have been up all night, and if you don't mind me saying, you look wrecked. Why don't you go and get a bit shut-eye? Your room is number twelve. Here is your key card."

Karl thanked Dermot, gave us all a wave, and said;

"See you all in a while." And went to his room.

Dermot then added;

"I have allocated a room for each of you. In your main wardrobe, you will find some fresh clothing along with all the other essentials."

He gave us our room key cards, and we all headed up to freshen up. I have to say my room was nice, and it had a great view. When I opened the wardrobe, I was amazed at what had been supplied,

I had a nice, possibly well needed, three-quarter length raincoat, two quite smart jackets, two pairs of chino trousers, two shirts, two ties, two pairs of brogue shoes, socks and underpants. To complement this, I also had some nice toiletries and a new electric razor. Now, I don't know who did the wardrobe shopping, but whoever it was had even got my sizes right.

While I took a shower and shaved, I mulled over my new identity. My new name was John West. Mr. West was a reporter for the West Midlands, Express, and Star. While I understood that these false identities were just given to us to avoid unwanted attention and to make it harder for the terrorist group to trace the members of S.T.O.P. I had to laugh as it reminded me of that famous tin of salmon.

As soon as I had finished showering, I dressed in my smart new clothes and went back down to the reception area. I was the first to arrive and was greeted by Dermot and Connor who immediately organised a coffee for me. We then sat and Dermot asked for his records if I would kindly recall what had happened to me and my late wife from the time we landed in Tenerife. Oh boy, was that a tall order. I did start, but within minutes, embarrassingly although I tried, my emotions got the better of me. So, we agreed to shelve this for the time being.

Next to arrive was Francisco Ruiz (Carlos). He had also raided his new wardrobe and was wearing a smart navy blue, slim fit suit and light blue shirt. He greeted us all in Spanish by saying, Buenos Dias Hombre's, I love the clothes and they fit great. Now have you seen Frau Hannah Schmidt yet? Well, we all knew who this was, Theresa Tarragon-Jones, and right on cue she arrived and looked every bit at a reporter from the German newspaper Frankfurter Allgemeine Zeitung. Hannah Schmidt had on a smart grey two-piece suit, white shirt, and some extremely nice black high-heeled shoes. In perfect German she said;

"Guten Morgen, wo ist der Kaffee?"

Francisco Ruiz (Carlos), looked Hannah Schmidt up and down and answered;

"Wow, wow, wow, you look stunning. Forget the coffee, we might want to go back to your room."

Giggling, Frau Schmidt went and sat by Carlos and said;

"Darling coffee first, Geschlechtsverkehr later."

That comment brought about instant laughter but, as I don't speak German, the latter went right over my head. Carlos could see I was lost, and slightly blushing he told me;

"B.J, Geschlechtsverkehr is German for sexual intercourse"

Karl then re-appeared and only caught the last bit about Geschlechtsverkehr is German for sexual intercourse. He said laughing;

"Folks, it sounds like I have been missing out on some weird conversations."

While we all laughed at this, I caught a glimpse of the García's heading towards us. Valentina looked extremely pale and was being supported by her brother. I rushed over to her and asked if she was OK? She shook her head from side to side, and with tears in her eyes, she replied;

"Everyone needs to hear this. Those who passed away on the Aer Lingus flight and those who died the main terminal building life's forces have been harvested. They are now all in the same realm as all the others. This means two things, one; the entity that is controlling their life forces has just become much, much stronger, and two; we now have hundreds of more souls to save. Sadly, with the short time that we have, we might lose this fight, and put all the souls in the other realm in jeopardy."

Now that was something we did not want to hear. A silence fell on all of us as we tried to comprehend the forthcoming battle Valentina was going to have, but sadly we were not spiritualists and all we could do is give her moral support. I did, however, have a question for her, and asked;

"Have you been able to contact Shelia to hear what she thinks of the new situation?"

Valentina took my hand and replied;

"B. J, with the influx of all these new life's forces, this other realm is in pandemonium. At the moment, trying to contact Shelia is impossible. I do however have a wild idea."

Still holding Valentina's hand, I answered for everyone by saying;

"OK, please put forward your idea."

She then continued;

"The last time I was able to contact Shelia, I was under the influence of a military-grade incapacitating agent. If we could replicate this and put me into a state of unconsciousness, I will endeavour to leave my physical body and travel to this other realm. Once there, I will try to contact Shelia, and together we will begin our plan to free all the trapped life forces. All you guys have to do is shut down the Zenneck power plants, jam the ELF waves, and stay safe."

Alejandro García jumped straight in, and looking with some concern at his sister, he asked;

"Valentina, as I understand it the incapacitating agent you were given was a modified version that was administered to you by injection in controlled doses. Do you realise that you might just have to be knocked out of the military-grade stuff and if this is administered to you over several hours it could be very dangerous for you? Next, we were going to time this so everything happened together. If you are having an out-of-body experience, how are we going to let you know when we are ready?"

Valentina then let go of my hand, stood up, looked at us all, and replied;

"Yes, there will be risks, but unfortunately Alejandro, it would seem our backs are against the wall, therefore to get the job done, I am prepared to take whatever military-grade incapacitating agent is available. Now to answer your other question. This is plan B, and plan B needs an element of luck. Now Dermot, how quickly can you get hold of some military-grade incapacitating agent?"

Dermot also stood up, and before we went any further, he asked for a show of hands to approve of what Valentina had proposed. We all knew we had no other option, everyone, including Alejandro García, raised their hand. With that done, Dermot said;

"OK, the clock is ticking, I will get my Army Ranger team to source some incapacitating agent. In between times, I would suggest that you all have a wander around the town centre and act like international reporters. Once we begin to close things down, the person or group who is now attacking Southern Ireland will want to know where the S.T.O.P team is?"

Both I and Carlos walked to the hotel's front door and quickly had a look outside. All we could see were dark thundery clouds, heavy rain, gale-force winds, and a town central area that was empty of people. I looked at Carlos and said;

"I think for my newspaper, I might write that with such atrocious weather, no electricity, communications, or internet, Donegal had become a ghost town.

Carlos began to laugh and responded;

"I'm sure it will make headline news. Please send me a copy of that, my editor will love it."

We both laughed and went back to see Dermot who already gathered that our journalistic careers were dulled by the weather. With a smile on his face, he put on a very strong Irish ancient and told everyone;

"Now then ladies and gentlemen of the press, it would seem the inclement weather has dampened your appetite to do a wee bit of reporting. Therefore, to get those juices flowing again, would anyone like to partake in a glass of Irelands finest Guinness?"

At that, one of the Irish Rangers brought in a tray with glasses of Guinness on it. We all took a glass, raised it in the air, and when directed by Dermot, we all said; "Slauncher" which means "health" in Irish and Scottish Gaelic. Now, if you have never tasted Guinness, it's an acquired taste. For me, Karl, Theresa, and our Irish hosts it was a beautiful, full-bodied drink. But for our Spaniards, it was a completely new experience and one that did not suit their pallet. While the García's were very polite, taking a sip and saying nothing. Carlos was a little more verbal. Laughing he inquired;

"Is this cold oxo gravy with marmite mixed in."

Well, we all howled at that review. However, our laughter was brought to an abrupt halt when the Irish Ranger came back in and announced;

"Ladies and Gentlemen, can I have your attention. We have acquired the military-grade incapacitating agent you requested, and have just been informed by the command that operation Stop will commence in ten minutes.

One of our Irish Rangers, who is also a field medic, will administer the incapacitating agent to Mrs. García and keep her in a state of unconsciousness for as long as needed. After that, the medic will stay with her until she fully regains consciousness."

Dermot thank the Irish Ranger, looked at us all, and said;

"OK, folks I hope you like the name operation STOP. We thought with you onboard it was highly appropriate. Now let's put it into action. Valentina, would you kindly head up to your room, Sargent Kathryne O'Brian is waiting for you."

It was spontaneous, but we all rushed over and gave Valentina a big hug. Calmly, she then took my hand, kissed me on the cheek, and said;

"B.J please don't worry; Shelia and I will do you proud."

Oh, and guess what, I got all emotional. For the millionth time, my eyes filled with tears. I just hated the thought of my beautiful wife being trapped in this other realm, alone and afraid. I wanted Shelia to escape. But on the other hand, my heart knew if this plan worked. this would be our final goodbye, and that was just heartbreaking.

Seeing my emotional distress, my Spanish buddy came over, patted me on the back, and in a sympathetic voice said;

"B.J let's hope we win this so Shelia and all other life forces can safely cross to the afterlife. Once she is safely there, it might be possible for Valentina to contact her."

I wiped the tears from my eyes, gave everyone a long-repeated nod. After that, Connor asked if we would all gather around.

Then just like a New Year's Eve, he began a final countdown. As seconds passed by slowly, I don't know what we all expected, but the tension around us was immense. He then called; "Five, four, three, two, one." And, absolutely nothing happened. We all looked at each other and sighed relief.

Chapter Twenty-six,
Outstayed welcome

After the countdown. several minutes passed and still, nothing happened?

Connor then surmised saying;

"Let's not think the worst, it may take a while for the military, air force, and navy everyone to co-ordinate all of the ELF jamming devises."

However, we knew something was working because above the noise of the storm outside, we could hear some loud shouting. We all cautiously went to the front window to see what was happening, and to our horror, a small mob had gathered in the town square. They had armed themselves with all manner of weapons, and were chanting;

"Kill all strangers."

As we crept away from the window, Carlos said;

"Our adversary knows we are trying something and is fighting back. The entity we spoke of is using mind control technology, and the only ones who can stop this is Valentina and Shelia."

Then, without warning, Connor lunged at Carlos, hitting him with a solid right-hand punch on his chin. As Carlos fell to the floor, I caught a glimpse of Dermot pointing his SIG Sauer M17 handgun at me. I dived for cover as three shots whizzed just over my head. Fortunately for me, Theresa Tarragon-Jones was just to the rear of Dermot, and with one mighty swing, she Karate chopped Dermot on the back of his neck. Amazingly this only stunned him, but Theresa followed up with one hell of a kick right into Dermot's bollocks, and he dropped to his knees. Then, without hesitation, she jumped on his back and applied a rear chokehold. Dermot tried to struggle, but Theresa held the hold until he passed out.

At the same time, Karl had rugby tackled Conner and brought him to the floor. Now, I had never heard Karl boast about his unarmed combat skills, but he had Conner face down and in one hell of arm lock. Gaining my composure, I looked over at Carlos and could see he was sparked out.

Looking at Karl, I asked;

"Where is Alejandro García?"

He replied;

"The last time I saw him, he was running towards the stairs."

We then both looked at each other and simultaneously thought;

"Oh shit, the Irish rangers."

Using a bit of ingenuity, Karl quickly pulled some electrical cord of a couple of table lamps and tied Conner and Dermot up with it. He then pulled off a table cloth, ripped it into two, and used the two sections to gaged both Dermot and Conner. While he did this, I went back over to Carlos, who thankfully was now conscious and rubbing his jaw. As he got to his feet, I quickly filled him in on what had been happening. We all then drew our handguns out ready for the next wave of attacks. We knew there were five Irish Rangers in the hotel, one was with Valentina, and we hoped Alejandro García would deal with her. However, now we had to deal with four highly trained elite soldiers and possibly a mob outside.

Karl whispered to us;

"This restaurant area is too big for us to defend ourselves from. Quietly head over to the lady's toilet area."

Karl had studied military strategy; therefore, he had a good idea of how the Irish rangers would man their assault. So, we did as we were told, and silently crept to the lady's loo. Once inside Karl explained;

"The Irish Rangers will first find us using by scanning the area with thermal imagining cameras. Once our location has been established, they will then begin their assault by blowing the door with an explosive device. That will be followed by a few flashbangs. Once they believe that we are disorientated, the four-man team will move in for the kill.

Now for our defence tactics. The cleaner's cupboard is locked and we need it open. Once open we need a bucket, Corrosive drain cleaners, bleach, ammonia, floor cleaner, and something strong enough to wedge the door shut. We also have four handguns with two 17-round magazines per gun. That's one hundred and thirty-six rounds. We will need these for phase two of our defence."

Karl guarded the main toilet door while Theresa tackled the locked cleaner's door. Within seconds using just a hair grip, she had it open. I then quickly rummage through the cleaner's cupboard. I did find a heavy-duty metal door wedge, some bleach, drain, and floor cleaner, but no ammonia. I guess nowadays with ammonia being toxic, it's off most cleaners and households list.

While I secured the toilet entrance door with the wedge, Karl unscrewed the caps of the bleach and drain cleaner and poured them into the bucket. He then placed the bucket close to the centre of the door and jammed a few live bullets under the door so that they faced outward. Then addressing Carlos and Theresa, he told them;

"Go to the last toilet cubical. Inside you will see a small window that leads out into the rear courtyard and garden. See if you can prise it open or quietly remove all the glass."

He then turned to me and said;

"B.J, we are ready, go join the others."

Karl's final action was to pour the floor cleaner onto the tiled floor. Once he had finished, he joined us, and seeing that Carlos and Theresa had successfully removed the glass from the window, he quickly enlightened us on this part of his plan;

"OK folks, I want you to take any no notice of what is going to be happening at the toilet entrance, that was phase one. Now let's concentrate on phase two. In a few seconds, we are all going to exit out of this window. Now, just in case the Irish rangers or any of the mob have snuck around the back, I will go first. But as you exit, have your handguns at the ready, with the safety off, and if necessary, shot to kill."

Karl then wriggles through the window. Theresa and Carlos then quickly followed, and as I began to exit, I heard a mighty explosion at the back of me. Instantly, my ears rang with sound, but I knew I had to quickly get out as the first explosion was the lady's toilet door being blown off, and if Karl was right, the next thing would be flash-bangs. With one mighty effort, I lunged through the small window opening and crashed onto the others who gallantly tried to break my fall. Although I had knocked everyone over, no one was hurt. We all quickly got up and collectively heard the thunder of the flashbangs.

As the smoke and fumes billowed out of the small toilet window, we got a whiff of Karl's chemical concoction. Instantly we all felt like coughing and as the bleach fumes hit our eyes they began to sting. It was time to go, but thanks to Karl's military expertise, our escape from the hotel this far had been successful.

We were also fortunate that the mob in the town's central area hadn't come around to the back of the hotel. Knowing that Karl's tactics would only delay the Irish Rangers, we thought it would be more prudent to put some more distance between us and them. So, ran across the garden area, climbed over the back wall that leads to a car park and Donegal Bay. Then keeping our heads down, we looked for somewhere that would give us good cover. As the tide was low, we hid behind the sea wall, and there my thoughts went to Valentina and Alejandro García. Sharing my thoughts with the others I said;

"Right now, our priority should be for Valentina's safety. She is the key to talking this entity done. We need to take the Irish Rangers out and get back into the hotel."

Karl answered by saying;

"You are quite right in what you are saying, but I am confident that while we try to deal with the Irish Rangers, Alejandro García will do everything in his power to protect her.

Carlos had been keeping an eye out for any unwanted activity and told us;

"Look over there, someone is waving from behind the hotel wall."

Cautiously we poked our heads up over the sea, and to our amazement, it was Alejandro García. He beckoned us over, but Karl said we needed to be careful as the rangers could be setting a trap. This was a catch twenty-two situation, so, asking the others to cover me, I volunteered to go over to Alejandro. Then, using a few vehicles that gave me some cover, I crisscrossed across the car park to where Alejandro García was. As he looked down from the wall, I could see that he had a gas mask hanging around his neck, and four assault rifles on his right shoulder. He smiled and said;

"B.J it is safe, Valentina is well, and I have taken care of the Irish rangers. However, the mob has grown and is still a big threat to us all. Let's get the others back to the safety of the hotel, as this battle is far from over."

I shimmed back up over the wall and waved for the others to follow. Once we back inside, I could see that Alejandro had a rough time, his lower lip was cut and the right eye was swollen. I was about to ask Alejandro how he single-handed managed to overcome all of the Irish rangers when he said;

"OK everyone, we need to act quickly. All four male rangers are un-consciousness Three of them were overcome by fumes, and me throwing a canister of an incapacitating agent into the lady's toilet. The other one was shot in the foot, and I knocked him un-consciousness. Anyway, before they come back around, they need to be tied up. However, you must be careful, as the toilet floor is still very slippery.

While you do that, I will go upstairs and secure my lady sparring partner. She and I went a few rounds, and the only way I could get the better of her is was with the aid of a fire extinguisher."

Well, with my questions answered, we were all set about our tasks. Fortunately, that did not take long. However, the only thing we could find to tie them up with was more electric wiring from the lamps dotted around the reception and restaurant area. As soon we had finished, we meet back in the reception area, where Alejandro shared out the assault rifles, handguns, and ammunition he had taken from the Irish rangers. Then he showed us a stash of other goodies he had attained by searching the ranger's quarters. The first was, twenty canisters of incapacitating agents the Irish rangers had as extra to those needed to keep Valentina un-consciousness.

To protect themselves and I guess us from a gas attack, they also had twenty full-face gas masks. Next on the list were four scoped rifles that fired tranquilizer darts, and to complement these rifles there was a big box of tranquilizer darts. Finally, he showed us an array of flashbangs, explosives, and hand grenades.

Our next course of action was trying to secure the hotel's front entrance. Making sure the door was locked was our first consideration. After that, we quietly made a barricade out of tables and chairs that would act as a secondary defence if the front door was breached. The front windows were difficult to secure, but they also worked to our advantage as they did not open fully. We planned to use the small openings to initially fire tranquilizer darts at any hostiles. However, if things got bad then regrettably, we would have to be shot to kill.

We knew through experience that the rear of the hotel could easily be accessed by scaling the garden wall. Therefore, trying to stop a mob would prove extremely difficult, so we split ourselves into three units. I and Carlos would cover the front of the hotel, Karl and Alejandro would cover the back. Theresa's job was to guard the stairs and replenished everyone's supply of ammo.

With all the previous noise and explosions in the hotel, we were amazed that the mob outside hadn't already been over to investigate what was going on. Perhaps the explosions were covered by the thunderous storm raging outside, who knows? But our luck broke when Dermot managed to slip his gag off and began yelling at the top of his voice;

"The strangers are in here. Kill them!

Before we could silence him, he yelled this several times, and with that, the frenzied mob rushed over and tried to smash their way through the front door. Fortunately for us, that proved quite difficult. Failing that, the mob turned their attention to the hotel's street-level windows. We planned to try to shoot some of them through the small opening, but this failed as the windows shattered over a hail of stone and large rocks. All I and Carlos could do was back off, and fire a few tranquilizer darts through the smashed window panes. However, the tranquilizer guns were way too slow to reload, so we lobed a couple of flash-bangs outside. That only gave us a minute or two, and we now had to implement our next plan. Get our gas masks on, and throw a few canisters of incapacitating agents just inside the windows. I called to Theresa;

"Masks on, masks on."

She acknowledged with a thumbs up, and then ran to the others and informed them. Once Theresa came back and put her gas mask on, we carefully rolled four canisters so they stopped by the skirting boards, and with a hiss, they began to release the incapacitating agent. With no regard for their own safety, the first of the mob tried to clamber through the broken windows. However, as soon as they inhaled the potent gas, they just dropped like flies. We stood well back and were amazed to see other frenzied people just pulling the limp bodies out of the way, and as they did this, those who were unconscious received terrible wounds from the shards of broken glass.

While we held off the frontal attack with more and more gas canisters, Karl and Alejandro were doing the same at the rear of the hotel. However, the bodies were now waist-high, and the mob was just relentless. Then some bright spark in the mob used a transit van and drove it at speed into the front door. Well, the door and frame just shattered into a million pieces under the impact, and a crowd surged through the opening and into the reception area. We immediately had to retreat, but for a few minutes more, we were able to hold back the crowd with the knockout gas. I looked at Carlos and whispered;

"We had a serious problem, between us all we only had one canister left."

He nodded and pointed to our assault rifles indicating that our next line of defence was to use deadly force. Sadly, I had to agree. By this time Karl and Alejandro had also retreated, and with our guns pointing at the mob, we all joined forces on the stairway. Karl took command and told us;

"Throw the last gas canister, and take the safety off all your weapons, we will give the gas a few moments, then I will fire a few rounds over their heads. If this doesn't stop them, then on my command fire."

Alejandro threw the canister close to the people at the front of the mob, and its potency soon took effect. However, to our surprise, the mob had gotten used to seeing the gas canisters and now had a plan. Several deliberately fell on the gas canister forming a human blanket and completely restricting its flow. Seeing this, Karl then fired three rounds just over the heads of the mob, but the thought of being shot or killed didn't frighten them.

Taking a deep breath, I aimed, and then a voice in my head yelled;

"B.J Stop!"

I instantly recognised the voice as Shelia's. I called at the top of my voice to the others;

"Don't fire, don't fire. "

Now, although the team was confused at me, without hesitation, they did as I requested. At the same time, we looked at the mob, in an instant they had turned from a raging sea of crazed humans into a calm millpond. We could see in their eyes, expressions, gestures, and a look of horror, that they had no idea how they got to the hotel, or indeed what they were doing there?

Carlos looked at me and asked the question everyone else was thinking;

"Mi amigo, how the hell did you know this crowd was going to stop their attack?"

Looking at the S.T.O.P team, I said just one word;

"Shelia."

Everyone nodded, and their eyes all looked up the stairway that led to Valentina's room. Now I could not say we all ran to her room, but I certainly got there as fast as my legs could carry me. Bursting through the door, I was surprised to see a clear plastic tent had been erected around Valentina's bed. Inside the tent was a device that held six canisters of incapacitating agents that slowly releases the gas. It was obvious that Valentina did not need to be unconscious any longer, so I unzipped the tent and turned the device off. Then while the others gathered around, I checked Valentina's pulse, and thankfully it was a steady fifty-eight beats. Seeing she was ok, I sat on the edge of the bed, removed my gas mask, took a couple of deep breaths to calm myself down, closed my eyes, and mentally I called out to Sheila;

"Are you there my love?"

Not getting any response, I tried several times, and then a mental vision filled my mind, it was Shelia. She smiled, waved at me, threw me a kiss, and then slowly the vision faded. I mentally called out;

"Don't go, I love you, please don't go."

As I opened my eyes everyone was looking at me. I tried to take a moment to compose myself, but I failed So with my body shaking, tears in my eyes, and trembling lips, I told them;

"She has gone."

Now I know at this point I was an emotional wreck, but Mi amigo Carlos on a scale of one to ten scored well over twenty.

He didn't just burst out crying, he fell to the floor sobbing and repeatedly saying;

"I'm sorry, I'm so, so sorry."

Taking sympathy for him, the team all rushed over to console him. It was then that it hit me that he still felt guilty about Shelia's death. So, I too went over and hugged my friend and said;

"Carlos, over the last few months, we have gone through an awful lot, and we have become not just good friends, but brothers bonded by our experiences."

Carlos stopped weeping and replied;

"Thank you for that B.J, but Shelia's death will always play heavy on my heart. I am sincerely sorry for what happened in Tenerife."

Wiping some of the tears from his eyes, he gave me a manly kiss on my cheek and said;

"B.J, I, no we, are happy to hear Shelia is no longer trapped in this other realm and has now finally crossed over."

He then paused and added;

"Since this started, our brotherhood has expanded into a family, the S.T.O.P family."

We all just looked at each other, and nodding, we agreed with these sentiments.

Chapter Twenty-seven, Mop up

With so many still unconscious from the gas and others with injures, Donegal's community hospital was overrun, however, Valentina was given priority and a private room. Further, her care was provided by a highly qualified army medical team who were on hand until she regained consciousness. Now, as you can imagine, our hotel needed some major repairs, so we packed our bags and moved up the road to The Abbey Hotel.

Once we settled in, we all meet up with Dermot and Connor in the meeting room. Needless to say, both men looked a little battered, but first on their agenda were some sincere apologies for attacking us. After that, it was down to business. Conner reported that the joint effort on jamming the ELF jamming waves had worked well. As he looked at his wristwatch, he stated;

"The good news is, the deadline for attacks on Cities in Southern Ireland has passed over an hour ago, and all is well in Southern Ireland. I have spoken with our Taoiseach and he has said that Southern Ireland will forever be in S.T.O. P's debt. He has also requested that when Valentina comes around and is ready to travel. he would like to meet you all in person so that he can personally thank you."

While all of this was really good news, I had another pressing issue in my mind. I needed to contact my daughters. As our mobile phones had been compromised, I asked Dermot if he had access to a secure line? He kindly obliged by lending me his secure mobile, and while the others continued chatting, I excused myself to my hotel room and then telephoned my girls.

Over the next hour or so, I filled the girls in on what had been happening since we left the hotel in England, meeting with the

British Prime Minister, our sudden fight to Southern Ireland, and what had happened since we had been here. I then concluded by telling them that Valentina was still unconscious and my mental vision of their mom waving goodbye. Now, the latter brought on the tears, and yes, that also included yours truly. We ended our conversation by saying how much we all missed mom and hoped that she was now in a much happier place.

When I returned to the meeting room, everyone was busy looking at the hotel's evening meal menu. That's when my stomach let me know it too was empty, and needed filling. The waiter told me the T-bone steak was excellent, so I ordered that with all the trimmings. Then just before the waiter left the room, Connor had a call from Donegal's community hospital that Valentina had regained consciousness, and she wanted to speak to us right away. The thought of food instantly left our minds. With a spurt on, we all piled into a Military Mini-bus that was on hand to transport us around Southern Ireland, then with a siren wailing, we headed at full speed to the hospital.

Valentina surprised us all by being up, makeup on, dressed impeccably and waiting for us in a small room that I guess is usually used as a doctor's surgery. She greeted us all with a hug and then sitting, looking quite relaxed, she began to tell us what she and my late wife had experienced. She began;

"Hi all, I am so pleased to see everyone is maybe a little battered but safe."

While she said this, she looked at her brother, Carlos, Dermot, and Connor. We all laughed at that. Continuing she added;

"Not long after I became unconscious, I could feel the life energy of those who had been killed on the Eire Lingus flight and those at Donegal's airport being pulled to this artificial alien realm. As I followed them, I could feel Shelia's presence, however, she was still trapped in now what I understand as one of three of these zones that hold people's life's energy.

When you are traveling outside of your body vocal speech does not work. So, I mentally called to Shelia that it was time to implement the escape plan. As it turned out, since our last meeting Shelia had constantly been working on this. She had already been communicated with others in her realm about what we were about to try.

They like Shelia were desperate to escape and without hesitation, they all agreed to unite their life's energy as one force. However, they wanted someone to spearhead this, and Shelia was chosen. Amazingly, as this new force looked for ways to escape, it detected many other life forces in two similar realms. Time as we know it does not exist when we pass to the other side, but putting this into an earthly perspective, in a considerable short time, Shelia convinced every life force across the three realms to unite.

Shelia's collective then sensed another vast realm that had incredible power. Now although the collective did not understand how it worked, they did understand that this was a power source that drew their life forces away from crossing over and captured their life forces into the three realms. In this nanosecond of clarity, the whole collective realised that to escape, they needed to shut down this energy force.

Once again using their collective power, Shelia directed them away from their captivity into a vast space that was filled with what could only be described as an unknown form of energy. Shelia surmised that as their life's forces are just energy, they as a collective would be able to absorb this other form of energy. It was agreed to try this, and as soon as they did this, the energy that had captured them was absorbed, and they were finally able to escape. One thing that Shelia and the collective did notice as they escaped was, the thing they had escaped from looked like a black pyramid?

Shelia then had one final request, and that was to use their energy to divide back into individual life forces. This too was agreed, and to her surprise, this worked. Now free, it allowed every soul captured to travel into the spirit world. However, before they did this, Shelia and each life force sent a mental message to a loved one that they were now safe."

Valentina paused for a few seconds, took a breath, and looking at all of us she said;

"Something you also need to know is, I did feel the presence of that person, alien, or entity that was controlling the ELF waves and the power from the pyramid. Now, all I can tell you is when the power was drained from the pyramid, the entity disappeared.

Also, I believe that we all have to acknowledge that despite everything that has happened to her, Shelia was the real hero in this battle. I would go as far as to say that she is a true member of the S.T.O.P team.

She then looked at me, smiled, and added;

"B.J this is just for you and his family. Shelia and I have now a special spiritual bond. That bond allows me to communicate with her in the spirit world. So, if at any time you want to pass on a message to Shelia or vice versa, I will always be here to do this for you, Shelia, and your family."

Those words were heart-warming to me. I gave Valentina a big hug and told her that the Jameson family would also be overjoyed at hearing this.

In light of what Valentina had said about the entity disappearing, we began to speculate on what would happen next? But then in truth, we did not know. All we knew is S.T.O.P would continue and we would be on the front line if we were called on.

Chapter Twenty-eight,
The other sides,
Epilogue one

It had been four weeks, one hour and thirty-five seconds since operation Southern Ireland has finished and Francisco sat and re-evaluated all that had been happening. Everything had gone exactly as predicted up to the artifact's power vanishing. He was even surprised that his supercomputer and new quantum computer could not analyse what had gone wrong. However, to Francisco's mind, every cloud has a silver lining, and he took full advantage of this hiccup.

Using his Fran-Freight transportation business, he had the artifact and some high Tec ELF transmitters secretly taken to the China Academy of Space Technology (CAST). There he planted the artifact and ELF transmitters in one of their research labs. To make his plan look authentic, he had a few of the Lab workers killed by having their heads explode after forcing explosive compressed air capsules into their mouths. His mercenary team then filmed this and leaked the footage to the press, media, and the worldwide web.

Consequently, the Chinese government came under heavy political fire for this. They responded by strongly denying any knowledge of this. Although the war was mentioned, luckily for everyone on the planet that did not arise. However, every country in the world imposed crippling economic sanctions against China. With the yen hitting an all-time low, and trade restrictions hitting hard, Francisco knew it was time to covertly step in. He utilized all his company's resources and services and was making an absolute financial killing from the Chinese government and multinational Chinese businesses.

For several years now, the Franco pharmaceutical company had done extremely well on supplying several vaccination drugs and a variety of covid relief tablets to help control the spread of the Covid 19 virus and its many variants. Now while Francisco didn't have anything to do with this particular virus, he did see a fantastic financial opportunity in developing a new virus and at the same time having a vaccine to control it. However, with lots of money still flowing in from covid 19, this was something for the future.

Now going back to the present time, Francisco wasn't even that perturbed about losing the alien artifact. He also wasn't the slightest bit concerned that every country in the world had deployed ELF high Tec jamming devices. His research had shown there were several more alien pyramids on planet earth, and with the aid of his supercomputer, several had been easily located. And yes, these alien artifacts were the power source for ELF waves. Nonetheless, he had discovered that they were also the power source for all the other alien artifacts NASA had discovered and he had been able to replicate them. While Fran-com supercomputer did not have the computing power to evaluate the power source connections to these other alien artifacts', his new quantum computer did. More pleasingly, the quantum computer solved this issue in a few hours.

With this new knowledge, alien artifacts, and quantum computer power, the world, and off-world possibilities were endless. He laughed and thought;

"I wonder how the S.T.O.P team will try to stop all of my future exploits."

Chapter Twenty-nine,
Eyes of the universe
Epilogue two

While Francisco continued to construct his devious plans, others who had been to the planet terra many eons ago had been monitoring the human's current activities. With some apprehension, they realised that human technology had advanced considerably. More concerning was, these humans were on the brink of accessing some of the accent technology that had been left on the planet. Now. if this was allowed, humans would soon be able to travel through the known universe and beyond. To these off-world beings, another major concern was some of this ancient technology would give humans a better understanding of other dimensions and how to cross into them.

It was therefore agreed that the old masters of planet terra should return and destroy all the technology they had left, and for the safety of this and other universes and other dimensions, they might have to annihilate this ape-like hostile race.

The end, or possibly the beginning of something big.

About the Author

James Moclair was born in England in nineteen fifty-one. Ever since he was a young boy, James has always had a passion for science and in particular science fiction. Over the years, he has read many great science fiction novels. He has also been a fan of Star Trek, Babylon five, Battle Star Galactica, and much other great science fiction series on television.

Further, James can also boast that he has never missed an episode of the world's longest science fiction program., Dr Who. For the big screen, James's memories are as a lad he loved Flash Gordon and Batman. Nowadays with C.G.I, superhero movies are even more spectacular. DC and Marvel movies just blow James's mind. His favourite science fiction film to date is Avatar.

For many years James worked professionally as a professional martial arts instructor. But James started practicing martial arts as a young boy over half a century ago! In slightly over five decades, James has achieved a Tenth Dan in Jujutsu and also holds numerous other high Dan grades (Black Belts) in various other martial arts.

James did not turn his hand to writing until the year 2004, and since that date, he has written three martial arts books that have then been self-published. After that, James turned his pen to his other passion, writing science fiction. His first book was called S.P.A.C.E (Special Populations and Cosmic Enigmas). He wrote a follow-up and this book was appropriately named T.I.M.E (Temporal Inconsistencies Mythological Entities). T.I.M.E deals with the consequences of meddling with time!

Now James's latest book, S.T.O.P (Stop Terrorizing our Planet) addresses things a little closer to home. This book has some rather interesting alien twists and even crosses over into the spirit world.

James also has many other interests and the first may not surprise you and that is, he loves fitness training. He's also a very keen fisherman and to indulge his passion, he lives in a riverside house. When James was just twenty, he bought an Omega wristwatch and this fired another interest. James now has an extensive watch collection and also has a YouTube channel where he reviews watches. Another way James relaxes is to play on his X Box or his V.R Headset.

www.ingramcontent.com/pod-product-compliance
Lightning Source LLC
Chambersburg PA
CBHW020440270626
47155CB00022B/751